ÆRENDEN
THE GILDONAE ALLIANCE

Kristen Taber

sean tigh
PRESS

For my daughter, my greatest creation

ACKNOWLEDGMENTS

I cannot publish a book without giving my utmost regard to my editors and beta readers, the great line of defense against errors. For catching those little (and big) things that slip through after my umpteenth read, I heartily thank Jessica Lux, Heather McBride, Karen Giera, Steve Giera, Brigid Gory-Hines, Trish Hanson, Amy Hedges, Jo Reed, Cheri Schueller, and Sabine Veasey.

CHAPTER ONE

THE WORLD streaked past, brown bark and evergreen mixed with the dirty sludge of winter. Meaghan leaped over the remains of a fallen spruce, and then dodged around a thorn bush. Her stride never broke. An ice patch appeared in front of her, pressing red and orange leaves into the ground, and she veered left to avoid it. She had almost missed this one, though heightened adrenaline had saved her at the last moment. She could not fall. She could not slow. Her life depended on it.

Wind burned her cheeks and whipped her hair behind her. She ignored it. She also ignored the way her breath seared her lungs. She pushed harder, further than she had before. And she focused, straining her ears and eyes. An attack would come soon. She expected it, though she wished she had Nick's sensing power to warn her when it neared. Without it, she had to rely on her training alone. She hoped it would be enough.

Up ahead, vines hung motionless across her path. They could be harmless, but she could not take the chance. Without changing her pace, she grabbed a stick from the ground and threw it into the curtain of green stretching in front of her. The vines reacted, snapping and curling around the branch until it crumbled into splinters. She swerved off the path, circled around the creeper vines, and then hurdled when she realized a log blocked her path. An inch shy of clearing it, she caught her foot on a protruding branch.

She hit the ground and rolled before springing back to her feet and pushing forward once more. Her ankle ached where she had broken it months before. Cold weather often brought a familiar pang to her old injury and tripping had increased that ache, but she could not allow it to stop her. She tightened her arms at her sides, increased her speed, and set her eyes on her goal—a white flag. Safety.

Her heart raced in anticipation. Her eyes locked on her prize as victory spread a smile over her lips. Then seconds before she reached it, a growl caught her attention from the trees. A figure dropped from the thickest limbs to her right. Wind swirled his dark brown cloak around him as he reached for her, skin stretching across skeleton thin fingers. Red eyes sought hers in an attempt to freeze her, and then a howl escaped his fibrous mouth when his power had no effect. She attempted to skid to a stop, but her feet continued to slide.

Ice took her legs out from under her. She landed on her back. Pain shot through her spine, and she struggled to reclaim her breath. The Mardróch jumped on top of her. His knees pressed into her chest and his hands crushed her arms into the ground. Snow numbed her skin, and in that moment, she realized the monster was not one of Nick's training holograms.

Why had she not smelled him? Her empath power coursed

through her, stronger than ever. The Mardróch should have triggered it well before she got close to him. Yet she sensed nothing. Not even while his breath brushed her skin.

And where was Nick? As her Guardian, he should have come running when the Mardróch attacked. He would not leave her to fight the creature alone—unless he had no other choice and the Mardróch had reached him first. The thought seized her before she banished it, refocusing on the monster's bony face instead. She had to figure out a way to escape before she could worry about Nick. She had to figure out how to breathe.

Gray shadowed the edges of her sight. The Mardróch tightened his grip, digging his nails into her wrists, and she drew her knees up in attempt to shove him away. One of her ribs gave instead. She cried out in pain before she could control the reaction.

The Mardróch's webbed mouth opened in a gaping grin. His eyes swirled a darker red with his pleasure, and she solidified her resolve. She tried again, and this time her boots met muscle. She pitched sideways, throwing the monster off, and then whipped her head around to search for the white flag Nick had used to mark the end of her course. Sometimes the flags led to real hiding places, but not today. Not this one. He had attached it to a rock.

She jumped to her feet. The Mardróch did the same, facing her. Electricity arced across his fingers. He grinned again, emitted a deep, rattling laugh, and she ran. She needed to get to the cabin. The crystals surrounding it would protect her.

She managed only a few steps before dirt exploded at her heels. She wove through the forest, placing trees between her and her pursuer. Wood splintered in front of her. Bushes erupted into fire at her sides. Heat burned her skin and seared the hairs on her arms. Her breath rasped and her ribs screamed with every step. Six more yards to go. Now five. She could see the cabin ahead, though the Mardróch would see nothing more than forest. If she could figure out a way to distract him while she crossed the border into the protected clearing, she would be safe. She only needed a plan.

She did not have the chance to form one. She made the mistake of turning her head to look for her attacker, slipped on another patch of ice, and fell to her knees. The Mardróch raised his hands, and then a streak of blue and white filled her vision.

CHAPTER TWO

"**WELL, YOU** almost made it."

The forest lurched around Meaghan again, dissolving into view at the same speed it had faded. She blinked several times. A pair of ocean blue eyes peered down at her, and then Nick's face came into focus. He knelt over her, a small vial in his hand. Empty, she had no doubt, as she tasted bitter potion on her lips.

"What happened?" she asked and pushed up to her knees. Although panic still worked its way through her veins, turning her blood into rapids, Nick's presence told her the Mardróch had not been as he seemed. A quick scan of the surrounding woods confirmed her suspicion. "Where is he? He was real. He…" her voice failed her and she swallowed hard.

"Killed you," Nick finished her sentence and frowned. A few strands of his sandy blonde hair fell into his eyes and he swept his hand across his forehead to move them out of the way. "Fortunately for you he wasn't as real as he seemed. Why didn't you use your knife?"

Her hand moved to her belt, where a leather sheath held an eight-inch blade. She had forgotten she had it. That made the third time in the past month she had run instead of using her weapon. No matter how hard she tried to retrain the way she thought, she could not seem to remember that death would stop her attacker better than any other method. The one time she had drawn her knife, she had not been able to use it against the man who chased her. It felt too much like murder.

"I didn't think of it," she confessed. "The Mardróch was an illusion?"

Nick nodded. "I put a hallucination potion in your water this morning."

"I see." She ran her fingers along her rib cage, searching for the break, but found no tenderness, not even a small amount of pain. "So everything was fake?"

"Yes." Nick stood. Taking her hand, he pulled her to her feet. "All of it easily fixed with an antidote, fortunately. You have to learn to defend yourself, Meg. They'll kill you if you don't kill them first."

She sighed. "I know."

"But you still don't strike." He held her gaze a moment longer until shame forced her to look away, then he turned and began walking back to the cabin. She followed him. When they reached the clearing, she trailed her eyes toward the sky. Red streaks greeted her along the horizon. The sun would be gone soon.

"Guardians use the potion to simulate real situations, to determine if a student is ready to graduate," Nick continued their conversation as if no silence had elapsed between them. "It took me two tries to pass the test."

Yet his displeasure that she had failed her first try broadcast across her empath power like a parental scolding. She stiffened her shoulders. "It wasn't exactly a fair test," she said. "I can smell Mardróch. I can't smell illusions. If he'd been real—"

"You'd be dead. The Mardróch would have heard you long before you sensed him. You're too loud."

She crossed her arms over her stomach, but he did not give her time to object.

"Furthermore, this isn't about fairness. It's about war and about survival. You can't count on being able to sense the Mardróch. They figured out a way to weaken the Guardian sensing ability. They could do the same with your empath power."

"They found an old spell to mute the Guardian sensing power. There aren't any Spellmasters left to create another spell to block my power. Caide and Aldin aren't strong enough to do it, even if Garon knew where they were."

"You assume they won't find another spell," Nick said. "The castle is full of old spells hidden by the royal family and their Guardians. Since Garon lives there now, I wouldn't count on luck to get you through."

Meaghan blew out a short breath to ease her frustration and stopped at the steps to the cabin. "Fine. You've made your point. I won't count on anything."

"That wasn't my point. You just can't count on being able to sense the Mardróch. You *can* count on your everyday senses. Garon can't take those away. Pay attention, be alert, and follow your instincts."

"My instincts are to run," she reminded him. "I haven't

experienced combat my whole life like you have. It's not easy for me to hurt someone, even if they are trying to hurt me."

"You think it's easy for me?" Nick asked. His eyes snapped to hers, and the strength of his anger overwhelmed her power for a moment before he controlled it. A second emotion flickered beneath the first, but she could not name it. "It isn't meant to be easy, but even if it was, it doesn't matter. All that matters is you learn to defend yourself. We can't rejoin the people from my village until you do."

She frowned. "I know you want to get back to your mother and the other Guardians, but—"

"Damn it, Meg!" His anger surged again. His hands shot forward and his grip bruised her shoulders. "This isn't about getting back there. This is about keeping you alive."

She stared at him and at the red blanketing his face, surprised by the depth of his anger. Her shoulders throbbed. Her throat constricted with panic. Then it hit her. His buried emotion flooded to the surface, followed in quick succession by a series of other emotions she had failed to detect. Worry, anxiety, fear, and grief tumbled within her and she understood.

"Nick," she began, not sure what to say, but stopped when he shook his head. He released his hold on her and, for the first time since they had arrived at the cabin, he used his power against her. He masked his emotions, drawing a barrier around them so she could no longer sense him. Then, turning from her, he crossed the porch and entered the cabin.

She followed close behind him. As soon as they cleared the

doorway, he pointed to the small table in one corner of the room.

"Sit," he said. "We have more work to do."

The command increased her own anger and she debated the satisfaction of fueling an argument, but decided against it when he cast her a warning glare. She slid into a chair, folded her hands on top of the table, and waited.

"Start the focusing exercises," he instructed, and though she had done them hundreds of times in the last few months, he recited the steps anyway. He began pacing the room and she knew he had stopped paying attention to her. She closed her eyes.

"Close your eyes," he said.

She inhaled and focused on her breath and then on the heat beside her lungs.

"Now inhale and focus on the point where your breath expands in your lungs, on the warmth there…"

She tuned out the sound of his voice, seized her power and held on to it. She had grown to recognize its warmth over the past few months. Although it seemed strongest by her heart, she could sense it even in the smallest cells of her body. She could command it along those cells, alive and ready, like electricity running along wires. Whenever she wanted it to work, she flipped the switch and the power poured through her—to her hands or feet or even to her legs, as she had discovered one day at the end of the fall season. She had been sitting cross-legged in the clearing not long after they had arrived at the cabin. The chill in the air had turned to ice, bringing death or hibernation to many of the plants surrounding them. Because she had no way to test her revival power, she had dispersed the energy into the ground.

At first nothing had happened, but then wildflowers began to grow beneath her legs and around her. It had been the last time she had seen pride on Nick's face. Since then, he only grew more frustrated with her progress.

It did not help that she had learned to control her revival power, but still had no clue how to command her empath power. She could not seem to shut it off. She failed at every technique he taught her. She focused on shrinking it, but the warmth stayed steady. She tried to contain it, but it escaped her hold. She tried ignoring the emotions, but they grew stronger until she paid attention to them. And each time she failed, Nick's disappointment overshadowed her own.

Today they would attempt a new technique Nick's mother, May, had shared with them. She used it for Guardian children who had the most trouble controlling their sensing powers. As Nick's emotions grew stronger within her, she would focus on them individually, peeling off each one until nothing remained, like stripping petals from a rosebud.

When Nick dropped his guard again, Meaghan allowed his emotions to overwhelm her, and then followed May's instructions. She focused on Nick's fear first, since that seemed to be the weakest emotion. Concentrating on it, she envisioned plucking a rose petal from a flower and let the imaginary petal drift to the ground. The emotion remained. She frowned and reached for it again. It strengthened, so she ignored it and moved on to the next emotion. Worry begged for her attention, so she latched on to it, then discarded it and waited. Nothing happened. One last effort on his anger produced the same result. Opening her eyes, she felt hope layer on top of Nick's other emotions, and shook her head in response.

He nodded, tucked his hands behind his back, and walked out the door, leaving disappointment behind him.

§

DARKNESS SETTLED across the night, casting long shadows through the woods and turning trees into ominous sentries set for war. Stars flickered above, but the moon chose to hide, holding its light hostage within the clouds. Nick tightened his cloak around his shoulders, blocking the wind from slicing his skin, but the garment failed to ease the chill that had settled into his mind. He knew he should find his way back to the cabin and to the fire Meaghan would have built by now, but his feet continued to wander.

He needed the solitude and the chance to settle his emotions again. He had succeeded in keeping them buried over the past few weeks, despite the news he had received from his mother, but Meaghan's failed field exam had dismantled that control. He had hoped she would pass the test so they could return to the protection of the Guardian army. Mardróch had been sniffing around the area over the past few weeks. It would only be a matter of time before they spotted the hideout. The cabin would stay hidden by the crystals, of course, but Nick could not hide all traces of his and Meaghan's existence. Training and hunting left them vulnerable to the acute senses of the vile monsters.

Much like the dark night did, Nick realized. He froze as low-lying leaves rustled to his left, the noise slicing through the still air in warning. Nick curled his fingers around the hilt of his knife and turned, poised to fight. A raccoon darted from underneath a bush.

"Mangy creature," Nick muttered and forced his body to relax.

The animal stopped to watch him, then turned and disappeared into the black forest. No sooner had its ringed tail vanished than another movement caught the corner of Nick's eye. A shadow stepped through the trees and Nick drew his blade, throwing it so it imbedded into the bark of a pine tree only inches from the shadow's head. He pulled a second knife and waited.

"That was stupid," a familiar voice said, then a large hand reached out to dislodge the blade from the tree moments before the moon broke through the clouds, glinting light off a pair of pale blue eyes. "You just gave me a weapon. If I'd meant to harm you, it would be in your chest by now."

"Your aim's not that good," Nick responded, slipping the blade in his hand back into its sheath. "Besides, I already sensed you didn't intend any harm. I just wanted to send a warning."

"So you aimed for the tree?" The man chuckled. "You've gained some skill with the knife then." The man stepped closer so Nick could view the weathered face and long, black and gray beard of one of his oldest friends. Nick accepted his knife, stowing it before the man engulfed him in a big hug. The man's eyes appeared misty when he let Nick go.

"Training Meaghan has been good for you, I think," he added.

"It has," Nick agreed. "It's nice to see you, Cal. How long have you been here?"

"All day. I wanted to watch Meaghan's progress. She's doing well."

"Well enough," Nick responded and continued walking. Cal kept pace beside him. "Thank you for the supplies," Nick said. "The timing of your deliveries is impeccable."

Cal shrugged. "It's been fairly windy this winter. It allows me to use my power to check up on you."

Nick nodded. An owl hooted in the distance, and the night settled around them. Cal tucked his hands into his cloak, a pensive gesture Nick recognized, but several minutes still passed before the older man spoke again. "Your mother asked me to give you the update."

And it would not be good, if the lines creasing Cal's forehead offered any indication. "Another village fell?" he guessed.

"Several. The largest at Oak Point. Only one person survived there, a woman who had an invisibility power."

"Oak Point Village had two hundred people living in it," Nick said, though he did not expect a response from Cal, nor did he receive one. Counted among the dead would be a childhood friend of Cal's, a Guardian named Sylb. "I'm sorry."

Cal kept his eyes glued to the ground. Nick watched brown leaves disintegrate beneath the man's oversized feet.

"The Elders receive survivors from the smaller villages nearly every day," Cal continued. "We can't refuse them."

"And each one could be a traitor," Nick realized.

Cal nodded. "The Elders continue to maintain a strict protective barrier. That helps. So does moving every six weeks or so."

"But it's only a matter of time before Garon finds you," Nick said. Cal nodded again and panic squeezed Nick's throat. "Then I need to double my training efforts. Meaghan needs to be ready to lead soon or there won't be anything left of her kingdom."

Cal glanced up. A frown burrowed into his beard. "You're already pushing her too hard."

"That's a matter of opinion. She's handling the pace fine."

"She's grown weary and she's lost too much weight. Even I can see that, so don't claim you can't."

Nick could not deny it, but he did not want to admit it either. Meaghan's copper eyes had begun to show strain, muting the gold that once sparked within them, and her deep brown hair and olive skin had grown dull, a reflection of poor nutrition. He had already talked to his mother about which herbs he could use to supplement Meaghan's diet, but more food and less training would be a better solution.

Cal stopped walking, prompting Nick to do the same, and Nick realized his friend had taken the silence as an admission of guilt.

"Training takes years," Cal said. "You can't expect her to complete it in a few months."

"In a perfect world, I would give her that time," Nick responded, clasping his hands behind his back. "But this situation is far from perfect. Meaghan's people need her, and even if they didn't, she needs the Elders' protection. The Mardróch are around."

"They haven't found you yet. I keep an eye on them, too."

"What good does that do?" Nick challenged. "You watch us through the elements, but most of the time you're too far away to help. And when you're here, you don't show your face. Or you didn't before today. Why now? Did you come to lecture me?"

"I'm here to help. You've done fine on your own, so I thought I'd butt out where I wasn't needed. But now—"

"Now you think it's time to step in, to tell me I'm wrong to train her the way I do." Nick narrowed his eyes. "Don't judge me. You aren't here every day. You don't see the way she struggles to make sense of this world. And you don't see the disappointment on her face when she can't control her powers or the fear in her eyes when she fights the Mardróch I inflict on her. I need to get her through this, and soon. Before it's too late."

"Before the Mardróch find her or before she hates you?" Cal asked, arching an eyebrow that told Nick he had guessed what the answer would be. "She isn't the only one who looks tired, Nick. I worry about you, too. That's why I'm here."

With those words, Nick's anger deflated. He continued walking, Cal now his shadow. The older man's voice softened when he spoke again.

"I know there isn't much you can do to slow down Meaghan's schedule, but there are other ways you can relieve her stress. You're proud of her accomplishments. I can see it on your face when she's not looking. Why don't you tell her?"

Nick dropped his gaze to the ground. "It wouldn't help. She needs to focus on improving."

"She's improving, and it would help her morale to hear it. She also needs to hear the other things you're not telling her. May says you've decided to shelter Meaghan from the weekly reports."

Nick shrugged. "Bad news won't relieve her stress."

"Maybe not," Cal said. "But showing you trust her will, particularly given your situation. It's only natural for her to care what you think about her, and to worry about it."

Nick grunted. "If you say so."

"I do. I have my fair share of experience with women. Besides, it doesn't really matter what you believe. The Elders want her to have the updates."

Nick's feet stalled. He stared at Cal. "Since when do you follow the Elders blindly?"

"This isn't about the Elders, lad, and you know it. This is about you keeping information from Meaghan. She can sort through it as well as you can, and she has a right to do so." Cal placed a hand on Nick's shoulder. "I know this is hard for you, but you can't hide these things from her. Just like you can't hide what you feel from her. This isn't a job any longer. This isn't about you guarding her."

"Of course it is. I'm her Guardian."

"You're her husband first. That's where your bond lies. And you're the King second. You may be a Guardian, but your instincts to protect her don't come from that any longer. They come from your other roles in her life."

King. Even hearing the word made Nick's stomach sour. He thought it best to direct the conversation to safer ground. "So what do I do about Meaghan's training?" he asked. "I don't have years."

"No, you don't," Cal agreed. "But maybe you won't need it. She's doing well in her combat training."

"She won't strike to defend herself."

"She will when the situation's real," Cal said. "Though honestly, if she's able to avoid it, it's best for her. Especially since she understands the emotional aspect of it, and will feel it more than

16

anyone."

"But if she doesn't learn how to do it now, she'll get killed. She'll hesitate or run when she has to do it for real."

"And you didn't?" Cal asked. "You were fourteen when you passed your field test. That's a young age to face the possibility of taking a life, but you did it. Did it help? Did it prevent you from panicking when it was real?"

Nick swallowed hard over the grief he still harbored for the first life he had taken. The woman's face haunted Nick's dreams. Her green eyes bore guilt into him at each battle. The knowledge she had been trying to kill him did not ease his guilt, nor did the memory of the searing pain he had suffered when her pyrotechnic power had turned his arm black. At first, he had given in to his instinct to run. When he finally followed his training, he had watched the woman's life leave her body, her soul die in her eyes, and wondered if it was worse to kill than be killed.

"No," Nick admitted. "It didn't help."

"But you eventually did it because you had to. She will, too."

Nick hoped so, but he did not have time to discuss it further before a feeling of urgency pulled on the corners of his mind. His sensing power had detected danger. He glanced toward the north, then back at Cal.

"Three of them," Cal said, confirming he had sensed it, too. "They're heading in the wrong direction, but I should go to be safe. Before I do, I have one more piece of advice for you."

"What?"

"Even if she's ready to fight, she won't be able to rejoin the others until she can control her empath power. You need to make her power your focus."

"I've tried, but none of the training techniques have helped."

Cal shrugged. "Of course not. Meaghan's not a Guardian."

"What do you mean?"

"I mean exactly what I said. Think on it and the answer will come. For now, I've left some packages on the porch. Give my best to Meaghan, and if you're going to continue to train her so hard, make her eat more. The herbs your mother wants you to use are vile."

Nick nodded. "I'll remember that. Thanks."

"No problem." And with those words, Cal turned and disappeared into the forest, gone as silently as he had come. Nick followed his example, threading his way through the trees toward the cabin. At the edge of the clearing, several rows of dried corn stalks caught his attention. Meaghan had found the remains of an old garden here, left by a former resident of the cabin.

Nick had thought the plants had long since died, but over the course of several hours, she had sprouted a feast for them. Corn, tomatoes, and peppers responded to the touch of her power, as did squash and onions. The vegetables had lasted several weeks, but the dried corn leaves and stalks were all that remained now. He ran his fingers down one, mesmerized by it. She had such amazing command over her new power, so why did her older power still elude her? The Guardian techniques had never failed before.

But Meaghan was not a Guardian.

Cal's advice tumbled in Nick's head until he had polished it into understanding, then an idea followed with such certainty it tugged a smile across his lips. With renewed hope, he gathered the dried corn leaves and whatever husks lay on the ground, and then made his way back to the cabin in time to watch the Mardróch's futile hunt along the edge of the clearing.

CHAPTER THREE

HE APPEARED to her in a haze. Abbott stood on the stairs, his presence a warning to Meaghan. She had fallen asleep in the cabin and woken up in the middle of May's living room. Meaghan's eyes met his, and then trailed over the other faces in the room. Each seemed poised, locked in stone while they studied her. Miles, the Head Elder, brought comfort and vague memories of her youngest years when he had helped save her from a burning castle. The comfort faded as his gray eyes bore uncertain distrust. Beside him, Sam kept vigil, still deciding her capability as Queen. Sharp wisdom cultivated from age and experience emanated from behind his deceptively soft face. To his left, her cousin, Angus, triggered her empath power with rage and hatred. Alarm blossomed, pushing those emotions aside. He should not be here, not after his betrayal.

But then, none of this should be. Meaghan scanned the living room again. She had watched May's house disintegrate in fire. And Abbott, the Dreamer who had delivered Vivian's vision of Nick's coronation, had since been murdered.

Her gaze returned to him. Smoke curled around his body. He remained oblivious to it and to the red marks that flames cast over his skin. The house had begun to burn again.

"She was never wrong," Abbott told her, and Meaghan realized he meant Vivian. Her visions had never been wrong. "She saw the truth. Always. She shared your future with me."

His decree choked air from Meaghan's lungs. Vivian, the woman who had raised Meaghan, had predicted her death. The coronation would be for the King, not the Queen.

The fire swelled, charging past Abbott and down the stairs, but Meaghan could not feel its warmth. The ice that seemed to encase her heart spread to her skin. She shivered. Abbott began to babble, his words as incoherent as they had been when she had first met him, and the cold grew stronger.

Her shivering turned to tremors. Her knees wanted to collapse beneath her. Then sturdy arms circled her.

Something hard pressed into her back and she shifted, turning on to her side, toward the warmth emanating from the person next to her. May's living room faded. The Elders' faces dissolved and in their place, dying embers greeted her. She drew her eyes across the wood floor of the cabin to the red blanket beneath her and Nick's bodies, then to Nick's face. His features seemed blurry in the increasing darkness.

"You had a bad dream," she heard him say, though it took her a moment to comprehend his words. The air had grown cold with the dying fire. As they did every night, they slept on the floor instead of their cots, using each other's bodies to ward off winter's breath. She had succumbed to another nightmare, a twisted version of the Dreamer's prediction of her death, and she closed her eyes, chasing away the image as best she could.

Nick's arms tightened around her. He drew her close and though she wanted to remain angry at him for the way he had left earlier in the evening, she could not find the will to turn away his comfort. She pressed her face into his neck and let him lull her back into sleep.

§

IN THE morning, a fire blazed once more in the small fireplace. Meaghan turned on her side, not surprised to see Nick gone from his side of the blanket. Long sunlight streaking across the floor told her she had slept late. She reached her arms over her head, and then stretched out her legs in an attempt to ease her stiffness with no success. The cabin's floor provided little comfort. Each morning, she felt as if she had aged a hundred years overnight. The feeling would pass soon enough, once her muscles responded to her daily exercise routine.

She rose and joined Nick at the table. In front of him, he had stacked two neat piles of dried corn husks and yellow leaves. She traced a finger along the edge of a husk. It still held the chill of winter. As did Nick's face, she realized when he looked up at her. His brows cast shadows over his eyes and it seemed any comfort he had extended to her in the middle of the night had disappeared today. She leaned back to frown at him.

"You didn't wake me," she said.

"You needed sleep."

"I need to train. I've lost a good hour now. How else am I

supposed to pass the test if I waste daylight? We don't have much of it right now as it is."

"You're not going to pass it if you run yourself into the ground either," he countered and stood. She grunted in displeasure, but he chose not to respond, crossing to the fireplace instead to remove a kettle from the ashes. He filled a teacup and brought it back to the table, placing it next to a plate she had failed to notice before. He slid both in front of her. A slice of brown date cake sat in the middle of the plate, but she ignored it in favor of the tea, surprised by the citrus flavor cascading over her tongue.

"Orange," she said. "We haven't had that in weeks."

Nick shrugged. "Cal brought more supplies."

"I figured. Did you see him this time or is he still hiding from us?"

"I saw him."

She raised an eyebrow and set the cup down. "Is everything okay?"

"Everything's fine. He wanted to talk to me about a few things."

"Like?"

"Like you have to eat more."

"Oh." She pursed her lips together, and then in spite of her desire to remain surly, laughed. "I don't know if I should feel comforted or disturbed that he's watching us so closely."

"Maybe both," Nick said. "Did you eat dinner last night?"

"I didn't feel like it."

"You still need to eat," Nick told her and nodded toward the cake. "Please."

She sighed and cut off a small chunk of the cake with her fork. After slipping it into her mouth, she followed it with a sip of tea, and then went after another bite. She ate half the cake before she looked back up at him. "Better?" she asked.

"Much. Thank you."

She set her fork down, picking up her tea with both hands in exchange, and he reached for a piece of corn husk. The pale yellow reminded her of the porcelain figurines her mother had loved so much and she looked away before grief overtook her. It had been months since she had last allowed her sorrow to grip her and she could not let it take hold now. She cleared her throat, dissolving the lump that had started to form.

"What are those for?" she asked Nick, glancing back at him and the pale leaves.

"Maybe nothing," he responded. "I'm having trouble with it, so I'd rather not say until it's complete."

In other words, he would never say. She had grown tired of his secrets. Every time he spoke with his mother by commcrystal, he told her the Elders had nothing new to report, but Meaghan had her doubts. Nick slept little, if at all, in the nights that followed each conversation. And it appeared the same code of silence would be applied to his talks with Cal. Standing, she used her growing anger to sweep the last of her grief away. "I guess I'll start training while you finish your 'nothing' then."

Without waiting for a response, she removed a set of knives and her cloak from a rack by the door and left the cabin. She did not break her stride as she flipped her cloak over her shoulders and fastened it. Nor did she slow down when she cinched the belt of knives around her waist. Only when she reached the edge of the clearing did she pause a minute to take stock of her weapons, running her fingers across the sheaths to count the blades. One was missing, an oversight but not one she would allow to delay her training. Most likely the knife had needed to be sharpened and Nick had pulled it to perform the task. Three others remained secured within their holsters.

She removed one of the dark gray knives to examine it in the sunlight, admiring its quartz-like surface and almost weightless heft. The knife, much like many of the battle-worthy weapons in Ærenden, had been made of allestone, a substance that withstood strikes alongside the strongest metals. When the set was full, all four knives remained within easy reach.

She put the knife away and began jogging, heading for the training course Nick had set up when they had first arrived. Each target looked innocent enough—a well-placed score mark in one tree, a manmade hornets' nest that looked real hanging from another, the spot where two dead trees crossed—but Meaghan could find each one by memory. She sought them out and attacked like the threats they represented.

The first came sooner than it had before and she smiled, feeling exhilaration from her increased speed. Frustration from yesterday's failure had pushed her faster, and though her lungs hurt some from the extra effort, she welcomed the challenge. Eying the target—a weathered knot halfway up the trunk of a hollow tree—she reached for a knife, and launched it. She hit the target, but only barely. Her knife lodged at its edge. She hopped up onto a stump below the mark to retrieve her knife and frowned. She would need to run the course twice today to ensure she hit the target properly the second time around. Removing the knife from the bark, she sheathed it, and then pushed forward. The next target lay a half mile away.

Tightening her arms at her sides, she pushed her legs harder, ignoring the cold that brought tears to her eyes. She liked this course. She liked the freedom of the run, the instinct of the hunt, and the mindlessness of the routine. She only wished she had taken to archery the way she had to her knives. She imagined it would add to the challenge of the course. But no matter how hard she had tried, she could not seem to grip the bow properly or get the balance right. Each shot became lost to directionless aim or fell like a rock to the ground, no matter how often she trained.

Puffing out her cheeks, she blew off renewed disappointment with a breath. Although archery had eluded her, she had proved halfway decent at wielding a sword. She had even come close to defeating Nick in a few sparring matches, and his pride had told her he had not faked the near-wins.

She slipped the knife closest to her left hand from its sheath. This one held a serrated edge and stuck better than the others in her set, something she had learned long ago worked best on the next target. Flipping it so she held the blade in her hand, she took aim, and then let it fly. The blade tumbled, end over end before sinking deep into the fake hornets' nest. The nest swung in the wind for a few seconds before falling to the ground and splitting open to release her knife. She scooped up the blade, returned it to its home, and then examined the nest. In fragments, with its wire cage broken open for display, it no longer blended into the woods. She debated hiding it, but did not want to delay her training. No one else but Cal had been within miles of the cabin over the last few weeks. Even the Mardróch lurkers had disappeared with the deepening cold. She made a mental note to come back for the nest after she had completed her route, and took off running again. She detoured around a fallen tree lying across her usual path, and then doubled back toward the cabin and her third target.

The wind whipped past, swirling pebbles and leaves within small tornadoes. She shielded her face with her hand, and then lowered it when the wind settled into a breeze. The air warmed by ten degrees. She released the clasp holding her cloak across her chest and tossed the heavy wool material over her shoulders, allowing it to fly behind her like a cape. She felt liberated. She felt alive. She plucked the serrated knife from her belt again, took aim, and let it fly. It sank into the center of a large knot on a tree ten feet away. Although the tree was not part of Nick's official course, it had become her personal target. The knot bore the white scarring of her triumphs, a constant reminder of how much she had learned.

She veered off her route, toward the tree to reclaim her knife, and skidded to a stop when a mix of exhilaration and agony crested behind her, coupled with a low, raspy noise. She mistook the noise as laughter at first, but when she whipped around, she recognized it as labored breath. Her pursuer struggled to breathe, forcing rattling air into his lungs.

He froze in his steps. For a heartbeat, Meaghan wondered if Nick had laced her breakfast with another potion, but then a sudden spike of anticipation came from the man in front of her and she knew better. This attacker was real. She swallowed her fear, and drew her last two knives, holding them steady in her hands.

The man, if she could call him that, stared at her with bloodshot eyes. His dark hair lay plastered against his head with sweat. His skin, although normal in places, had turned ashen in others. When he raised his hands and blue electricity fizzled on the edge of his fingernails, her panic spiked with the realization of what he was—a creature both human and Mardróch. His nose had begun to twist and sink. He parted his mouth, revealing partial webbing at the corners, and then cast his hands toward her, howling when lightning sparked back across his palms.

Anger emanated from him, then determination. Meaghan tightened her fingers on the hilts of her knives and debated her next move. Although she suspected she could outrun him, she could not risk turning away. She needed to see if his lightning bolts started working, which left her only one option. She had to fight.

She waited a beat, stepped back, and then began circling as she kept her eyes pinned on his. He did the same, drawing a sword from a scabbard on his back and pointing it at her. A tilted smile crossed his face and then he charged, lifting the sword up and driving it down toward her head.

Crossing both of her knives, Meaghan blocked his blade. The impact shot through her forearms, resonating pain, but she gritted her teeth against it and pushed back, forcing him away. He circled his sword through the air and took another swing at her. She sidestepped him, but did not have time to avoid the blade's next strike. It met her side, slicing through her sweater and biting into skin. A cry escaped her mouth before she had time to control it. Sticky warmth rolled down her skin, soaking her clothes, but she could not allow it to distract her. Her attacker charged once more and she dropped to the ground to roll out of his way.

Jumping to her feet, she faced off with him again, maintaining the same careful steps as before. This time, she did not give him the chance to make the first move. A fast step forward, a quick flick of her wrist, and she drew blood. A long gash opened on his forearm.

He howled again, a noise similar to that of a lone pack wolf, and swung his sword toward her with his uninjured arm. She ducked, driving her other knife into his shoulder. He teetered back, yanking the hilt of her knife from her hand, and then retreated. Stopping a few yards away, he pulled the knife from his body, and tossed it behind him.

Down to one weapon, which would be useless against a heavy sword blow, she passed the knife between her hands, determining which would be the strongest. She settled on her left. Although her right was dominant, she feared the gash in her side would inhibit her movements. She lifted the knife, preparing for a kill. One perfect throw, a strike to the heart, and he would be felled. A miss and she would be defenseless.

She tensed, preparing to run if the latter happened, and then froze when a low whistle streaked past her ear. A moment later, her attacker dropped to his knees, an arrow imbedded deep in his stomach.

CHAPTER FOUR

A SECOND arrow found its way into his skull, silencing the man's terror forever. He fell backward. His eyes remained open, staring at the white feather quill between them, and Meaghan held back the sickness threatening to charge from her stomach. She tightened her grip on her knife, unsure of what she would be facing next. Certainly, someone who had just saved her life could not be dangerous, but her heart still raced, and her brain still held on to fear, so she turned in preparation for a fight. A hand clamped down on her wrist.

"Meg, it's me." Nick's voice came through before she recognized his face. She succumbed to his arms. His fear washed over hers and she realized he had used his power to block hers during the attack.

He tightened his hold on her, drawing her closer, and then froze when she whimpered. Stepping back, he lifted his left hand. His fingers and part of his sleeve dripped with blood. His gaze snapped back to hers. "You're hurt," he said.

"It's okay," she told him, though she could not seem to stop shaking. She wanted to crawl into bed, to hide from the world in the cabin, but another instinct overrode the desire. "There are others around," she told him. "I can smell them, but I can't tell how many there are. Can you?"

Nick nodded, but said nothing about it. Instead, he pushed up the hem of her sweater and frowned. A jagged gash ran from the bottom of her rib cage to her hip.

"Nick," she begged. "Tell me how many."

"Two," he said. "They aren't close. We have time to get back to the cabin."

"We need to hide the body."

"There's no time. I'll come back after—"

"No," she interrupted, grabbing his arm. She could not stand the thought of the Mardróch finding the dead man, and in turn, stalking the cabin until she or Nick gave its location away. She could not stand the thought of wondering if another creature might be around each time she ran this route. "It has to be now. There's a tree with a hollow trunk not far from here. That way," she pointed into the woods. "It should be big enough."

The wind swelled, whipping through the forest at a speed that only added to her fright. She stared through the boney arms of a bare tree into a darkening sky. Angry clouds gathered in warning of a fast approaching storm.

Nick drew her cloak around her shoulders, securing it before he pressed his lips to her forehead. "I'll hide him," he promised. "Go back to the cabin and make jicab tea. I'll be right there."

She nodded. When she had almost reached the clearing surrounding the cabin, she remembered the hornets' nest. Although it would not be as obvious as a dead body, she had no doubt anyone hunting for her or Nick would not miss the clue. She detoured toward it. Now that her fear had started to ease, her side ached. Her muscles stiffened, and her feet moved like heavy rocks. When she reached the nest, she leaned down to pick it up and regretted the movement. Pain shot across her rib cage, driving her to her knees.

For a moment, she could not breathe or think. She forced her mind back to her task, grabbing the nest before struggling to her feet. The forest sounded distant, as if the thick clouds above had filled her ears. She shook her head to clear the sensation. The world spun, and she gripped the low limb of a tree to keep from fainting. She concentrated on the distant clearing until the feeling passed, and then began walking again. She struggled to place one foot in front of the other. When snowflakes fell, small and infrequent at first, she barely noticed them. Only when they cascaded as thick flakes, melting against her cheeks and gathering on her wool cloak, did she realize the storm would not pass in an afternoon.

She exited the woods into the clearing and the protection of the invisible barrier, but she did not feel safe. She had to reach the cabin. Grass passed beneath her, at first brown and then white as ice took hold. She planted her boots with careful steps until she had reached the door to the cabin. The knob refused to budge. She removed her gloves and grabbed hold with both hands. Metal froze to her skin. Her arms shook with the effort. But this time, she managed to force the door open. Relieved, she slipped inside and shut the world out behind her.

Her cot commanded her attention. She took a step toward it, and then paused. Somewhere in the cloud expanding through her brain, she heard Nick's voice. He had told her to do something once she arrived, but she could not remember what. Her mind refused to focus on anything but sleep and the warmth of her blankets. She went to them, lay down, and slipped into darkness.

§

THOUGH NICK had sewn a wound more times than he cared to count, he had never had to do it under these conditions. He needed sutures and potions. He had a needle and fishing line, plus a small bowl of alcohol to sanitize them. He scanned the items beside Meaghan's cot, then took a deep breath and forced it out to ease his frustration.

Wind howled, whistling through the cracks in the door and creaking the roof in its best effort to get inside. Nick turned a wary eye to the closest window and frowned at the wall of white greeting him. It would be at least a day before the storm let up, and longer before the snow melted enough to allow travel to Neiszhe's village. Until then, he had no other choice. He had to stop the bleeding.

A log popped in the fireplace, and Nick turned his attention back to Meaghan's wound. Red stained the white bandage he had applied after he returned to the cabin, but it had not soaked through. That eased his mind some, though her pale skin and slow pulse did not. He could not delay any longer. Taking a deep breath, he threaded the fishing line through the needle, and started working.

Her blood flowed freely once he removed the bandage and he ignored it as best he could, piercing her skin with steady hands that belied his nerves. The tip of the needle met only the slightest resistance before slicing smoothly through with a flash of silver. Nick quelled his stomach, then turned the needle back around for another puncture. It seemed unnatural to knit skin as he would a tattered piece of cloth, and despite years of performing the task, he had never grown used to it.

He focused on pulling the edges of Meaghan's wound tight and closing it with slow and steady hands. As he had expected, he did not get far before her muscles tightened. A fraction of a second later, she gasped. He dropped his arm over her chest, pinning her to the bed before she could jerk upright. Her eyes opened wide, her pain and fear strong enough to trigger his sensing power. He waited for her to look at him before he spoke.

"You're still losing blood," he said, his tone calm and emotionless. Though he wanted to comfort her, he needed her to obey him first. "I have to finish or you won't live. Do you understand?"

Her breathing hitched, ragged underneath his arm. She curled her fingers into the blanket, gripping it until her knuckles turned white, but he kept his eyes pinned on hers, waited for her to nod, and then continued speaking in the same even tone. "I can give you some jicab root to chew, if you want."

She shook her head. Her struggling stopped, and he loosened his grip. "If you don't take the root," he told her, "no matter how much this hurts, you have to stay still. Are you sure you can do that?"

Her eyes slipped closed. For a moment, he thought she had passed out again, but then she forced a whisper past her lips. "Finish it," she said. Tears escaped the corners of her eyes, coursing silent trails down the sides of her face, and he refocused his attention on her wound. She tensed with each puncture, with each pull and knitting of skin. Her hands tightened on the blanket, but otherwise, she remained motionless. He worked as fast as he could and when he finished, he left her to pour a cup of tea. Returning to her side, he slid a hand down her face, soothing the tears away, and waited for her to open her eyes again. Pain and confusion clouded them when she looked up at him and he realized it would be some time before he could consider her fight with death won.

"I have jicab tea for you," he said. She nodded and struggled to sit up, but hissed with pain from the effort. He eased an arm under her shoulders, lifting her so he could slide pillows behind her back. Even the small amount of pressure had her wincing. "Drink, Meg. You'll feel better after you do."

She followed his instruction and then managed a feeble smile. "I guess I shouldn't have asked you to hide the body," she whispered.

He returned the smile. The tea had dulled her pain enough so he could no longer sense it. "I would have preferred not to, but you were right. The Mardróch arrived soon after I finished. They missed me, but there's no way they would have missed a dead man."

"Mardróch," she whispered, closing her eyes. "I got the nest. I was afraid they'd find it."

"I saw it on the table."

"What was that thing?" she asked. Her words had started to run together, and it took him a moment to realize she meant her attacker. "Who," she corrected. "Who was he? He seemed familiar."

"Did he?" When she did not respond, he moved his hand to the

35

top of her head. Her breathing slowed in sleep, so he leaned down to kiss her on the forehead and then eased her shoulders up again, removing the extra pillows before he lay her back down.

He recovered the half-finished corn husk project from the floor where he had dropped it when he had sensed her danger and began working on it again. Though he had no doubt she would be lost to sleep until tomorrow, he felt just as certain rest would not find him for quite some time.

CHAPTER FIVE

NICK FINISHED his project before lunchtime. After cleaning up the mess he had created, he decided to make a soup, hoping he could tempt Meaghan into eating when she woke. He found a stockpot and rooted through the shelves for anything useful. Their supplies consisted mostly of nuts, dried beans, and a mix of root vegetables. Cal delivered meat on occasion, usually venison jerky or salted fish, but they had not been so lucky this time. When Nick had unpacked the supplies, he had found only a large bag of silten. The silver grain had the texture of sand, and lacked flavor, but it had almost as much protein as meat. It would sustain them well enough.

Unfortunately, it would not work in soup. It turned to mush when it sat too long in water. He doubted Meaghan would mind, though. She could barely choke down the grain when she felt well. If he wanted her to eat more while she healed, he would need to go hunting when the storm cleared. A day's outing should at least produce something more palatable he could roast.

For now, he would have to do the best he could with what they had on hand. Dried herbs and a few cubes of powdered chicken stock would make a good broth. Carrots and potatoes would round out the flavor and fresh-melted snow would give them plenty of water. He picked up two metal buckets and stepped onto the porch. Snow continued to fall, draping a blinding curtain across the air and coating the ground with at least a half foot of snow. He filled the buckets with the soft powder and brought them back inside, setting them by the fireplace.

While they melted, he chopped the vegetables and added them to the pot. A cup of beans joined the mix before he brought the pot to the fireplace, added the water, and hung it over the fire to cook. Once it began simmering, he moved to Meaghan's side to check on her. A hand to the forehead told him she had not developed a fever. He hoped that meant he had cleaned her wound well enough, and the alcohol had disinfected his makeshift medical tools properly, but it was too soon to tell. Infection in these situations posed as much danger as the wound.

He frowned at the rough tear the sword had made in her sweater, and at the blood crusted over a section of blue yarn, turning it brown. Next time she woke, he would need to change her. He replaced her bandage with a fresh one, pleased to see the sutures still held, and then searched the cabin for something to occupy his time.

The evidence of their activities over the past few months overwhelmed him. Weapons hung from the walls. Supplies filled the shelves. The backpack that had travelled with them from Earth remained packed in one corner of the room, ready for another journey. Fishing poles and traps took up another corner. Their lives focused on training and survival, not entertainment. For the first time since he had returned to Ærenden, Nick wished for a television set.

He picked up the backpack and opened it to see what they had left. A small amount of jicab remained in the outside pocket. The last time he could recall using it had been to speed up Dell's death. It still hurt to think of the man. That day had not been the first time Nick had met the Mayor. Two years before, he had accompanied his mother to Dell's small village at the end of the ravine. Dell had been so grateful for a Healer's help in dealing with an outbreak of Green Spot Fever that he had insisted May and Nick stay in his house instead of the village's guest cottage. Over the course of the week, Nick came to understand why Dell had earned the title of Mayor, a position only granted to those who performed extraordinary duties.

Dell's power to transfer perspectives from one person to another helped him bring peace to warring villages by forcing the villagers to acknowledge each other's emotions and experiences. Dell's last village had been one of the worst in the kingdom, but within a year of his arrival, the villagers had grown from openly fighting in the streets to working alongside each other to rebuild the damage they had caused. The Town Hall, half-burned to the ground when Nick visited, had been one of the final reminders of the village's old troubles. Fortunately, Dell's legacy had continued after his death. The villagers had survived, defeating Garon's soldiers a day after Nick and Meaghan had passed through.

Nick put the jicab away, and then opened the main compartment of the backpack to see what else he could find. An emergency kit seemed mostly spent. The velvet pouch that had once held Adelina's amulet lay next to the plastic kit. He picked it up and rubbed the soft material between his fingers. Meaghan wore her mother's amulet around her neck now, as her mother once had. It seemed the safest place for the necklace now that it contained the Reaper Stone.

He frowned. They still knew too little about the stone. The Elders had warned Nick through a recent commcrystal communication that the stone would grow heavy with use and drain energy from its bearer until a spell relieved the stone of the powers it harvested. The spell had long ago been lost, and they all feared using the stone would put Meaghan in danger.

Nick tucked the pouch away, ran his finger over the red wool blanket he had taken from the barn their last night on Earth, then bumped his hand against something hard. He dug below the blanket to find the book his mother had given to Meaghan. No more than a small journal of fifty or so parchment pages secured by a dark brown leather cover, it did not look like much, but it contained some of the strongest magic in the kingdom. It bore the words of a Writer and as such, it held the power to transport a reader to the place and time it described.

He brought it with him to Meaghan's cot, and then sat on the floor in front of her to read the story. Although he had heard tales of Meaghan's parents before, he had never experienced them in the same way the Writer's book allowed. He smelled the dank earth floors and felt the rough stone walls in the dungeon where they had met and fought for the first time under the watchful guard of Nick's mother. He saw their surprise and horror when a prophesied wedding united them in the same way it had him and Meaghan. And he understood their hope in what the wedding might bring. Once the story ended, he flipped through the remaining pages. Each one had turned yellow with age and each stared blankly back at him. He set the book aside before standing to check on the soup.

When he lifted the lid on the pot, a rush of steam escaped, carrying with it the tantalizing scent of herbs. He leaned into the steam, inhaled deeply, and then stuck the vegetables with a fork. They still felt too firm, so he reseated the lid and returned to the floor.

Picking up the book again, he cascaded the pages under his thumb so the words blurred beneath his eyes as he thought. Ed had been a lot different than Nick had expected. Nick's mother had shared stories of the King's card games or the times he had disappeared into the woods, but Nick had never known much about Ed's life before he had become King. He had been devoted to his former tribe. Nick wondered if they had survived.

Ed's people had faded into the past for most of the kingdom, but for Meaghan, they represented another level of grief, the last of her family lost to Garon's rebellion. All lost except for Angus. Adelina's undeserving cousin had survived the raid on the castle only because he had been visiting a village on the other side of the kingdom at the time.

Nick chased the unpleasant thought away by rereading his mother's experience with her first charge. She had never told him this story. He had no doubt she preferred to think of Adelina as the close friend she had become over the years, instead of the woman who had loathed her new Guardian. And Adelina had been more stubborn and headstrong than his mother had admitted. Much like Meaghan. Nick turned to look at her.

Meaghan resembled Adelina in many ways. Her dark brown hair flowed like silk to her shoulders, appearing almost black in certain lights, the same as her mother's. Their copper eyes appeared identical. Even the height and shape of Meaghan's lean body mimicked Adelina's. Her skin differed, of course. Meaghan's olive tone blended the heritage of both parents, and parts of her looked distinctly like her father. The proud set of her jaw, the prominence of her high cheekbones, and her endearing smile reflected the former King.

Nick turned to the first blank page in the book and ran his fingers over it. Nothing about these pages made sense to him, but the reason for including them had been lost to history, along with the identity of the Writer. It did him no good to dwell on it. He started to close the book, and then paused when gray splashed across the page. At first, he dismissed it as a trick of light, but when he opened the book wide again, the gray darkened into black. Letters formed into lines and at the top of the page, a single title appeared, *Chapter Two*.

As soon as his eyes fell on the words, they transported him out of the cabin and into a forest. He caught his breath when Ed's horse brushed his arm as the King rode past.

CHAPTER SIX

ED KICKED his heels into his horse's sides, forcing the animal to go faster. They fled through the forest, spraying dirt and moss from the soft floor in a trail of anger and aggression, the perfect match for Ed's mood. He forced out a breath. His horse did the same. They both sailed over the hollow remains of an oak tree in the middle of the path. Then, after landing with a heavy thud on the other side, they continued their flight. Since he had discovered the news early this afternoon, he had ridden, chasing escape deep into the forest, blind to tree limbs, bushes, and obstacles. He did not care where he went, only that he continued to move. Fast. He needed speed. His heart catapulted in response. His blood rushed in exhilaration. But his head refused to clear, despite the miles separating him from the castle.

Why should it? In the months since they had wed, Adelina had riled his anger more days than not. She had pushed his frustration to the edge of explosion. She tested even the will of his control—a feat few others had accomplished.

Of course, few had made him feel so useless. While she insisted he live the role of King, she refused to allow him to do anything of importance. She refused to share updates. She made decisions without consulting him, even when he had insightful knowledge or input on the matter, and she discarded any attempts he made at trying to perform his full duties. She only seemed to want him for two things. She wanted him to attend dinners and parties, to mingle with the people and entertain their curiosity about the barbaric man from the north. And despite how little she seemed to think of him, she wanted him to give her an heir.

It infuriated him. He could offer so much more than a face to please the masses and a body to fill her bed. It had taken some time for him to adjust to the thought of being King, but now he wanted the chance to prove his worth. He had ideas to better the kingdom— architecture for the villages and spells for protection he thought might work better than their current practices. And he had solutions for problems she had yet to encounter, tactics for dealing with people she had yet to master. But she never gave him the chance.

As for fulfilling his duties as her husband, the matter proved to be more confusing. Despite her aggravating treatment of him, he had fallen in love with her. Her skill as Queen mesmerized him. Her strength, courage, and wisdom far surpassed any story he had heard of her. And her kindness toward her people, the passion she felt for them, overwhelmed him.

At least, the passion she felt for all of her people but those in Ed's tribe.

His feelings for her had waned with the news he had received today, but until he received confirmation from her lips, he refused to abolish them entirely.

The same love tying him to his doubts kept him from bedding her—that, and the prophecy by which they had wed. He wanted her, but their wedding bothered him. Ed had spent many hours and days analyzing the purpose for it. In the end, he could only see one possibility for why a man of no stature would be bound to a woman of the royal line. He needed to create a child with the Queen. Another man could easily be King, but Ed's lineage, combined with the Queen's, would create a unique blend that could not exist if natural attraction had been allowed to take its course. As a nomad, the thought of tying his heart to a woman with roots would never have crossed his mind. But now that magic had altered the course of his life, the thought consumed him.

Given the speed at which their wedding had taken place, he doubted it would be long before they fulfilled the prophecy's purpose. As much as he wanted Adelina, he needed to ensure they created a child out of love. It mattered to him, so he waited. He rebuked her advances in the hope she would someday love him in the way he loved her.

He sighed and reined his horse to a stop as a light materialized on the path in front of him. The light solidified into a figure. Ed's muscles tightened in dread, and then relaxed when a different face than he had expected frowned at him. He grinned in response.

"You were supposed to be at dinner with the Elders half an hour ago," the man said.

"I'll go if you want," Ed responded. "But more likely than not I'll strangle Adelina before dinner's through. I'd rather not end up back in the dungeon."

"Like you wouldn't escape the moment the guards turned their backs," the man said, and Ed heard the hint of laughter in his statement. "But you and I both know you wouldn't kill her with witnesses around."

Ed chuckled. "You know me too well, my friend. Why did they send you instead of Malven?"

This time the man outright laughed. "Because he'd kill you as fast as you'd kill Adelina. That's three times this week you've slipped his guard. You make him look like an idiot."

Ed shrugged. "He doesn't need my help with that. Besides, he can come with me any time he wants. He only has to keep up."

"You know no one can ride a horse as fast as you."

"That's not my problem," Ed responded before he dismounted. He stretched a hand out and the man clasped it, his smile welcoming Ed from a week's worth of beard growth. "It's good to see you again, Cal. The beard's new."

"It is." Cal ran a hand over his chin, disturbing the rough bristles. "We were ambushed and I'm afraid the battle didn't leave much time to shave. I may keep it. Even if my wife isn't so sure of it yet."

"I'm beginning to think it's best to ignore women. They're about as useful as a dranx on a bird watching trip."

"Do I really want to know what happened between you and Adelina?"

"Not really," Ed answered. "This way when they call you to testify, you don't have to fake innocence."

Cal raised an eyebrow, and reached out to stroke the horse's mane. "Alisen wasn't so easy on me in the beginning either. I lost my heart to her the first moment I saw her, but she made me work to earn her love. She was worth it." Moving his hand to the horse's muzzle, he patted it twice before turning back to Ed. "Adelina will be too. She's just a little guarded."

"Guarded isn't the word I'd use to describe her," Ed muttered. Tightening his hand on the horse's reins, he started walking. Cal flanked him. "Shall I assume your homecoming means the band of outsiders has been defeated?"

Cal shook his head. "Not yet. I brought Adelina the update, but I'm scheduled to return to the border tomorrow night."

"What update did you bring?"

Cal clasped his hands behind his back and remained silent. Ed understood the action and his anger grew deeper. "She told you not to tell me," he guessed.

"Ordered me," Cal corrected. "*Told* me has some leeway to it. Ordered means I'll be stationed in Zeiihbu for six month stints if I disobey. I like you, but I like seeing my wife more."

"Traitor."

Cal's smile held no remorse. "Are we going to keep walking or shall I teleport you back? You're a good twenty miles from the castle at the moment. As much as I'd like to give you the time to calm down, I suspect it won't help."

"You're right. It won't," Ed said and halted the horse with a slight tug. "I don't want you to get in trouble, but please tell me if they're okay. She can't object to that."

"Who?"

"My people," Ed responded. He turned his focus from Cal to the north, and to the mountains of home. "The Famine Curse killed nearly half our population. I know she called on them to fight. She'll wipe us out if she's not careful."

"How did you—?"

"Please," Ed interrupted, bringing his gaze back to Cal. "Tell me."

"They're," Cal hesitated, then gave in. "Fine. They've suffered no casualties."

Relief lifted a weight from Ed's chest he had not known existed. He inhaled a deep breath and held it, savoring the fresh air before letting it go. It only took a moment for determination to displace his relief. "They shouldn't be fighting," he said. "I'll put a stop to it before their fate changes."

"You need to have this conversation with Adelina," Cal said. His words carried no hint of reprimand, but rather, a warning, and Ed understood Cal would not follow the conversation any further. Cal turned to the horse and laid a hand on its neck. "We should head back to the castle before it gets too late. I suspect the Elders are already gone."

"My first good news of the day."

A grin returned to Cal's face. "I don't think they're your fans, either. They asked the Spellmaster to work on a spell to block your power in case they have to throw you back in the dungeon."

"I'll keep that in mind. Although I had a contingency plan in place the first time I wound up in the dungeon, just in case they already had such a spell."

"That doesn't surprise me. What was it?"

Ed narrowed his eyes at the Guardian. "Do you think I'd tell you? You work for the Elders."

Cal roared with laughter. The horse spooked and started to rear before Ed regained control of the reins.

"I live to upset them," Cal told him. "So what was it? Do you know a secret passageway or something?"

"I wish. That would have been much simpler than fighting my way out, but a lot less fun." He mounted his horse again, and then looked down at Cal. "You do know that I intend to ride the horse back, don't you?"

"Of course," Cal said. "What were you planning on fighting with? Or better yet, how were you planning on getting out of the cell without your power?"

"With a key. I stole one, and a knife, when I took my instrument back. I hid them inside the wall of my cell. They would've been easier to retrieve with my power, but I made sure I could still get them without it."

"Clever," Cal said. "I'll tell the Queen you'll be back in an hour. Don't make me hunt you down or I won't be happy."

"You won't have to," Ed promised. "If you ever wind up in the cell, the spot on the wall is marked with my initials."

"I won't discount the possibility." Cal chuckled, then teleported away.

Ed pointed his mare toward the castle and spurred her into a run, soon disappearing into the dark forest.

§

ED FOUND it hard to hold on to his anger while he watched Adelina. A fire glowed warm in the fireplace, turning her cheeks a pale shade of pink. Flames reflected in her eyes, bringing the copper in them to life so that it danced in response to the flickering light. She sat on the couch in front of the fireplace, her feet curled up beneath her, a cup of tea clutched between her hands. Yet the beauty of the scene had not muted his emotions as much as the weariness that lined her face and weighed down her shoulders. He rarely saw her vulnerable and it stalled the verbal attack he had intended to launch.

He entered their living quarters through the open patio doors. She had not heard his approach, and had not realized he stood in the room with her. For a moment, he watched her. For a moment, he wondered why he needed to battle with her tonight. Then she turned her head, noticed him, and the anger in her eyes refueled his own. She set her cup down on the coffee table. Her shoulders squared, and she made the first attack.

"What did you think you were doing?" Though her voice remained low, the harsh tone in it made the depth of her anger known. She stood. The stiffness of her spine matched the stiffness on her face. "The Elders—"

"I don't give a damn about the Elders."

"You should." She crossed her arms over her chest and glared at him. "Keeping peace in Ærenden depends on a symbiotic relationship with them. They represent and rule the Guardians, nearly a quarter of the population. What do you think would happen to our roles as leaders if they decided we didn't have the people's best interests in mind?"

He scoffed. "It's your role, not mine."

She uncrossed her arms to plant her hands on her hips. "It took me a month to convince them to hold your coronation, and even though they did, they still consider you on probation. They're just waiting for you to screw up so they can dethrone you. Are you trying to give them an excuse?"

The thought had never occurred to him. He frowned, wondering if losing his position would be such a bad thing. He wondered, too, if Adelina might be happier if her husband returned to his old life on the other side of the kingdom. Rather than offer the option, he thought it wiser to say nothing.

"You're impossible," she muttered. "How am I supposed to trust you to do anything if you skip out on the simplest things? Why don't you ever do as you're told?"

"I'm not a puppet," he snapped. Her face flushed increased anger, and he narrowed his eyes, casting the words he knew would add fuel to her fire. "My *Queen*."

"I hate that," she hissed. Her hands shook at her sides and she tightened them into fists. "You're not one of my subjects. We're—"

"Equals?" he finished her sentence. They had fought this argument before. "Hardly. You hide me in a corner until you think I might be useful, and then you parade me in front of your subjects like some freak of nature. I'm not a toy, Adelina. I have more to offer than banal conversation at dinners."

Adelina threw her hands up, and turned from him. He circled her so she faced him again. "If we're truly equals, then why do you keep things from me? Why do you send my people to slaughter without the courtesy of at least telling me you intend to destroy my kind?"

"Slaughter?" she echoed. Her eyes widened. "Where did you get—"

He grabbed her arms, silencing her. "You thought I wouldn't find out? That I wouldn't know about your betrayal?" The last word tasted bitter to him, laced with the hate surging within him. She had not needed to confirm anything. Guilt lined her face. "How could you? These people are my tribe, my kinsmen. When you wipe them out, you wipe out my culture. You wipe out my history."

"I wouldn't do that," she protested.

He dropped his hands and looked away from her, focusing on the open patio door and the direction of home.

"I couldn't." Desperation filled her voice. She gripped his arm. "Ed, you have to believe me."

"No, I don't." He glanced back at her, not bothering to mask the anger in his scorching glare and she dropped her hand. "A letter came for me today from my cousin. He told me how happy he is that he fights for me, that the tribe has joined the army for me. How could you send them to battle using my name? How could you let them think I'd sacrifice them?"

Adelina shook her head. "I didn't."

"You didn't what?"

"I didn't tell him it was your idea," she whispered. "He must have assumed that."

For a brief second, he debated if he could throttle her and escape without being caught, but he banished the thought. It had never been in his nature to murder, and he would not give in to that urge now. He would not let her change him. Crossing the room, he entered his bedroom. He could hear her footsteps behind him, but ignored them in favor of focusing on an old duffel bag. He began filling it with clothes.

"What are you doing?" she asked.

"I won't allow you to kill my people," he responded. "I'm taking them from your kingdom. We can survive in the Barren Lands."

"No one can live in the Barren."

He did not respond and she pressed her fingers to her temples, a telltale stress reaction. He had seen it many times before, though she would never use it around anyone but him. Usually he allowed it to calm their fights, but this time he refused to care. Grabbing a cloak from a hanger, he added it to the top of the bag. He travelled light. A single outfit, besides the one he wore, would suffice. Now he just needed supplies. He opened a drawer to remove a small medical kit, grateful Adelina's Guardian had insisted each room have one, and tossed it on top of the cloak. Then he closed the bag and hitched it over his shoulder.

"Ed, please," Adelina said, placing her hand on his wrist. He shook off her touch and stepped around her, but froze at her next words.

"I'm sorry."

He turned around to stare at her. He may not have known her long, but he knew her well enough to realize that no matter how desperate she became, or how wrong she was, she rarely apologized. She loathed showing the weakness.

"Let me explain."

He eased his bag to the floor at his feet. "Fine, but be wise about what you say."

"I should have told you. I just," she hesitated and sank down onto the bed, "I just didn't want you to worry."

"I'm not a child, Adelina. I can handle being worried."

She nodded. "I know."

"Then why did you keep this from me? And why did you drag my people into your fight?"

"I didn't." She drew her hands to her temples again. "Your cousin sent me a letter. Since the outlaws first appeared, they've driven your tribe away from two settlements. Your people were already fighting them."

"Outlaws?"

"A soldier in the army recognized one of them. The men are criminals, banned from the kingdom as part of their punishment. No one expected them to survive, but they did. They've made their way back across the borders."

Ed frowned and sat down next to her on the bed. "How long have you known about this?"

"Which part? Your tribe or the outlaws?"

"Both."

"I just found out about the outlaws today. I received the letter from your cousin a month ago."

"A month ago," he echoed, and cursed. "I had a right to know about this the minute you got that letter."

"I know," she repeated, but kept her gaze pinned to her lap. "He wanted to help, and frankly, I wasn't in a position to turn him down. In the beginning, there were only about forty outlaws. I thought rounding them up would be easy, but we couldn't catch them. The few times we found them, they overpowered our soldiers or escaped without leaving a trace. At first we thought they had figured out a way to revive their powers, allowing them to teleport. Then I realized their tactics were similar to those of the Zeiihbu armies."

"The wilderness gives them power in a way," Ed said. "It's not difficult to avoid someone or fight a person who doesn't know the territory. And for those of us who live within the forests and mountains, the wilderness is as easy to navigate as your village streets." He raised a finger to her chin, guiding her to look at him. "That's why you enlisted my people in the army. I understand the strategy, but it wasn't the right thing to do."

"I didn't enlist them," Adelina insisted. "At least, not in the way you think. Half my army is there to protect them."

"My cousin would never agree to that. The tribe wouldn't either. They can protect themselves."

"I have no doubt they can, but I didn't want them to die trying. I asked them to serve as scouts."

"Scouts?"

"Yes. Because they know the wilderness so well, they're able to find the outlaws without being seen. Once they do, they report locations back to the army." She paused, and he realized she waited for a reaction. He nodded for her to continue. "I told them everyone starts in the army as scouts. They seemed to accept that reason."

Ed studied her for a moment, noted the sincerity in her face, and the anger and anxiety that had clutched him all afternoon dissolved. In its place, respect grew. Removing one of her hands from her lap, he brought it to his lips. "Thank you," he said.

The corners of Adelina's lips turned up. "You'll stay then?"

"As soon as I've helped capture the rest of the outlaws, I'll return. My tribe won't tolerate having the army around much longer." Releasing his hold on her, Ed stood. "What's the protocol for commanding my Guardian to the border?"

Adelina's smile fell. "You can't be serious. You can't go to the border. You have duties here."

"Parties and dinners?" he asked and frowned. "Those are hardly duties, Adelina. I have a responsibility to my people and I intend to honor it. Even if it means the Elders strip me of my title."

Adelina's eyes widened. Her mouth tightened into a hard line, and he tensed for a fight, but it never came. Instead, she nodded one last time, and left the room.

CHAPTER SEVEN

"**THIS NEEDS** some of your spirit," Ed muttered.

Cal chuckled and lifted a tin cup to his lips, taking a hearty gulp. Ed's sips held less zeal. The camp cook had called it coffee, but Ed had his doubts. He grimaced when thick sludge hit his tongue. Oil might have tasted better. Or mud.

"I don't see why you're in such a good mood," Ed continued. "There's nothing around here but wilderness."

Cal refilled his cup and set the kettle beside the fire. A steady drizzle had not seemed to dampen the flames or the man's mood, but it had done nothing but sour Ed's. He peered through the hazy rain drops at the endless rows of muted brown and green trees and frowned. He wanted to be anywhere but here. He wanted to be home with Adelina. The realization both surprised him and darkened his sense of unease.

"I thought you grew up here," Cal responded.

"In the mountains," Ed said. "It's a lot nicer up there. The terrain varies. There are lakes, other people."

"Other people?" Cal asked and raised a knowing eyebrow. "Or are you thinking of one person in particular who, incidentally, isn't in the mountains."

Ed grunted, and set his cup aside. "I'm just tired of seeing your ugly mug."

Cal only chuckled again in response. Ed sighed and drew his eyes back to the forest. Time had not quite switched from morning to afternoon, yet semi-darkness filled the sky and blanketed the ground with thick clouds. Soldiers held posts along the edge of the thicket, each man tense in anticipation and vigilance.

"Have you heard from your cousin?" Cal asked, keeping his tone light, though he set his cup aside. A shadow had darkened the blackness of the woods to their right.

Ed stood and stretched, feigning the movement to better view the woods. "I sent the tribe home."

A lie, they both knew. Ed's cousin and a few of the tribe's best men hid in the trees, waiting. Two more shadows joined the first. Cal leaned back in his seat, his action casual, though it put his sword within reach of his hand. The Guardian's eyes trailed to the mid-line of a close pine and he nodded.

Four men dropped from the trees and an instant later, the same number of synchronized arrows flew in the direction of the shadows. Ed's tribesmen were fast, but the enemy appeared to be faster. Only one arrow found its mark. A guttural scream pierced the foliage. Then the other shadows streaked into the forest.

Ed did not hesitate. Grabbing his sword from the ground, he charged after them.

"Ed!" Cal's command roared through the air and he ignored it. He had promised he would not fight this time, but it had been a promise he had never intended to keep. He would not allow anyone else to fight his battles for him.

He crossed the tree line and darkness enveloped him, cutting his visibility down to an arm's length. Cal's panting came from behind, though far enough away for Ed to know he outpaced the Guardian. His eyes adjusted and shadows gave way to details. Pines flanked him. Bushes and scrub brush blocked most paths. And two men practically flew in front of him, their speed almost unnatural.

Ed pushed his muscles harder. He could not let them escape. He had missed them on their last attack, and he refused to make that mistake twice. The trail up ahead forked and one of the men banked to the left. Ed did not bother to pursue him. A tribesman sat in wait from a tree along the enemy's path. The man took no more than a dozen steps before he fell to the ground, an arrow protruding from his back.

Ed jumped over a bush and veered to the right, pushing through thick underbrush after the second man. Branches scratched his arms and tore at his face, but his focus held strong on the last traitor. Ed knew these woods. He had explored them over the past few weeks, learning their secrets and shortcuts, and he had seen his chance.

He pushed his way onto an overgrown path, cut through a blanket of vines with his sword, and then broke through the trees into a small clearing. The last man exited the forest into the same clearing only a few steps ahead of Ed.

Adrenaline pushed Ed's speed faster and with a calculated strike, he caught the enemy. The sickening crunch of bones breaking, the warm spurt of blood, and the hollow cry that followed told Ed his blow had been fatal. The man crumpled to the ground and Ed skidded to a stop beside him.

Sunlight had broken through the clouds, highlighting the ashen face of his enemy, though he barely had time to process the scene before a primal howl echoed through the trees. Instinct tightened Ed's hands on the hilt of his sword. He raised it and turned, ready to fend off an animal, but the reaction came too late as agonizing pain seared through his shoulder. He barely saw the wood handle of a spear and the gray face of his attacker before he collapsed to the ground.

§

"PUT HIM on the bed."

May's voice broke through Ed's unconsciousness and he pried open his eyes to find the redheaded Guardian staring at him from across Adelina's bedroom. Hard muscle pressed against his side and he looked up at Cal's stern face.

"Welcome back," the Guardian said with no hint of happiness. "You're an idiot."

Ed opened his mouth to object, but cried out instead when Cal dropped him on Adelina's bed with no hint of even attempting delicacy. Pain streaked through his body and Ed sought the source of it, remembering what had happened as soon as he saw the wood spear protruding from his shoulder. It rose only a foot into the air, rather than several feet as it had before.

"What the hell happened?" May continued and Ed focused on her again. "He's in bad shape."

"He only has himself to blame," Cal muttered. "He chased after the outlaws and ran right into a trap. He'd be dead if I hadn't caught up with him."

"You should've moved faster," Ed complained. "As my Guardian—"

"*Acting* Guardian," Cal snapped. "If I was your real Guardian, I would've been able to sense you instead of wasting time tracking you through the woods."

"What are you talking about?" Adelina's voice came from the doorway and Ed's gaze shot toward her. She looked pale. Her hand shook as she placed it against the jamb. "Where's Malven?"

"He's—"

"Now's not the time," May interrupted. "Adelina, we need your help. Stand beside Ed."

Adelina nodded and moved across the room. Ed tried to focus on her, but failed when May pulled him forward to look at his back. His world spun. He thought he might throw up from the agony of the movement, then May eased him back again and his stomach settled.

"The spear didn't pierce all the way through," May said. "We need to pull it out, but that will cause more bleeding. He'll need accelerated healing."

"Is it really that bad?" Cal asked.

May nodded, flicking somber eyes toward Ed, and panic welled within him.

"What's...?" he started to ask, but lost his words when May's fingers prodded the edge of his wound. His stomach surged once more and he clamped his mouth shut to avoid the full reaction.

May studied his face for a moment, and then frowned, turning her focus back to Cal. "He should be in more pain," she said. "Did you give him jicab root to chew?"

Cal coughed. "Of course not. It's illegal."

"The truth, Cal."

"Yeah, maybe," he admitted. "He was screaming. I couldn't stand to see him like that."

"Good. It will help with this. He handles the root better than most."

Cal shrugged. "He's used to drinking."

May shot a glare in Cal's direction, but the small smile cresting her lips belied the reprimand. "Adelina," she said, turning serious again. "Please help me brace Ed while Cal removes the spear."

Although Adelina's hands still shook, she held them firm against Ed's chest and uninjured shoulder. May placed a hand on his other shoulder, to one side of the spear, and then used her free arm to pin him down at the waist. When she nodded to Cal, the Guardian wrapped his large hands around the spear's wood shaft and Ed could no longer control his panic. It boiled within him, filling every fiber of his body so his breathing came rapidly and his muscles turned to stone. He closed his eyes, preparing for intense pain, and then opened them when none came. To his surprise, everyone stared at him.

"Are you okay?" May asked him. "You're shaking."

His gaze met hers. He wanted to tell her to continue, but could not find the courage. He barely found the strength to bring air into his lungs.

"Ed," Adelina whispered. "Talk to me."

He forced a long breath and held it. He had faced death many times in his life, and pain more times than he could count. Yet he had never been so terrified. Adelina slipped a hand into his, and he clung to it.

"Just tell me what's happening," he finally said. "I need to know."

"Everything will be okay," May responded and the kindness in her voice surprised him. She had never offered it to him before. "I'm not going to lie to you. There isn't enough time for me to heal you if I use my normal power so I have to speed up the process. It's tricky and it's going to hurt."

"So you're saying I might die?"

"Not in my hands," May said and her voice held an authority that rivaled Adelina's on her best days. He nodded, accepting the decree. "Have you ever been healed by magic before?"

"Only the natural way. I broke my arm once."

"And it probably took weeks to heal, right?"

Ed nodded. "Seven weeks, if I recall."

"I could have healed your arm in only a couple of hours," May told him. "But the aches you felt when your arm healed over those seven weeks would have been compounded into the same two hours. And the healing power itself burns in the process."

"How long does it take to heal an injury like mine?"

"In an ideal situation, four to five hours, but your wound is less than ideal. You'll bleed to death if I don't heal you faster."

"How fast?"

"The majority of your healing will take half an hour. The rest I can finish in an hour."

Ed swallowed hard over the understanding. Four hours of already intense pain condensed into thirty minutes, plus an hour for good measure—excruciating would not begin to describe it. He tried to focus on something more pleasant. His mind circled to Adelina, to the touch of her skin against his, and he intertwined his fingers with hers.

"If you feel the need to pass out," May continued, "don't fight it. Are you ready?"

He nodded, though he did not feel at all prepared. May glanced up at Cal and the man gripped the end of the spear once more.

"Now," May said and with the single word, she introduced him to a new form of punishment. He could manage the pain when the spear tore from his body. A scream escaped him, and then it was over. But he had no breath left for screaming once the true agony began. Her power pulsed through him. He felt certain she had figured out a way to rip his muscles from his bones using fire, and then he drowned in darkness.

§

HE AWOKE twice. The first time, a wash of hot pain rolled through him. Compared to before, he found it tolerable, and guessed May now used her normal power. He let it overtake him, lost still to some of the black waves that had removed him from the world when the first round of healing had started. He remained half-trapped within it, and welcomed the serenity. He could see nothing, but soon the voices floated past. Adelina's entered the abyss first. It resonated stiff and angry. The second voice he also recognized well. It held calm against Adelina's emotion, logic against her fear. It belonged to their advisor, Garon.

"My lady," he said. "Please understand. You have meetings. The Elders have an issue they need to discuss, and you have disputes to settle."

"I already told you," she responded. "I'm not leaving his side."

"I know this isn't easy, but he's in good hands. May said he's healing well. He probably won't even be awake before you return from your duties."

"I've made my decision," she insisted. Ed smiled, recognizing the ice in her voice. If he had money to bet right now, he would lay it all down on the wager that she crossed her arms in front of her. He would also bet that Garon had already begun to squirm under the intensity of her glare. "Give my apologies to the Elders and the villagers," she continued. "I'm not budging."

Garon sighed. "I don't think apologies will do. The Elders are already mad enough, after what Ed did to Malven."

"What do you mean?" May asked.

"From what I hear, Ed made Malven bet his guardianship away to Cal in a card game."

"He did *what?*"

"It was a joke," Cal said. "And it's not like I could've kept my so-called winnings. Only the Elders can transfer a guardianship."

"A joke or not, it was irresponsible," Garon snapped. "And it put Ed in this situation. Malven's a capable Guardian. More so than you, it appears."

"Ed's injury wasn't my fault," Cal said, his voice rising with his anger. "Malven's the one who put him in danger. If he hadn't teleported back here to whine to the Elders—"

"Enough, both of you," May commanded. "You can argue about this later."

Cal grunted, and then silence filled the room. A few minutes later, Garon spoke again, the animosity gone from his voice. "What exactly happened to him, anyway? I thought the outlaws had been defeated."

"For the most part," Cal responded. "But there are still a few to round up. Ed chased a couple of them into a trap this morning. I doubt they would've gotten the best of him, but these guys are different."

"How so?" Garon asked.

"I don't know. It's hard to explain. They seem stronger and faster than a man ought to be. And they don't look right. Their skin is the color of ash."

"Red eyes," Ed thought, although when the room grew quiet, he wondered if he had actually spoken.

"You need to leave," May said. "You've woken him."

"What's he talking about?" Garon asked, and the panic in his voice surprised Ed. "There's no such thing as a man with red eyes."

"There is now," Cal responded. "They look like dranx." The heat stopped coursing through Ed and Cal spoke again, "Come on, we'd better leave. The last time I saw May with that look on her face, she took after me with a knife."

"I didn't," May muttered. "But I will if you don't stop agitating my patient. His heart is racing."

The heat started again and Ed lost awareness once more.

The second time he woke, night had blanketed the room in darkness. He felt a pressure on his chest, another on his left shoulder, and no pain in his right. He rolled the shoulder, smiled when it responded without protest, and reached across his chest to determine what had caused the pressure. His hand found skin, then fingers. He traced them and the pressure on his shoulder stirred.

"Adelina," he whispered. "Is that you?"

"You're awake," she responded.

Her voice trembled and he reached for her cheek, frowning when she captured his hand and pulled it away.

"Adelina," he said, tightening his hand around hers. "If we can't share our feelings, how can we expect to share anything else?"

She took in a surprised breath, and then she nodded against his chest. He released her hand to seek her cheek once more. When he found the wetness he had expected, he followed his fingers with his lips.

"It's okay," he told her. "I promised I'd come back."

A sob escaped her throat. She clutched her fists against his skin, and then cried until her tears had dried. When silence enveloped the room again, he grazed a kiss across her temple.

"Why do you shut me out?" he asked. "Why won't you lean on me when you need someone?"

"I can't."

"Why not?"

She shook her head.

"Adelina, please. Tell me."

"Because," she hesitated. Her voice softened, and he had had to strain to hear her. "Because this isn't your home. You've made it clear you want to return to the mountains and I know it's only a matter of time before you do."

The truth sliced through him, as swift and painful as the spear that had pierced his body. He had longed for the freedom he had known with his tribe, and he thought he had hid that longing from her. He thought he had accepted his new home, his new role with dignity. But the only person he seemed to have fooled was himself. Joining the army at the border had made him aware of that. He had relished visiting his kinsmen and the land where he had grown up. He had even toyed with the idea of breaking his promise to Adelina. The idea had only lasted about a day before he began to miss her.

He drew his fingers to her brow and wished he had her gift to see in the dark. "If you feared I wouldn't return, why did you let me leave?"

"Because you needed to be there," she said. "You needed to protect your people. I understand that."

"It's why you fought in the Zeiihbu war, isn't it?"

"Yes. But going to the border meant more than that to you. You're a nomad at heart. I can't change that, and I'd rather let you go than hold you here against your will."

"Is that how you see me?" he asked. "Can't I be more than that? Can't I be the man who stays by your side, and the one who travels to ease his wanderlust?"

"Is that possible?" she asked. "Can you really be both?"

"If you let me. Adelina, I want to be here with you, but I need this to be my home. I need to be King by your side. And I need to perform my full duty for your land to be mine."

"It's not an easy job."

"Easy is boring."

She laughed, shifted beside him, and then her lips pressed into his neck. The softness of the gesture thrilled him.

"I love you, Adelina."

"Do you?"

"Of course." He buried his hands in her hair, and drew her head closer. "Since the beginning, you've left me little other choice."

"Good," she said. "I thought I was the only one."

He smiled, and though he could not see her, he had no doubt she did the same.

CHAPTER EIGHT

THE INTIMACY of Adelina and Ed's story surprised Nick. He would have felt like a voyeur if he had not recognized parallels between the past and the present. Cal had not changed much, except for the length of his beard. Nick's mother still commanded her healing power with the same strength and assurance. And Garon still cared more for controlling those around him than for understanding their needs, though Adelina and Ed had been blind to that failing in their advisor. They might not have remained that way if Ed had caught up to the red-eyed men he had chased.

Nick sighed and set the book aside. Despite the skirmishes on the border, it had been a peaceful time in the kingdom. It amazed him how fast things had changed. Not even twenty years later, the border seemed to be the only safe place to hide.

He stood and moved to the fireplace to check the soup. The broth boiled with such force that the lid rattled, letting steam escape up the chimney. A taste test revealed the soup had finished cooking, so he grasped the handle of the pot with a towel and moved it to the table, then sat down to eat. The howl of the storm kept him company until he spooned up his last bite, then Meaghan stirred and the noise of the storm disappeared behind a wash of her pain.

"Nick?"

He returned to her side. Her eyes opened, though they appeared unseeing, clouded with the pain he had sensed. She struggled to rise to her elbows, and he placed his hands on her shoulders, easing her back down.

"It's better if you don't move," he told her. "Do you want more tea?"

She nodded. He filled a cup and brought it to her. After propping her up with pillows, he helped her drink, easing the hot liquid past her lips until her pain subsided. When she nestled back against the pillows and closed her eyes, he stood, intending to leave her to sleep, but stopped when she grabbed his arm with tight fingers. She opened her eyes again, and he realized why her strength had surged. Fear widened them.

"Please," she said. "Stay with me."

He sat back down. "What's wrong?"

Her grip moved from his arm to his hand. He intertwined his fingers with hers.

"I keep dreaming about what happened," she whispered. "Every time I close my eyes, he's there."

Nick nodded. He had suspected as much. "He's gone now. He won't bother you anymore."

"That's not true. He always will." Tears filled her eyes and she looked away. "Who was he? Beneath the Mardróch, I saw a man. He seemed familiar."

Nick drew her hand into his lap, and then pressed it between his palms. He had recognized the man, too, and the realization of what Garon had done had torn at Nick. But it had also made it easier to fire the final arrow. In the end, releasing the man from his prison had been as much of a sympathy killing as Dell's death.

"His name was Vaska," he told Meaghan. "You met him in my village."

Meaghan's eyes returned to his, widening once more. "I remember him from the party," she said. "He played with the band, some sort of instrument that looked like a shell."

Nick nodded. "A whelk horn."

"He didn't seem like the same person."

"I know," Nick said. "The Mardróch spell doesn't just change a person's powers. It changes features. It robs humanity."

"Was he the traitor then? Did he let the Mardróch into the village?"

Nick shook his head. "No. If he had, he would have been a full Mardróch by now. The spell usually only takes a day to work, but he had only half-turned. He fought it."

"That's why I felt him instead of smelling him," Meaghan realized. "He was in agony."

"Most likely from fighting the spell," Nick said. "He would have lost in the end, and probably had started to or he wouldn't have attacked you, but he still fought it."

She closed her eyes tight enough to crease her eyelids. Tears escaped, coursing down her cheeks in straight rivers. "He threw my knife away," she whispered. "He could have used it against me, but he didn't. Did he have to die? Couldn't we have helped him?"

Rather than answer, Nick pressed his forehead to hers and released the block on his emotions so she could feel the depth of his grief. She lifted an arm and wrapped it around his neck.

"You helped him the only way you could," she realized. "Could others from your village have been turned to Mardróch against their will?"

"It's possible, but I doubt it." He traced a hand along her arm before removing it from his neck. "Garon's army captured Guardians and tried converting them when the war started, but the tactic didn't work as well as he'd hoped. Much like Vaska, they fought the change. Some even managed to kill a few Mardróch before the army disposed of them. Since then, Garon has adopted a no prisoner policy."

"So why did they try to convert Vaska?"

"It's hard to know," Nick said. "But there's no point in speculating. Garon's reasons rarely make sense." He stood and moved to the table, then filled a bowl with soup and brought it to her. "You need to eat."

Meaghan eyed the soup at first and he thought she would refuse it, but when he sat next to her again, she accepted the food and ate in silence. Only a spoonful remained when her eyelids drifted closed.

Nick removed the bowl from her hands, leaving her to sleep as he set about completing long overdue tasks. He sharpened the knives, tightened the string on his bow, and swept the cabin floor. After he checked the progress of the storm, not at all surprised to see over a foot of snow on the ground, he placed the soup pot outside so it would not spoil, and then curled up on his own cot and succumbed to a dreamless sleep.

§

THE NEXT morning, faint sunlight woke him, bringing a smile to his face. He turned on his side. Meaghan lay motionless in her cot, except for the steady rise and fall of her chest as she breathed. She had slept through the night. He took that as a good sign and hoped she would stay asleep through most of his hunt. Tossing back the blankets, he rose to verify her skin remained cool to his touch, and then rebuilt the fire before grabbing his bow and arrows and heading out the door.

No trace of the storm remained in the cloudless sky, though an endless sea of white still blanketed the ground, pushed by wind into small hills and valleys. On the porch, snow lay smooth as an undisturbed lake. He stepped into it, sinking mid-way up his calves. His boots kept the cold at bay for now, but the reprieve would not last long. Dipping his hands into the snow beside the door, he searched for the pot he had set out the night before. When his fingers brushed metal, he dug the pot from its icy burial and lifted the lid. The soup had frozen solid. He took it inside the cabin and hung it over the fire to defrost before heading back outside.

He ventured down the porch steps, barely distinguishable from the drifts surrounding them, and then braved his first journey into the new-fallen snow. Here, where no roof offered protection against the full brunt of the storm, he sunk past his knees before finding hard-frozen earth. Soft powder seeped into the lining of his boots, soaking through his socks and melting into his pants. Despite his desire to escape the cold and return to Meaghan before she awoke, he planted his steps with care, watching for hidden danger. A buried log or boulder could sideline him with a sprained ankle, leaving them to the mercy of Cal's bland supplies. Although it would not kill them, Meaghan would heal faster with fresh meat to entice her appetite.

He headed north, toward the body he had hidden the day before. Although the snow had not fallen as deeply in the forest, a snowdrift hid the hole in the tree, granting him reprieve from figuring out another grave. The frozen ground would not allow any digging for some time.

Turning east from the tree, he spotted fresh tracks in the snow and followed them. Two of the paw prints appeared to be about the size of one of his hands and he realized they belonged to a larger animal—a wood lion, perhaps, as he doubted anything smaller could make its way through snow this deep. He ventured half a mile further into the woods, following the trail, and then discovered its source. A white cat bounded ahead of him, focused on its prey. It pounced through the snow, its tail flicking back and forth in anticipation as it watched a bird flit from branch to branch.

The cat resembled a lynx in size and build, and it held a special power enabling it to mimic its background. The snow had turned it white, but its natural coat appeared brownish-red, earning it the name ambercat.

Because their primary power made them nearly impossible to spot, and a secondary power disguised their movements with artificial silence, years could elapse between sightings. Nick doubted he would have seen this cat, if hunger had not driven the animal into carelessness.

He stopped and slipped an arrow from his quiver in preparation. The cat remained focused on the blue jay's movements. The bird jumped from the branch. Nick waited, watching for the cat's leap straight into the air, and then became the predator. His arrow flew straight into the ambercat's heart, dropping it back to the ground. The bird disappeared into the sky, unaware of its luck.

As the cat's blood stained the fresh snow, turning it a deep shade of pink, Nick worked fast to field dress and skin the animal. When he had finished, he stowed the carcass in his burlap sack, and then hid what he could not use in a hollow log.

After burying the stained snow in a fresh mound of white, he paused to survey the area. Once satisfied he had not left any evidence of his kill, he made the slow trek back to the cabin. Although his legs had gone numb from the cold, and the effort of wading through heavy snow had made him tired, he did not relax until he stood on the porch once more, protected by the sapphire glow of the crystals.

He would need to process the cat after lunch. Until then, it would keep best outside, so he draped the hide over a railing to dry, and then hung the bag from a hook in the porch ceiling.

Satisfied with the results of his hunt, he opened the cabin door, ready to thaw out his clothes by the fire, but did not get the chance before a solid force shoved him backward into the snow.

CHAPTER NINE

NICK SAW the flash of skin above his head. Clothing flew by, hinting at denim and the deep blue of a thick sweater. Sun glinted off an allestone sword. Then all signs of the person disappeared. He jumped to his feet and tore across the field, forcing his way through the snow with as much speed as he could muster.

They were halfway to the edge of the forest when he caught up with Meaghan. She spun around to face him, and he tackled her, barely missing the edge of her sword as she swung it through the air. They tumbled, rolling in the deep drifts as she bucked against him. White blurred his vision. Ice bit his skin. Snow burrowed under his collar and inside his sleeves. Finally, he came to rest on top of her. She cried out in pain, and then went limp.

She had tried this ploy once before. He remembered it and anticipated what came next. She pushed once more against him, trying to throw him off with her knees. He tightened his hold, pinning her arms at her sides with his legs, her shoulders to the snow with his hands. Then he dropped his head next to hers, hoping somehow his voice would get through to her. Her eyes appeared blank and uncomprehending.

"Meg, you're safe," he said. "You're safe. I have you."

This time when she stopped struggling, it was not an act. Tears streamed down her face. Climbing to his feet, he looked for her sword, but found no hint of it along the compacted snow where they had fought. His eyes fell on a trail of red etched into the white and his throat constricted. The sword would have to wait. He scooped Meaghan into his arms and carried her into the cabin.

He set her down on her cot. Her eyes remained closed. Shivers rattled her body, chattering her teeth. She tightened her fingers at her sides, clenching them into fists. They had turned blue from the short time she had been in the cold, as had her feet.

"Meg," he said, stroking a hand across her forehead. "Open your eyes for me, please."

She did not respond and it took him another moment to understand why. She slept. Not just now, but when she had run into the field. Dreams had driven her, nightmares that roused her consciousness to the point of movement, but not to the point of reality.

Fortunately, he had arrived when he did. If he had not, she could be in the woods by now. It would not have taken her long to freeze. Or worse, she could have found the Mardróch her dreams had spurred her to fight.

It seemed it would be best not to leave her alone until the impact of Vaska's death had eased from her memory. She shivered again, curling her arms against her chest, and then winced in her sleep. He remembered the bloodstained snow and pushed up her sweater to check her wound. As he had suspected, she had popped a few stitches, though her bleeding had not seeped through. The old injury had not been the source of the blood in the snow. He cleaned and bandaged the wound, then pulled off her sweater and tossed it into the corner so he could examine her skin.

He found no injuries on her stomach or sides. Checking her back, he found nothing there either. She stirred, still asleep, and raised her hands to his neck. Her fingers still held the chill of outdoors, but the rest of her body had warmed. When she pressed her lips against his shoulder, he brought his arms around her in turn. Her body yielded to his touch, then conformed to his caress. He drew his hands up her spine, relishing in the shudder the movement produced and in the sigh that escaped her throat.

Then his fingers reached the nape of her neck where her skin yielded to sticky warmth. He pulled his hand away. Red coated his palm, and he released her to look at the blood staining the pillow where she had laid. When he glanced back at her face, she stared at him, her eyes wide in wakefulness.

"What...?" she started to ask, but fell silent when he took her chin in his hand and turned her head. Just below her hairline, he found the wound. She must have hit a rock when they rolled over the ground. The blow had broken her skin. He pressed his fingers to a lump the size of a walnut and she hissed.

He stood, picked up a bucket, and then went outside to collect snow. When he returned, she drew her knees up to her chest and circled her arms around them. Her eyes locked with his and her cheeks flushed red. From embarrassment, he realized, and retrieved a sweater and a small cloth bag from one of the boxes under the cot where they stored their clothes. He handed the sweater to her.

"Your other sweater was ruined yesterday," he told her.

She accepted the explanation with a nod. She started to lift the garment over her head, but stopped when he placed a hand on her wrist.

"I need to clean the blood from your hair," he told her. "You can put it on after that."

She nodded once more, and then leaned forward so he could sit behind her. Using the fresh snow, he washed the blood from her hair and from the wound so he could see it better. Her bleeding appeared to have stopped. Relieved, he finished cleaning the wound, and then helped her draw the sweater over her head and down her body.

"I was fighting with someone," she said. "I dreamed there were Mardróch and when I woke, you were gone. I thought they had you, so I ran after them." She shifted, and then winced, lifting her hand to rest it against the wound in her side. "It wasn't a dream, was it?"

"Some of it was," Nick responded. He fixed a compress from the bag and more snow, and then pressed it to the lump on her head. "The Mardróch aren't around today. I went hunting this morning."

"And the person I fought?"

"Me. Only it wasn't much of a fight. I tackled you to keep you from running into the forest."

She sighed. "I don't know what I was thinking."

"You weren't. You were reacting. Watching someone die like you did with Dell isn't the same as seeing someone killed. We all react to it differently." She did not respond, so he pulled her against his chest and wrapped his free arm around her waist. "I couldn't sleep for days after my first battle."

"I didn't kill him," she whispered.

"But you had a hand in his death."

Meaghan turned to stare at him, her eyes wide with hurt. Nick rested a hand on her shoulder.

"I didn't say that to be cruel," he told her. "It's something you have to face, because you're reacting to it. The fear and grief you feel are normal. And if you actually have to kill someone, you'll react to that differently, too. Although I hope that never happens."

"I thought you wanted me to," she responded. "That's the purpose of the final field test, isn't it?"

"No, it isn't." He lifted the compress to the back of her neck again. "The purpose is for you to defend yourself. You accomplished that in the woods yesterday, so I think it's safe to say you've passed the test. Hold this," he said, and let go of the compress when she did as he asked. He stood and walked to the fireplace. The fire had dwindled to embers, so he rebuilt it and then checked on the soup. It had overcooked, turning the vegetables into mush, but it would be edible. He stirred it, and then glanced at Meaghan. She looked tired, and he wondered if she had slept as well last night as he had initially thought.

"I made something for you," he said and crossed the room to retrieve her gift from a bookshelf. He tucked it behind his back and returned to her. "You've mastered the physical training. Now it's just a matter of mastering your empath power. Once you do, we can return to the protection of the Elders."

The shadows on her face darkened. "We've tried everything," she reminded him. "I can't get it right."

"I have another idea. Hold out your hands."

Meaghan knit her brows in confusion, but extended her hands anyway. He placed the gift on top of her palms. The doll did not look like much, but he had done his best with the supplies he had been able to muster. Corn husk and leaves formed cylindrical arms and a body, as well as a ball for a head. Shredded yellow husk fashioned a skirt. Brown thread mimicked hair underneath a husk hat. Berry juice from the dried fruit in the date cake stained black eyes and red lips, and two hands clutched a bouquet of tiny, white wildflowers that Meaghan had dried in the fall. The doll only extended from the top of Meaghan's hands to just past her wrists, but she still spent several minutes studying it.

She touched the tip of her index finger to its pearl button nose and smiled. "It's beautiful, but I don't see how this will help me control my power."

"I'll explain when you're feeling better," Nick said. "For now, think of it as a gift. I wanted you to have something special from me."

"Thank you."

He nodded and then returned to the fire to dish out two bowls of soup.

In the early afternoon, Meaghan slept while Nick prepared the ambercat to roast. Although he could not cook it all at once, the meat would keep on the snowy porch for some time, so he cut the animal into segments. The hind pieces would make sweet, tender roasts, and the rest would work well in soups. He had been fortunate enough to have ambercat twice before. The first time, Cal had trapped one for Nick's birthday, the last birthday they had spent together before Cal went into hiding. The second time, a friend of Nick's mother had been generous enough to share it with them. He had also taught Nick how to prepare a fresh kill.

Once the roast hung on a spit over the fire, Nick sat at the table to read the Writer's book again. He turned the page to chapter two, but found only blank paper. He flipped another page, and then a third. When those also appeared blank, he closed the book and reopened it. Nothing. Frustrated, he set the book aside, and then looked up to find Meaghan propped on her elbows, watching him.

"It happened to you, too?" she asked.

"What do you mean?"

"The book. A story appeared for you. Now it's gone."

"How did you know?"

"It happened to me a few weeks ago. What was your story about?"

He told her in as much detail as he could remember, and then frowned. "I'm not sure why it's gone."

"Maybe because there was something in it you needed to read," she said. "And I didn't."

"Or the book is compromised in some way. I think it's time to contact Mom."

Meaghan nodded, and then turned to stack a couple of pillows behind her. Nick took the opportunity to remove a long, smoke-colored crystal from his medical kit. Pressing it between his palms, he held it until it glowed, then set it next to Meaghan on the cot.

"You should have called me earlier," a voice broadcast through the room. "I've already heard the news from Cal."

"What news?" Nick asked.

"That Meaghan was attacked. Should I assume her injury wasn't bad?"

"She's still healing. I'm sure Cal told you we had a snowstorm, which is why he isn't able to provide a better update. I stitched Meaghan's wound, but it'll be at least a week before I can get her to the village."

"A week? With the number of Healers floating around this kingdom that seems almost barbaric." May's voice grew faint, then muffled. Nick recognized she spoke to someone else and waited. She returned a moment later. "I've asked someone to send a message to Cal. Until you can get Meaghan to Neiszhe's village, make her a poultice out of the green powder in your medical kit. It'll work best if you mix it with snow. Apply a thin layer to the injury over the stitches. If you want to do that now, I'll wait."

Nick raised an eyebrow at Meaghan and she shook her head in response. "She's fine at the moment," Nick told his mother. "We actually needed to talk to you about something else."

"Oh?" May's tone broadcast she felt nothing could be more important than the Queen's health, but she refrained from saying anything more about it.

"Yes," Nick said. "What can you tell us about the Writer's book?"

"Not much. Adelina's family had similar books created for

important events. Most of them were destroyed with the castle, but this one hadn't been finished yet."

"It was Adelina's idea?" Nick asked.

"It was mine. When Meaghan was born, I thought it would be nice to have a record of Ed and Adelina's wedding, so I talked to Ed about it. He had somebody in mind he wanted to use instead of the royal family Writer, so he took care of it himself."

"Did you know the Writer?" Meaghan asked. "Was it a woman with green eyes and brown hair?"

"I don't know. Ed never told me. In fact, when he died, the book still hadn't been completed, so I thought it was lost. About two years after we moved into the new Guardian village, it showed up on my doorstep."

Nick frowned. "I'm not sure I understand."

"I woke up and found it at my front door, wrapped in a white cloth."

"I see." Nick stood and went to the table to retrieve the book. He returned to his seat on the cot, opened the book to the first blank page and stared down at it. "Where did your story appear?" he asked Meaghan.

"Toward the end," she said, flipping the pages until she arrived at one and smoothed her finger over a creased corner. "I earmarked it. It was short, only a few pages long."

"Mine was here," he told her, turning back to the place his chapter had appeared. "It said 'Chapter Two'."

"The one I saw said 'Afterward A'."

"It may be going in order then. If it was finished after your parents died—"

"If what was finished?" May's voice interrupted from the commcrystal. "Do you want to tell me what you're talking about?"

"The book," Nick responded. "Stories have been appearing. I'm worried it might be a ploy to mislead us."

"What do you mean by 'appearing'?" May asked. "There's only one story."

"And a lot of blank pages," Nick said. "The stories are appearing on the blank pages, and then disappearing. Meaghan and I have each seen one."

"So you think Garon is planting stories to confuse you or to get you to do something?"

"I wouldn't put it past him. I'm just not sure how he could have gotten the book to you in the village when he didn't know where you were."

"He wouldn't have had to know," May responded. "He would only have had to convince another Guardian to deliver it. That person may not have realized he was doing something wrong."

"True," Nick decided. "So how do we know for certain what this is?"

"Start by telling me what you read."

Nick told her the story that had appeared to him. His mother interrupted several times to ask specific questions about trivial items, such as which side of the bed Ed lay on, and what type of stone comprised the spearhead, but fell silent when the story ended. After a few minutes, she spoke again.

"It's true," she said. "All of it. Adelina and Ed never told Garon anything more than what he heard and saw during the healing. Only the four of us knew everything."

"They told you what happened after you left?" Nick asked in surprise.

"Everything," May repeated. "Ed and Adelina both felt strongly that Meaghan was the reason for their wedding. They told Cal and me because they wanted us to understand the importance of protecting her. It was," May's voice cracked, "an emotional day for us when we found out about Adelina's pregnancy. They told us the whole story that day."

"So this can't be Garon's doing," Nick realized. "He couldn't have known those details."

"I doubt it," May responded. "But we can't rule anything out. What story appeared for you, Meaghan?"

"It wasn't a story," Meaghan answered. "Not really. It was my father sitting beside a woman with brown hair and green eyes. They talked about the wedding while she took notes. I assumed she was the Writer."

"That's as good a theory as any," May said. "Did either of you do anything unusual to trigger the stories? Maybe ask the book for more?"

"Not that I recall," Nick said.

"Me neither," Meaghan answered, and then frowned as she picked up the book. She flipped to the creased page and ran her fingers over it. "I was thinking something though. I've probably read the first story twenty times since you gave me the book. I have every detail memorized. After I read it the last time, I thought it would be nice if I had something more to read, something about my parents. The story appeared then. It stayed for a few days, but as soon as I decided to show it to Nick, it disappeared again."

May grunted. "Well, it's odd for certain, but I don't think the book poses any threat. Just be wary of new stories, and report anything suspicious to me."

"All right," Nick agreed and picked up the crystal to shut it off, but paused when his mother spoke again.

"It's too bad we don't have any Seers or Dreamers around. They'd be able to tell us something about this, but no one has showed either of those powers since Abbott. I wish he hadn't succumbed to the potion again. He could have been invaluable to us. Instead, his betrayal cost so much."

Meaghan's head snapped up. *"Betrayal?"* she mouthed at Nick.

Nick kept his eyes glued on the crystal.

"Anyway," May said, "let Meaghan rest. Don't forget the poultice."

"I won't," Nick promised and cupped his hands around the commcrystal.

It turned dark again, but the dense gray clouding the crystal did not come close to the blackness shadowing Meaghan's face.

CHAPTER TEN

NICK FOCUSED on mixing the poultice. It had been years since he had last used it, and his memories of the medicine were not fond. Too much liquid and the green powder had no effect. Too little and it turned to cement before it could be mixed. He had already forgotten what the powder did, but if his mother recommended it, it would help. So he focused on getting it right, and used the task to avoid looking at Meaghan.

He did not have to see her face to know the storm in her eyes had brewed to a full hurricane. She wanted answers.

As he stirred green powder into a bowl of snow, Cal's advice came back to him. As King, Nick had a duty to share what he knew with her. The title still did not sit well with him, but it did not change the facts. Protecting Meaghan from the news would only hurt matters for the kingdom in the end.

The poultice began to turn, solidifying into a stew and he stopped adding powder. He kept stirring. Something about his current situation nagged at him, though he could not seem to place it. He snuck a glance at Meaghan. She caught him, and responded to his curiosity with a glare. She had a right to be mad, but he had to make her understand he meant no harm by his actions. Much like Adelina's decision to protect Ed in the past, it seemed like the right thing to do.

But the decision had been wrong. Instead of protecting him as she thought she was doing, she had made it more difficult for him to become a part of his new home. Nick doubted his behavior had any less of an impact on Meaghan.

The poultice thickened to a pudding and he stopped stirring. He brought the bowl to Meaghan and stood over her.

"Turn on your side," he told her.

She did as he asked. He removed her bandage, and then began applying the poultice with a spoon. She winced, but did not complain.

"You were right," he said after a minute had passed. "There were details in that story I had to read. Or rather, there was something I needed to learn."

She peered at him from below raised eyebrows, waiting for him to continue. He scooped up more of the poultice, focusing on her wound rather than her face.

"I've been keeping things from you," he said. "I've known for some time about Abbott's treachery."

"I see." She hissed and he could not tell if her injury or his statement had caused the reaction. He dared a glance at her. Her eyes appeared hard, but pain shadowed them.

"The poultice should work soon."

"I'm not a child. I can handle it."

Nick nodded, realizing she had meant the news, not the injury. He dropped his gaze back to the green goop. It had turned hard and white around the edges. He began applying another layer.

"Those were almost the exact same words your father said to your mother when he found out she kept news from him," he said. "She was wrong to want to protect him in that way. And I'm wrong to do the same." He returned the spoon to the bowl. After spreading the poultice into an even layer with his fingers, he taped fresh bandages over her wound. "How does it feel?"

"Cold," she said. "It tingles. What does it do?"

"If I remember correctly, it prevents infection and numbs the wound. It may do more, but it's been a long time since I've used it."

She sat up and lowered her sweater. "Nick, tell me the truth. What happened to Abbott?"

He took her hands in his, facing her, and the truth. "He let the Mardróch into the village that night."

"He," Meaghan started, but could not seem to find any other words. Her grip tightened on his hands. "He couldn't have," she finally mustered. "Why would he?"

"To destroy you. The Elders believe he took the potion to gain access to the village through a Healer."

"That's not what your mother said. She's one of the Elders."

"They make decisions based on majority. Mom thinks we didn't clear all of the potion from Abbott's system. It's possible he let them in while crazed."

"But you don't believe that," Meaghan said and narrowed her eyes. He realized she had used her power to sense the doubt plaguing him. "No matter which theory they subscribe to, all of the Elders believe Abbott started the attack, but you don't. Why?"

Nick shrugged. "I should. He's the one who attacked Max and Cissy."

Meaghan shook her head. "The potion would explain why he went after Max, but not his betrayal. Letting the Mardróch in would take planning."

"I know." Nick stood and moved to the fireplace. The roast had some time left to cook, but it had begun to emit an aroma that foreshadowed a tantalizing feast. He could not find the will to enjoy it. "None of it makes sense. Garon has no qualms about murdering, but he doesn't like to waste Mardróch if he can help it. The attack on the village cost him five of his monsters. It would have been far simpler for him if you'd abdicated. You would've been unprotected."

"Yet Abbott helped talked me out of it," Meaghan said. "I understand your concern. We'll have to be cautious when we return to the others. If you're right, the real traitor could still be there." She folded her hands in front of her, more relaxed than she had been at the start of the conversation, but her face still looked taut and her knuckles appeared white. "What else haven't you told me?"

Nick glanced back at the fire.

"You said you were keeping *things* from me," she continued. "Plural. What else?"

"Updates on the war, mostly. Battle outcomes, villages lost. Garon's become more aggressive. The Elders have set up several refugee camps in the caves to accommodate the displaced villagers."

"They're in that position because of my return," Meaghan

guessed, and did not wait for confirmation. "I'm fed up with this, Nick. I'm tired of hiding while Garon slaughters thousands. It's time I defended them."

Nick raised an eyebrow. "How? You know nothing about wars. And I know only a little more than you."

"A wise person once told me a good leader doesn't do everything on her own. She finds people who can help."

Nick chuckled. "I may have said that, but I didn't mean for you to take over the war."

"Perhaps not, but it's part of my job. Our jobs," she corrected. "And if Garon is destroying the kingdom because of me, then we have to stop him."

The determination in her eyes, and the steel in her voice brought a smile to his lips. He had expected her to be upset about the news or to feel responsible for Garon's actions. He had not expected this. "And how do you plan to do that?"

"I intend to learn how to control my empath power. Starting tomorrow, if you're up for it."

"Then what?"

"Then," a mischievous grin spread across her face. "I guess you'll find out. You're not the only one who can keep secrets."

CHAPTER ELEVEN

MEAGHAN DID not keep her secret for long. That night, as they lay in their cots, their bellies full, and the night blanketing the room in darkness, she whispered her plan to him. It seemed simple enough. If she could make it work. Nick had his doubts.

Before she could attempt it, though, she needed to heal so they could travel. Until that happened, he had one focus. After a breakfast of cold roast and bread, he retrieved the cornhusk doll from the shelf where he had put it the night before and brought it to Meaghan's cot. She sat in the middle of the bed, her legs crossed in front of her.

"I thought we'd try visualization again," he said, sitting beside her. "But instead of shutting off your power, I want you to move it."

"I don't understand."

"I think you're having trouble learning the Guardian techniques because your power can't be shut off. Some sensing powers can't be."

She blew out a breath in frustration. "Do you realize what that means, Nick? If I can't shut it off, I won't ever be able to live around others."

"Not necessarily." He picked up the doll and traced his fingers across its corn husk brow. "The Elders and I made the mistake of assuming it could be shut off because you sense emotions from everywhere in exactly the same way a Guardian senses magic or danger. Because we've been focused on faulty logic, we never bothered to see if any other tactics might apply."

"Meaning?"

"Meaning you aren't the first Empath, and you're certainly not the first one who's wanted to live around other people, so there has to be a tactic that applies to you. I think focusing will be the key."

"I've tried that. All I focus on is my power when we do those exercises."

"Focusing *on* your power isn't the same as focusing your power," Nick said, and then stared down at the doll when Meaghan knit her brows in confusion. She had to understand the concept for his plan to succeed. His eyes slipped from the doll's face to the floor, and then the water bucket. An explanation came to him.

"Think of a sensing power as a river," he told her. "We all have the ability to see the objects a river carries, like rocks and twigs. In the same way, we can see the things our powers sense. Guardians can focus on and differentiate between types of magic, for instance, and you can do the same with emotions. Is that clear?"

She nodded. "Sure, but it still sounds like the same type of focusing."

"That part is the same," he agreed. "What's different is how the power is managed. Using the same analogy, if we want to control a river, we have two options. We can block its flow or we can redirect it. Most people with sensing powers can block them, essentially by building a dam. For others, the power can't be controlled. It has to flow continuously—"

"Like a Seer's power."

"Exactly. But unlike a seer, I think you have the ability to redirect your power, to focus it on one point. A specific person or," Nick placed the doll in her lap, "something else entirely. The doll isn't ideal in every situation, but it's a good start. Once you gain control of diverting your power, you can figure out what object works best for you."

Meaghan's eyes fell to the doll. "Do you really think this can work?"

"Nothing's certain. It's been over a century since your power last appeared. What knowledge remains of it is vague, but I think this technique has a better chance of working than the others."

Meaghan stared at the doll for a second, and then nodded. "All right. Let's give it a try."

He stood. "Great. Focus on your power. I'll walk you through it."

She closed her eyes and he began pacing the room, his feet shuffling over the floor in a steady rhythm. He waited for her to nod in acknowledgement that she had located the warmth of her power, before stopping in the middle of the room and facing her.

"Can you tell the difference between your powers?"

She shook her head. "Not really. When I activate my revival power, I focus on the warmth and it does as I tell it."

He had suspected as much. He latched his hands together behind his back as he moved again. "In order for this to work, you need to be able to separate your powers. Focus on my emotions. What do you sense?"

Her brows knit together in concentration. "You're nervous about this," she said, "and hopeful. You're also afraid, but there's a calm about you that settles the other emotions. It stems from relief. Why do you feel relief?"

"No guesses?" he asked, and then chuckled. "I thought knowing the source of emotions was your super power."

"You make it sound like I'm a carnival psychic," she complained and opened her eyes. Insult dragged a frown over her face. "It's not like I can't figure out the source of most emotions if I pay attention. I only guess when I'm reasonably certain."

"And you're almost always right," he told her. "I've gotten used to that, and frankly, I find it amusing."

"Is that so?" She set the doll aside. "I'm glad you find me so entertaining."

Her sarcasm erased the smile from his face. He sat down next to her and placed a hand on her thigh. "I'm only teasing, Meg. You've actually developed a talent for understanding the source of people's emotions. It's impressive."

"So you tease me about it?" She crossed her arms over her chest. "That hardly seems fair."

"I suppose it isn't," he said. "But I didn't mean any harm. I guess I just feel a little more relaxed today, more like I used to before all of this happened."

His eyes held hers, and she nodded in understanding. "Before we left Earth," she said. "Before the stress of being King and Queen and the constant fear of being hunted."

"Yes, before." He lifted his hand to her neck and drew her closer so he could press his forehead to hers. "Do you remember what it was like when we spent time together? When I used to be able to tease you and it made you laugh?"

A wistful smile flickered over her face and for a moment, he thought he also detected longing in her eyes. It used to be there whenever they spent time alone in his apartment, when they sat this close, and when his fingers touched her skin the way they did now. He leaned in and tested her lips, then dove deeper, feeding his need. She responded with the same frantic passion as she had the first time they had kissed on Earth, and then she withdrew from him with the same speed she had the last time he had tried to kiss her, the night they had moved into the cabin.

It had been his choice to push her away in the beginning, when he thought giving in to his attraction would destroy them both. And it was her choice now. He had long ago destroyed what had been building between them and he had to pay the price for his decision. The realization tore through him, dragging pain with it, but he stifled the emotion and stood.

"I'm relieved you're okay, that's all. I was worried I would lose you for a while." He picked up the doll from the bed and handed it to her. "We should get back to work. Focus on my emotions and tell me if the warmth changes."

She closed her eyes, but opened them again a moment later. "It's hard to tell when you're burying most of your emotions. Maybe if you—"

"That won't work," he decided without letting her finish the thought. "You need something stronger, more defined. Close your eyes again."

She frowned, but conceded to his request. He moved across the floor to their stockpile of weapons, picked up a knife and did the only thing he could think of to cause intense emotion. He gripped his fingers around the blade and pulled.

Meaghan gasped. Her eyes flew open and within them, he saw the intensity of his own pain. Red welled over his palm. He squeezed his hand into a fist, slowing the flow of blood. It oozed between his fingers.

"Nick," Meaghan protested. "What are you—"

"Focus," he commanded. "Or this is a waste."

She snapped her mouth closed and nodded, then squeezed her eyes shut.

"Does it feel any different?" he asked.

She nodded again. "My revival power emits steady warmth, but my empath power feels more like a lighthouse beacon. It moves as if it's searching for something."

"It pulses," Nick guessed.

"Exactly."

"Good, now grab hold of it. Do you have it?"

"Yes."

"Open your eyes."

She did and turned them toward Nick. He wrapped a towel around his hand and nodded at the doll. "Slide your power," he instructed. "Shift it like you do with your revival power."

She looked at the doll. Minutes passed. Creases grew along her forehead. She shifted on the bed, and then leaned forward, almost glaring at the doll. He remained silent. When a half hour elapsed, he found a seat next to her on the bed. Her eyes flicked to his, then found the doll once more and he said nothing.

Her hands came together. Her knuckles turned white with the intensity of her grip. Sweat beaded on her brow and rolled down her cheek. Finally, when the color drained from her face, leaving her pallor waxy, he gripped her shoulder.

"You need a break," he said.

She sighed and closed her eyes. "Every time I think I have it, it slips away. It's like trying to grasp the skin of an eel. I can only move it so far before it escapes my hold."

"And my emotions?"

"They dulled, but they never went away."

Her words brought him hope and with it, another emotion he made sure not to stifle. Meaghan narrowed her eyes before opening them wide to stare at him.

"I don't understand," she said. "You're proud, but I failed. The technique didn't work. It—"

"Worked." He grinned. "You need more practice, but you made it move. Meg, you made it work."

CHAPTER TWELVE

OVER THE next few days, Meaghan and Nick kept the same schedule. They feasted on ambercat and the remainder of their supplies until little remained of either. Meaghan pushed her power further, testing the boundary of her will and her exhaustion until Nick forced her to sleep. She felt more confident with each new attempt, her pain diluted and her injury forgotten as her power commanded more of her attention.

On the fourth day, she waved off his effort to get her to rest, ignored his prompts for lunch, and then glared at him when he attempted to talk to her.

"Meg," he tried again. "You can't do this all day."

"Quiet," she told him, refusing to remove her eyes from the doll. "I almost—"

A knock came at the door, cutting off her words. Startled, she jumped from the cot and Nick chuckled at the reaction.

"Only one person knows about the cabin," he reminded her.

"Right." She laughed and raised a hand to her chest, placing it over her heart. "I just didn't sense him." Her eyes grew wide. "Nick," she said, but did not have to say anything more. He swept her into his arms and into the air. When he brought her back down to her feet, he planted a kiss on her forehead.

"You did it," he said. His eyes held hers. Pride shone within them, but she did not feel it. Her focus remained on the doll. He lifted a hand to her cheek and for a moment, she thought he would lean into the distance between them, but another knock came and he released her. He crossed the room to open the door.

"It's about time," their visitor complained before engulfing Nick in a hug.

"Nice to see you, too, Cal," Nick responded, his voice muffled by the thick material of Cal's jacket. "Trying to suffocate me?"

"Don't think you don't deserve it. You two gave me enough of a scare." When Cal let Nick go, he raised an eyebrow at Meaghan, studying her as he ran a hand over his beard. "You don't look like you're dying."

She cast him a bewildered smile. "Were you hoping for something different?"

"You know better than that," he responded. "I was watching you on the wind when you fought that half-monster. It's no flesh wound you took. I kept hoping the wind would return so I could check on you, but it never did."

"You couldn't use our fire to spy on us?"

"Not without something to connect me to it. The cabin walls keep out precipitation and earth. I could have used your smoke to get into the cabin through the chimney, but still air isn't useful to carry remote visions." He paused, narrowing his eyes as he scanned them down her body. "You really don't look as bad as I expected. You're not healed already, are you?"

"She's getting there," Nick answered. "The snow is too deep for her to make it to Neiszhe's, but I was hoping we could attempt it by the end of the week."

"I was hoping we could attempt it now," Cal said. "If we don't get Meaghan to the village sooner, Neiszhe will be intolerable. She gets grumpy when she doesn't get enough sleep, and she's been up worrying most nights."

"About?"

"Her," he nodded toward Meaghan.

Nick shrugged. "I'm not going to object to getting Meg to the village sooner. What's your plan?"

"We teleport. There's a crystal cave not far from here—"

"A cave?" Nick interrupted. "Please tell me you're not serious. It took us days to travel here from Neiszhe's village."

Cal rubbed the back of his neck and shot a sheepish grin in Nick's direction. "Vivian told me it was necessary. She was right, wasn't she? You wouldn't have met Faillen or saved his son otherwise."

"I suppose not," Nick conceded. "So how do you propose getting Meaghan to the cave?"

"We carry her, at least on this end. The storm wasn't as bad by the village. The snow's already melted. She can walk well enough there."

"I could walk on this end, too," Meaghan said, then frowned, insulted by the conversation taking place around her. "I don't need anyone coddling me."

Cal chuckled. "I have no doubt of that, and I also have no doubt you'd reinjure yourself trying to prove you don't need our help. You'll be carried and that's the end of it."

He turned from her, but she refused to accept his decree. For the first time since she had left Earth, she had begun to regain control over her life and she did not want to surrender it so soon. She raised her voice to get his attention. "I don't appreciate you coming in here and telling me what to do. I'm a lot stronger than I used to be. Unless you intend to knock me unconscious—"

"That can be arranged." He glared at her over his shoulder, and then left the cabin. Meaghan took a step forward with the intent of continuing the argument, but Nick raised his hand, stopping her.

"Neiszhe isn't the only one who gets grouchy with lack of sleep," he said. "And Cal's used to dealing with your father. He'll follow through on his threat if he feels it's necessary."

"But I'm perfectly capable of walking."

"I have no doubt." He covered the distance between them. Placing his fingers under her chin, he lifted it so he could smile down at her. "I'm proud of you for controlling your empath power, but now isn't the time to corral it. Release your focus on the doll, and tell me what Cal is feeling."

She did as he asked, letting her power roam again. Nick's calm flooded through her first, and then Cal's strong emotions followed. "He's frustrated, anxious, and worried."

"About you," Nick said. "We all know you can make it to the village on your own if you need to, but the terrain isn't safe. The snow is still deep, by a couple of feet in some places. And the wind knocked down a lot of trees and branches. If you try to make it through the forest with your injury, you could pop your stitches. I wouldn't be able to stop the bleeding."

And he could not fix her stitches in the woods, which meant she could bleed to death. The thought chilled her and she crossed her arms over her chest.

"All right," she conceded. "I understand."

"Good," he said. "Let's go tell Cal."

They found Cal crouched on the porch, examining the ambercat pelt. Nick had cleared the snow off a section of the porch and laid the pelt flat, then crusted the exposed side with a thick layer of salt. Cal flipped up a corner of the pelt so he could run his fingers over the fur.

"This is beautiful," he said. "How did you manage to get her?"

Nick shrugged. "Luck."

"How can you be sure the animal was female?" Meaghan asked.

"Female ambercats are hunters," Cal answered, looking up at her. "Males stay close to their dens, watching the young. As a result, only females have developed the power to camouflage their coats." He flipped the pelt over again so she could see what he meant. Everywhere he touched, the fur turned the color of his skin. She gasped.

"Amazing, isn't it?" he asked, letting go of the fur. "This would make beautiful gloves. They'd be invaluable in the wintertime."

"That was my intent," Nick said. "I thought I'd bring it to the tailor in Neiszhe's village."

Cal nodded his approval, and then a hopeful smile spread across his face. "Any meat left?"

"We finished most of it," Nick replied, reaching up to remove a bag from the hook in the ceiling. "But I saved the best roast for last. It'll be enough for four people."

"Fantastic. I'm already starving." Cal rolled up the pelt, then tucked it under his arm and stood. "Grab what you need for a few days in the village. It's time to head out."

§

TIME HAD a way of warping perception, allowing moonlight and sunlight to merge, and tricking the mind into believing days had become weeks. Meaghan had naively fallen for the illusion, letting it convince her that it had been long enough since she fought the Mardróch for her body to heal. Her trip through the forest proved otherwise.

Every jostle brought agony. Every shift of Cal's arms and every step sharpened her pain. When he grew tired and traded her to Nick, his elbow bumping her in the side in the process, she had to bite her lip to keep from crying out. She wished she had taken the time to drink a cup of jicab tea as Nick had suggested. Her ribs ached. Her head throbbed. She struggled to keep her eyes open. And the thought of controlling her power became no more than a fleeting wish.

She clutched the doll in her hands, but her power refused to listen to her command. Nick seemed to realize her waning strength and began using his blocking power soon after leaving the cabin. When Cal's worry and anxiety became too much, she reached out for Nick's power, focused on the peace it brought her, and closed her eyes, only opening them again when Nick's pace slowed. He crossed a small river, long since frozen into a sheet of ice, and entered into a thicker part of the forest. A few recognizable landmarks caught her attention, but otherwise, everything blended together, lost to trees so dense she could not tell if day held the sky or if dusk had descended over them.

Cal turned right. Nick followed. They reached the opening of a low cave, ducked to enter, and then stood tall again when the small entrance yielded to a vast cavern. A stream of light cut through the darkness from a hole in the roof, brightening the front of the cave, though it did nothing to warm the space. The temperature seemed to have dropped ten degrees within the confines of the rocky earth. Meaghan shivered.

"This way," Cal said, banking to his left. A moment later, they stepped around a wall and entered another, smaller cave. This one appeared to be no bigger than the cabin. Every surface but the floor glowed with white crystals. Meaghan shielded her eyes. The world dissolved, and then came back into focus when they teleported into a larger crystal cave. The familiarity of the new cave did not escape her, though it had been many months since Meaghan had last seen it, and the potent effects of raw jicab root had dulled her senses during the initial visit.

Nick sat her on top of a rock as Cal moved underneath a hole in the ceiling. Picking up a wooden torch from the floor, he lit it with a match from his pocket.

"I thought it would be best to keep a torch here after our near brush with the Mardróch," he told them. "It's saved me more than once. They've searched this area at least twice a month since you went into hiding."

He whispered a rhyme, directing the fire to blaze, then closed his eyes and lifted the torch above his head. Smoke escaped through the hole and with it, his power. A few minutes later, he lowered the torch. Waving his hand over the fire, he put it out. "We're good," he said. Turning toward a boulder resting along one wall, he waved his hand again. The boulder slid to the left, revealing a small opening.

The last time she had crawled through the tight tunnel, she had been nursing a broken leg and a sprained ankle. The short distance through the mountain to the outside had been agonizing. This time the pain in her side made her movements difficult, but she emerged on the other side without suffering. She also managed to walk to the village, rather than riding along in Cal's arms like a pesky child who could not keep up. Rows of colorful cottages and houses appeared in the distance, growing larger in welcome as Meaghan trekked across the open field.

When they stepped onto the main road, villagers greeted Cal with familiar waves while Meaghan and Nick received the same curious stares as before. Cal met each person with a courteous nod, but kept a fast pace, leading the way through to a small cottage near the end of the street.

As soon as they turned onto a narrow, cobblestone path, the front door for the cottage opened. A woman rushed toward them, her black hair streaming behind her as she ran, and her smoke-colored eyes dancing with joy. Launching herself into Cal's arms, she pressed her lips to his.

"It's good to see your face, love," she told him when they parted. "It's been too long."

"I know," he whispered. "I missed you too, Neiszhe, but our reunion will have to wait." Drawing his hands up to her cheeks, he kissed her again before nodding toward Meaghan. "You have a patient."

Neiszhe turned her head. Although her eyes met Meaghan's and then flicked down her body, Meaghan realized the woman did not see her as much as she used her power to sense for an injury. When her gaze alit on Meaghan's side, she pressed her lips together, and then sighed. "You're worse than May told us."

"It's not that bad," Meaghan responded, and covered her side with her hand.

Neiszhe shook her head. "I disagree, but it shouldn't take long to fix. Come inside and we'll get started."

Relief washed through Meaghan before she checked it. Her wound burned from the trip and she wanted to take Neiszhe up on the offer without a second thought, but Neiszhe's face looked tight and pale, her eyes tired, and Meaghan had her doubts that lack of sleep had contributed to the slight tremor in the woman's lips. Meaghan tugged her power away from Nick's, commanding it to follow her will. It took all of her focus, but she managed to train it on Cal's wife before the dozens of other emotions in the village broke through her resolve. She reached for Nick's power again.

Though her connection with Neiszhe's emotions had been brief, it had been long enough. She tilted her head, studying the woman before trailing her attention to Cal. Given what she had sensed, she had expected to see worry or concern on his face, but he remained calm. A moment later, she understood why. He did not know.

Meaghan's gaze returned to Neiszhe. "Can you even do the job?" she asked. "Is it safe?"

"Of course. Why would you think," Neiszhe started, then drew her hand to her stomach. Her eyes widened. "How did you know?"

"My power," Meaghan responded, but said no more when Cal placed a hand on Neiszhe's shoulder, and turned her so she faced him.

"What does she mean?" he asked. "Is something wrong?"

"It's nothing," Neiszhe told him. "We should get Meaghan inside if we want to—"

"I don't believe you. You look pale."

"I'm fine," she insisted. "I'm just—"

"Distracted," Meaghan said, offering Neiszhe a cover. She had not intended to worry Cal or to give away his wife's secret. "She missed you. I thought her emotions might impact her power."

"Neiszhe's one of the best Healers in the kingdom," Cal responded and his tone conveyed both anger and a warning Meaghan did not miss. "I don't appreciate you insinuating she'd be anything less than professional."

"I'm sure she didn't mean it that way," Nick said, stepping in front of Meaghan. "How long has it been since you were home last?"

"Don't change the subject," Cal growled, crossing his arms. "Meaghan's out of line. I expect an apology."

Neiszhe sighed. "It's all right, love. Answer Nick's question."

"Fine." Cal dropped his arms, though his eyes remained heated and locked on Meaghan's. "Six weeks, give or take a few days."

"You gave us the impression you'd spoken recently," Nick said.

Cal shrugged. "We talk through the fires when there's wind. There's been a lot here over the past few weeks."

"But it's not the same as seeing each other. Why has it been so long?"

"You aren't the only ones who are targets. The Mardróch have traced me back to my home twice over the past three months. It's easy enough to change caves, but here," Cal hesitated, looking around at the people as they hurried by, at the houses surrounding them. "I don't want to think about what those monsters would do if they followed me here."

"They're able to trace you because you're moving around a lot," Meaghan whispered. She grabbed Nick's hand as the weight of her words settled over her. "Because you're helping us. We've put you in danger."

"You haven't," Cal said. "I choose to help. Not because of who you are, but because I loved your father, and Nick's. It's not just you, though. My power makes me a target. I can't exactly make it go away."

"I guess not," Meaghan conceded, though she did not feel any less guilty. Weariness washed over her and she closed her eyes, only opening them when a pair of hands bracketed her shoulders.

Neiszhe stared back at her. "Let me heal you."

"No," Meaghan protested. She brought her hands to Neiszhe's wrists and held them there, commanding the woman's attention with the gesture. "You can sense my injury. You know I'm not in danger."

Neiszhe tightened her grip. Meaghan could also see protest tightening her face, ready to form on her lips when she parted them, but Meaghan did not let the woman speak.

"I insist," she commanded, and then lowered her voice so only Neiszhe could hear. "Please let me do this for you. You need time with Cal."

Neiszhe held Meaghan's gaze, and then nodded. "If you insist, my lady, then I have no choice." She squeezed Meaghan's shoulders, then let go. "But you'll drink a pot of jicab tea before you sleep."

"That isn't necessary."

Neiszhe's lips curved into a smile. "It's the only way I'll agree."

"You shouldn't be agreeing at all," Cal muttered. "Meaghan might think she's entitled, but she has no right to treat you like—"

"Be quiet, Cal," Neiszhe's soft voice cut through Cal's building reprimand. "Or you'll say something you'll regret."

"She's out of line," he blustered in response. "I hardly think I'm going to—"

"You will," she assured him. "Now come along. If you want to be my hero, you can start a fire in the kitchen so we can brew tea. I don't have the patience to light the stove today."

She turned and went back inside, leaving Cal staring after her in bewilderment.

CHAPTER THIRTEEN

"DO YOU want to tell me what happened this afternoon?" Nick asked. He threw one more log onto the fire, and then straightened up, turning from the fireplace to face Meaghan. She lay across the bed in the guest cottage, holding the cornhusk doll in her hands. He had expected her to fall asleep by now. Though curiosity had bugged him since their bizarre conversation with Neiszhe, he had refrained from asking Meaghan any questions while he built the fire, giving her the quiet she needed to rest. But when it became obvious his expectation and reality would not meet anytime soon, he allowed his curiosity to take over.

Setting the doll down at her side, she smiled at him. "I'm not sure what you mean."

He crossed the room to sit next to her on the bed. "You know exactly what I mean. You should have allowed Neiszhe to heal you. Why didn't you?"

"I wanted her and Cal to have time together," Meaghan responded. "It isn't fair they have to be apart so much." Picking up the doll again, she touched a finger to its hair. "I can't seem to master this technique. My hold only lasts a few minutes, and then the emotions flood through."

"You're injured," he reminded her. "That makes things a lot harder. Even if you weren't, controlling your power won't happen overnight. It's going to take time."

She frowned at him. "How long?"

"It's hard to say. Based on how fast you learned to control your revival power, I'd guess a few weeks."

"Weeks," she echoed and closed her eyes. "I want it to be sooner. We're putting Cal in danger."

Nick lowered his lips to her forehead. When she opened her eyes again, he stroked a thumb across her brow. "Danger is part of life," he said. "We can't change that. And we can't change Cal. He won't stop protecting us even after we return to the Elders. He'll still be away from home. He'll still be doing what he feels is right."

"He needs to be here," she told him. "He may not want to change, but he'll have to soon. He won't have a choice."

Nick withdrew his hand from her face. "What do you mean? What do you know?"

She sat up. "It's not anything bad. At least, Neiszhe seemed to be happy about the news. I suspect Cal will be, too."

"What news?"

"They're going to have a baby."

"They...what?" Nick shook his head, disbelieving her words. "Meg, Cal's fifty-four."

Meaghan shrugged. "And he wed a younger woman. It happens.

He may be older than most who become fathers for the first time, but it doesn't change the fact he'll be one."

"Maybe," Nick conceded. "But I don't see how you could know about it. Only Healers can sense a pregnancy."

"Apparently not. I can sense the baby's emotion."

"What emotions?"

"Not emotions. Emotion. Just one, contentment. Although I imagine there'll be more as the baby grows."

Nick frowned. "So you're basing your diagnosis on a single emotion you sensed from Neiszhe?"

"Not from Neiszhe, from her baby."

"You can't be certain of that. It wouldn't be a stretch to say Neiszhe feels content when she's with Cal. And if it came from her direction," he hesitated, unsure of how to finish his sentence without insulting Meaghan.

"Then there's no way I could isolate her emotions from her baby's," she finished for him. "Is that what you think?" He nodded and she laughed. "I can tell what direction emotions come from, even when I can't see who they're coming from," she reminded him. "And when I'm with several people, I can tell who's feeling what. Why wouldn't I be able to distinguish Neiszhe's emotions from her baby's?"

"Because telling people apart is different. They're separate from each other. Neiszhe and her baby share the same space."

"True, but the baby's contentment feels different. It's hard to explain, but it's faint, primal, I guess."

"Undeveloped," he offered, finally understanding.

"Exactly."

"That's incredible," he said, studying the conviction in Meaghan's eyes. It erased any lingering doubt from his mind. Somehow she had learned to differentiate the smallest signals her power gathered. He never would have expected her to gain such command over her empath power in a few years, let alone in the few months she had been in Ærenden.

He reached his hands up to bracket her face, and then grazed his lips over hers. "You should get some rest," he said. "There's a festival starting tomorrow. Neiszhe will heal you in the morning and by afternoon you should be able to practice controlling your power around crowds. For now," he placed his hands on her shoulders and eased her down on to the bed, "sleep."

Without protest, she let him draw the blankets up to her chin and promptly did as he had asked.

§

"WHAT A day to be out of spirit," Cal exclaimed the next morning after Nick and Meaghan had arrived at Neiszhe's house. He held his chest high, his eyes sparkling as he greeted them and Meaghan felt giddy with Cal's contagious excitement.

"It seems a toast is in order," he continued, clapping Nick on the back. "It's the perfect day for it."

"It's a bit early to be drinking, isn't it?" Nick asked.

"Not when there's cause for celebration," Cal responded. His gaze fell on Meaghan and he scooped her into his arms, crushing her in a tight hug. Pain shot through her side, but she gritted her teeth against it.

"You knew," he said when he set her back down. "I thought you were being, well," he shrugged. "Your mother could be spoiled sometimes. She got bossy when she didn't get her way."

"I didn't want to give anything away," Meaghan said, bringing a hand up to her wound. The pain increased. "I thought Neiszhe ought to be the one to share the news."

Cal chuckled. "Well, you had me fooled. I thought I'd have to lecture you today, but Neiszhe set me straight. Not soon enough, though. I owe you an apology."

Meaghan shook her head, but could not manage the words to go with the gesture. Her ribs burned too much to allow much breath. Her skin felt wet beneath her sweater. Nick's arm came around her waist.

"Meg," he started, but Cal interrupted.

"She looks pale. Is she okay?"

"I don't think so." Nick's voice seemed distant. Meaghan shook her head to clear the haze surrounding it.

"I think I'd better get Neiszhe," Cal said, and without waiting for a response, disappeared into the kitchen. Nick guided Meaghan to the couch. She sat, grateful to relieve her shaking legs, then felt panic rise when Nick lifted her sweater and cursed.

"You need to lie down," he told her. Worry painted his face. She glanced at her side, saw red, and allowed him to pull her down. She closed her eyes. Something soft pressed against her wound, swelling her pain.

"I have tea," Cal's voice came from across the room. Heavy footsteps moved toward the couch. "What happened?"

"She's bleeding again," Nick said.

"She had stitches," Neiszhe's voice came from beside Nick. "I sensed them yesterday."

"She popped some a few days ago," Nick told her. "The wound seemed to have healed enough so I didn't redo them, but—"

"I broke more when I hugged her," Cal realized. "Damn," he muttered. "I'm an idiot. How bad is it?"

The cloth moved for a second, and then the pressure returned. Meaghan opened her eyes in time to see the panic on Neiszhe's face.

"Has she had any tea?" she asked.

"Not yet," Cal responded.

"Get some into her. She'll need it for an accelerated healing. I'll be right back."

Cal nodded and Neiszhe rushed from the room, exiting the house through the front door.

"Where's she going?" Nick asked.

"To get help," Cal said, setting a mug down on the coffee table. "Keep applying pressure to the wound. I'll prop her up so she can drink."

Nick nodded and Cal lifted Meaghan by the shoulders. Sitting down on the couch beside her, Cal used his body to brace her back, then handed her the mug. She gulped the vile liquid down as fast as she could manage, ignoring the heat scalding her mouth, and soon reaped the reward of her effort. The pain in her side dulled, soothed by a numbing warmth. When she set the mug down, Cal spoke again.

"I reached May through the fire last night," he said. "I wanted to confirm Neiszhe would be okay to heal Meaghan under the circumstances."

"What did Mom say?" Nick asked.

"That basic healing would be fine, but if things got complicated, Neiszhe wouldn't be able to complete the job without putting the baby in danger. She recommended a backup plan just in case."

"Good thing for that," Nick muttered. He shifted his hand, applying more pressure, and Meaghan winced. He picked up the mug and handed it to her. "There's a little left."

She nodded and sipped as Cal spoke. "Neiszhe's been training an apprentice. He'll do the healing, but so you know, he and the other villagers think Meaghan is Neiszhe's cousin. It's the story we used after you left last time. We told them her name's Adara."

"Easy enough to remember," Nick said. "What's my story?"

"That may be more difficult to remember. You're her husband. Your name's Nick."

Meaghan's laughter came so swift she spit out the last sip of her tea, spraying the side of the couch. "Ow," she protested as her hand came up to cover her side. Her fingers met Nick's, and the towel he used to staunch her blood. "Don't make me laugh."

Cal grinned and stood, easing her back down to the couch as the front door opened. Neiszhe entered, followed closely by a young man. Thick, red curls topped his face, giving him a cherubic appearance. He brought a hand to his mouth to chew on already short fingernails while his green eyes darted around the room. When they fell on Meaghan, he smiled, flashing dimples in her direction.

She swallowed her nerves, and wondered if he was old enough to control his power, let alone manage an accelerated healing. When Cal chuckled and patted her on the shoulder, her cheeks burned with embarrassment. Apparently, her face had given away her fears.

"Mycale's not as young or inexperienced as he looks," Cal assured her. "And Neiszhe will be sensing his progress the entire time. You'll be fine."

"He's right," the young man said and despite the nerves he had displayed when he first entered the room, his voice held steady. He approached the couch and knelt beside Meaghan. "It just takes me a minute to adjust to feeling pain from someone else."

"I can understand that," Meaghan said, but refrained from saying anything more about it. He could not know how well she understood his reaction or how well she could empathize with the oddity of processing someone else's emotions. Only the Queen had an empath power, and right now, she needed to be someone else. "How long have you been healing people?"

"My power first showed up when I was five. My father's a Healer, so I've helped him since. Let me have a look at your wound." Mycale took the towel from Nick and lifted it, then pressed it back down. Closing his eyes, he spread both of his hands over the towel. A look of concentration passed over his face. "You have three cracked ribs," he told her, "and your wound is severe, but those stitches saved your life. I'll need to take them out to do my job, though."

"I'll get some scissors," Cal offered and left the room.

"When I remove them," Mycale continued, "your bleeding will get worse. Do you know what accelerated healing is?"

"I've heard of it," Meaghan said without having to lie. Nick had explained it to her when he told her the story of her father's healing.

At the time, she thought how horrible it sounded, but now it seemed even worse.

"But you've never been through it?"

"No."

"Have you been through a regular healing before?"

"Once," Nick told him. "She had a broken leg."

"Then you understand the pain involved in the healing process," Mycale said. "This is a lot worse. It won't be easy, but I find it's more tolerable for my patients if they have the steady contact of a loved one."

Mycale shifted down to clear room on the floor beside Meaghan's head. Nick filled the vacated spot. Taking her hand in one of his, he rested his other palm against her brow. For a moment, his fear swelled as his hold on his power slipped, and then the emotion disappeared. She met his eyes and found strength in them.

Mycale began removing the stitches. Nick's fingers tightened around Meaghan's hand, and a moment later, pain cascaded through her. She dragged breath in and out of her lungs, and then gritted her teeth to keep from screaming. The effort did not last long. Cries ripped from her throat before she could control them. They raked through her, joining with the fire springing from Mycale's hands. When even that outlet no longer alleviated the agony squeezing her mind, she sought solace in the same darkness her father had found so many years before.

CHAPTER FOURTEEN

LESS THAN six hours later, Meaghan basked in the sun's waning warmth, amazed at how fast things could change. This morning, a chill had soaked the air, clinging to her frozen skin as she walked from the guesthouse to Neiszhe's cottage. Now, the day felt renewed. As did she. Her fingers sought her side, pressed, and found no pain.

"You're not bleeding," Nick's voice broke into her thoughts.

She turned to face him. "I know that."

"Then stop poking at your side."

She scowled, but her agitation eased when he chuckled in response, letting her know he had been teasing. Bringing an arm around her waist, he planted a kiss on her temple, and then skimmed his eyes over the scene in front of them. She followed his gaze.

The main road for the village teemed with people, their voices overlapping in excitement. Lines snaked past booths set up in front of houses, offering food and drink. A vendor offered some sort of pink meat on a stick to Meaghan's left and the sweet aroma awakened her appetite, but before she could take one, her attention jumped to another item and then a third, each more tantalizing than the last. Young kids slurped seeds from the rind of a yellow and white striped fruit. An old man devoured a thin green pancake stuffed with grilled vegetables. A woman clutched one of the largest turkey legs Meghan had ever seen. Teenagers chowed down on multi-colored popcorn kernels. And everyone seemed to have a goblet in their hands. When a few people staggered by, she guessed Cal would not have trouble making a toast tonight.

Interspersed among the crowd, tables provided places to congregate and eat. Musicians played and danced. Jugglers dressed as clowns entertained groups of children. A fire starter designed elaborate shapes in the sky, sparking and fading flames so that smoky paintings remained behind. And three men who appeared to be triplets hovered overhead, performing acrobatic feats.

"How are you feeling?" Nick asked.

"Good." She reached behind her back to feel for the doll she had tucked into her belt. Hidden by her cloak, only she and Nick knew it existed. Her focus remained intact, steadier than it had ever been before. It seemed Nick had been right about her pain distracting her from gaining control.

"I'll keep my power on all night," he told her. "So don't try to overdo it. Use my power to block yours whenever you need. And Meg," he focused his full attention on her, broadcasting his seriousness in both his gaze and his tone. "I need you to make a promise."

"What?"

"Don't try to use your power on anything but the doll. I know you'll want to at some point tonight, but I'd prefer you master this part of the technique first."

"All right," she agreed, and then turned her head when she caught a familiar scent. "Roast lamb," she said in longing. "This festival is so impressive. I don't even know where to begin. What's it for?"

"The birth of our kingdom," Nick said, and began guiding her through the crowd. His voice remained at a whisper and she realized everyone who grew up in the kingdom would know the festival. The fact Meaghan knew nothing about it would give away their identities if they were not careful. "The Founders' Festival celebrates Ærenden's beginning and the first King and Queen." He stopped in front of a booth to pick up two wooden goblets, and then pressed one into her palm, forcing her to grasp it. "Try this."

She raised an eyebrow. "What is it?"

"Founder's juice. It's a mix of several different types of berries. It's only made for the festival."

She sniffed the deep red fluid, wrinkling her nose when a sour-tart aroma greeted her, followed by the scent of strong alcohol.

Nick chuckled. "Just try it, all right? I'm not going to poison you."

She lifted the goblet to her lips. A thick liquid coursed over her tongue, first burning it, and then settling into soothing warmth. The taste blossomed, both complex and familiar, and she lowered the goblet in surprise. "It tastes like spiced wine, but darker, more like blackberries than grapes."

"That's a good description," Nick agreed. "But be careful. It has more alcohol than you're used to, and you haven't eaten much."

"We should fix that," a voice came from behind Meaghan. She

turned, smiling in recognition when Mycale's grin greeted her. He slid his hands into his pockets. Even though he slouched some, he towered over Meaghan by almost a foot. "I'm famished myself. Accelerated healing takes a lot of energy."

"I imagine so," she responded. "Thank you for that. I was sorry to see you left before I woke."

"It's my pleasure." He nodded toward a booth across the street. "Shall we get food? The baker just put out fresh envelope pies."

Nick led the way through the crowd. Locating the baker's booth, he grabbed three small, white bags from the counter, then handed one each to Meaghan and Mycale. Meaghan set her goblet down at a table close by, and opened her bag. Steam escaped, carrying the scent of pastry and meat with it.

Nick tore his bag down the middle, and then folded over the paper so he could use it to hold the pie. Meaghan mimicked his movements, revealing the envelope shaped pastry nestled inside. She took her first, tentative bite, sucked in a breath of cold air to keep from scorching her tongue, and then savored the flavor. The ground meat tasted like a sweeter version of beef, spiced with cinnamon and nutmeg. A berry exploded in her mouth, overwhelming her senses with memories of pumpkin pie, and she realized the baker had laced the meat with spice berries. She took another bite, tasted currant, and smiled. The envelope pie offered a savory and sweet combination that had her devouring it in half a dozen fast bites.

"This is amazing," she said.

Digging into the bag, she pinched up the last of the crumbs and dropped them into her mouth. She cast Nick an embarrassed smile when he raised an eyebrow at her, not bothering to mask the amusement dancing within his eyes.

"What type of meat was that?" she asked, tossing the bag into a nearby trashcan.

"Bison. Do you want another one?"

She shook her head, though she felt more than a little tempted. "There's too much food to try. I don't want to miss anything."

Mycale chuckled. "You act like you've never been to a Founder's Festival before."

"She does this every year," Nick said, covering her slip with a wave of his hand. "It's her favorite holiday."

"It's everybody's favorite holiday," Mycale responded. "And it's hard not to get excited this year, given the recent turn of events."

Meaghan nodded, pretending to know what he meant.

"Besides," Mycale continued, offering her a sheepish smile. "A lot of it's new to me, too. My village is half this size, so our festival isn't nearly as good."

"Where are you from?" Nick asked.

"A village by the Zeiihbu border," Mycale answered. "In a valley below Clear Mountain."

Nick raised an eyebrow. "You're a long way from home. Isn't it customary for Healers to apprentice at a village nearby?"

Mycale's hands slipped back into his pockets. He rocked on his heels, and Meaghan realized the motion stemmed from nerves. Despite the promise Nick had elicited from her, she refocused her power from the doll to the young man in front of her. She sensed his nervousness, as she had expected. But she also sensed deceit. The added emotion concerned her and she decided to keep her power focused on Mycale until his intention became clear.

"It is," he confirmed. "But my dad's the only Healer in the area. I suppose I could have apprenticed with him, but I wanted the chance to explore the kingdom."

"During a war?" Nick pressed. "That's risky. I wouldn't have expected the Elders to approve your request."

Mycale shrugged. "I don't answer to them. I'm not a Guardian."

"Yet you're training under a Guardian."

"I didn't have much of a choice," Mycale said, and irritation emanated from him, though he did not show it. "There aren't many Healers who aren't Guardians, and since Cal served with my father in the royal army, Neiszhe offered to apprentice me."

"Is it rare for a Healer not to be a Guardian?" Meaghan asked.

"Apparently," Mycale said. "Though I didn't realize it until the time came for me to apprentice. My father and I are the only ones."

Nick cocked his head, studying the younger man. "But you said your father was in the army. He has to be a Guardian."

"He was once, but he isn't anymore. He hasn't been since soon after the war started."

"Wait," Nick said, frowning. "You mean your father is Darvin?"

Mycale's eyes grew wide. "You know my father?"

"I've heard stories."

"What have you heard?"

"Nothing of significance," Nick told him. "I know he's the only Guardian to ask the Elders to strip him of his powers, though no one knows why. Is that true?"

"Yes," Mycale confirmed.

"I thought as much. Everything else I know is based on rumor. You wouldn't want to hear it."

"I'm sure I already have," Mycale said. He pulled his hands from his pockets and tightened them into fists. "People say he worked with Garon to kill the Queen and King and later regretted it or that he secretly knew my mother before they wed and didn't want to admit he broke the rule. They also say he went crazy, killing everyone in sight, but the Elders didn't have enough proof to throw him in jail. Are there any new ones?"

Nick shook his head. "That pretty much covers it."

"My father's a good man. He wouldn't do any of those things."

"If Cal let you work with his wife, I'm sure he wouldn't," Nick said and laid a hand on Mycale's arm. "You came here hoping to learn the truth, didn't you? You thought Cal would know the reason your father had his powers stripped."

"Yeah, maybe," Mycale confessed. "But he didn't know." His deceit disappeared, replaced by shame. Relieved his emotions had not represented any threat, Meaghan refocused her power on the doll. Although she had managed to keep the crowd's emotions at bay, her vision had begun to haze from the energy it had taken to perform the task. She closed her eyes. The world tilted, and then hands gripped her shoulders, steadying her.

"That's odd," Mycale said. His voice came from next to her ear and she realized the hands belonged to him. His hold tightened. "I sense exhaustion. That doesn't make any sense. Did she rest before she came here?"

An arm looped around her waist, and Mycale's hands disappeared. "All afternoon," Nick muttered. "I think I'd better take her back to the guest cottage."

"I'm fine," she protested and forced her eyes open. "I want to stay. I don't want to miss the festival."

"You should have thought of that before," Nick said, and the anger in his voice told her he realized what she had done.

"Before what?" Mycale asked.

"Nothing." Nick shifted the pressure of his arm, pulling Meaghan away from the crowd, toward the cottage. "She's had too much juice, that's all."

"She's not drunk," Mycale protested. "I'd be able to sense that. It feels more like she ran through a training course."

"She's just tired," Nick said, quickening his pace. "I'm going to take her—"

Mycale locked a hand on Nick's arm, forcing him to stop. "You aren't taking her anywhere," he insisted and the crowd around them backed away, clearing a circle in anticipation of a fight. "She's still my patient. I refuse to let you put her in danger."

"She's not in danger." Shaking off Mycale's hand, Nick started moving again. A hush fell over the crowd as a dozen pairs of eyes locked on Meaghan. "I'm her husband. I know how to take care of her."

Mycale moved around them, and then stood his ground, blocking their path. "She needs medical attention. You can't help her with that."

"Looks like we have our first juice fight," a loud voice boomed from across the street. The crowd parted and Cal made his way through. Though his words sounded slurred, evidence of his own celebratory drinking, he maintained complete control of his movements and the anger sparking heat in his eyes. He grabbed Mycale by the scruff of the neck. "How much have you had, lad?"

"I haven't had any. Nick's trying to—"

"Not a sip," Cal said and chuckled. Those in the crowd closest to him did the same. "That's always the story of new drinkers, isn't it?" More people joined in on the laughter. "I guess I'd better take him back to Neiszhe's to sober up." He turned his focus toward Nick and faked a grin. "Her too?"

"Looks like it," Nick responded, adding levity to his own voice. "Adara can't hold her juice."

"Must run in the family. Neiszhe can't either. Come along," Cal said and ignoring Mycale's sputtering, he dragged the young man down the street.

§

"I'M NOT drunk!" Mycale protested when Cal finally let him go. He brought a hand to the back of his neck and rubbed at the red marks Meaghan had no doubt would bruise by morning. "I swear. I didn't have anything to drink. Neiszhe, tell him."

Rather than respond, Neiszhe stood in the doorway to the kitchen, shaking her head. Her eyes darted from Mycale to Cal, and then to Meaghan as Nick deposited her on the couch.

"Tell him," Mycale begged again. "He thinks—"

"He doesn't," Neiszhe said when her eyes came to rest on the young man. "Cal knows drunk. He doesn't need me to tell him who is and isn't." She returned her gaze to her husband. "What happened?"

Cal shrugged. "Your guess is as good as mine. Everyone was having a good time, and then Nick and Mycale decided to get into a fight. The crowd was ready for the entertainment, so they dropped whatever they were doing to watch. I had to come up with a reason for the spat so no one would gossip about it."

Neiszhe crossed her arms over her chest.

"Okay, so they won't gossip as much as they would if they'd guessed the truth. Drunk is a regular excuse for the festival. I figured it was the best way to go."

"We didn't *decide* to get into a fight," Nick said. "I was trying to get her out of there and Mycale felt it appropriate to stop me."

Mycale's cheeks flashed almost as red as his hair. He spun around to face Nick. "I wouldn't have needed to if you had let me look at her. We don't know what happened to her. Until we know, she needs to be under the care of a Healer. It's my job to protect her."

"I know how to protect her far better than you ever could. You have no idea how much danger you put her in by—"

"And this is why Healers and Guardians are usually one and the same," Cal interrupted.

Mycale's attention shot to Cal. His eyes grew wide. "What did you say?"

"When you first arrived, you asked me why there are no other Healers who aren't Guardians. This is why. The power evolved that way to prevent Healers and Guardians from killing each other. Both positions instill protectiveness. You got the power from your father because he was a Guardian. Otherwise, you wouldn't be a Healer."

"I don't understand." Mycale's gaze traveled back to Nick. "But that means—"

"He's her Guardian," Cal finished for him.

Mycale's brows knit together. "Why would you lie to me about that?"

"We did it to protect them, and you. But now you know and your life will depend on keeping their secret."

"What secret?" Mycale backed up against an armchair and lowered into it. "Why would my life depend on me not telling anyone he's a Guardian?"

"Because he's May's son," Neiszhe responded when everyone else remained silent. She let out a long sigh then pressed a hand to her stomach and addressed Cal. "There's a pot of jicab tea ready on the stove. Would you get it for me, please? Bring three mugs. It looks like Meaghan needs some. I'm feeling nauseous, and I'm fairly certain we're about to put Mycale in shock."

Cal nodded and disappeared behind his wife into the kitchen.

"May," Mycale echoed. "Do you mean the Healer who visited my father last year?"

"One and the same," Neiszhe said.

"So that would make Nick…oh no," Mycale's eyes jerked toward the couch, then widened. "You called her Meaghan. She's Queen Meaghan."

"And there you have it," Cal said from the kitchen doorway. He moved around Neiszhe to place a tray on the coffee table. On top of the tray sat four mugs and a tea pot. "So now you know why we're not concerned about her current bout of exhaustion. This isn't the first time her empath power has gotten the best of her."

"It didn't," Meaghan protested. Her dizziness had subsided and she smiled with pride for her accomplishment. "It went better than we expected. I held control the entire time."

"Is that so? Then why aren't you still at the festival?"

"Because she took a risk she shouldn't have," Nick told him. When she opened her mouth to argue, he shot her a look that silenced her. "She tried focusing her power on people instead of the doll. She wasn't ready, and after her healing, she didn't have the energy for it."

"Headstrong and foolish," Cal decided. "Maybe you're not a whole lot different from your mother after all."

Meaghan narrowed her eyes into a glare in response, but he ignored her in favor of pouring tea into mugs. He handed the first to her. "Drink up. After the fiasco tonight, you'll need to head back home. Remember that when you're traipsing through two feet of snow instead of enjoying the rest of the festival."

Cal's words erased her pride. She risked a glimpse at Nick, saw the disappointment on his face, and felt even worse for breaking her promise. They could have had a few days around other people, but now they would have to go back to the cabin, and their solitude. She stared into her cup and realized it was not just foolishness that had gripped her, but selfishness.

One look around the room confirmed how miserable her actions had made everyone. Cal looked weary and angry. He had seemed excited to spend time with Nick. Now he would not have the chance.

Neiszhe not only appeared nauseous, but worried. She cast her eyes toward the source of that worry—Mycale. Her intent had been to keep her apprentice out of the danger Meaghan had forced upon him. Meaghan's mug shook in her hands, spilling hot liquid onto her skin. She closed her eyes, ignoring the sharp pain it brought.

"The tea's not going to do you any good if you don't drink it," Nick said. When she did not respond, he draped an arm around her shoulders and drew her close. "We need you to think about these things because you put yourself in danger when you do them. But we don't want you to feel this bad."

She heard Cal chuckle and opened her eyes. "We've all done it," he told her. "You're getting the crash course on power management, so things are a little more difficult for you, but you can't make mistakes we haven't made. And I guarantee you'll never make a mistake as big as I did."

She shook her head. "I'm sure your mistakes never put people in danger like mine do."

"Oh no?" He raised an eyebrow. "Do you really think the elements are safe to control? Or I should say, to lose control over?"

"I hadn't thought about it."

"I hadn't either when I first started training with my powers. I wanted to learn everything at once, but the instructors insisted I learn to manage the elements one at a time, starting with earth and moving up to wind. I was certain they didn't know what they were talking about. I couldn't create wind, but I had been told I could harness it and one blustery day I decided to give it a try. I grabbed hold of the wind, commanded it to follow where I wanted it to go, and for a while, it did."

"Then what happened?" Neiszhe asked.

"I wasn't strong enough. The wind started swirling together, and the next thing I knew, it had taken on a life of its own. My tornado lasted five minutes and destroyed three buildings." He raised an eyebrow and a half-smile at Meaghan. "I highly doubt your empath power can do that."

Meaghan laughed. "I guess not, but I'll be more careful from now on, just in case."

"Pay attention to Nick," Cal said, turning serious again. "He's a good teacher, but you have to listen to him."

"I will," she promised. "You've made your point. I just wish I'd learned it before I ruined our visit."

"It's not ruined," Nick told her. "The timing's right for your plan. I think we should make the detour before we head home."

"What plan?" Cal asked.

"Stop by the guest cottage tomorrow and I'll tell you. We'll hide out there during the day and take off at nightfall. It should be easy enough to sneak out during the festivities. How long is the festival this year?"

"A week," Cal answered. "In honor of the Queen's return. Although, to be honest, I'm not sure how many people will still be conscious enough to celebrate after more than a few days of eating and drinking."

Nick chuckled and stood. Offering Meaghan a hand, he pulled her to her feet. "I'll take Meaghan to the cottage. She needs sleep." He turned to Mycale. "I trust there are no objections this time?"

Mycale shook his head. "I'm too confused to object."

"Don't worry," Neiszhe said. "I'll explain it all, but first," she handed her empty mug to Cal. "I'll take a refill. It's going to be a long night."

CHAPTER FIFTEEN

THE VILLAGE retreated behind them. Meaghan turned and cast a longing glance toward the rows of charming houses. After nightfall, the villagers had strung lanterns along the streets, which now cast a glow into the sky. Laughter floated across the air, mixing with the first notes of a spirited song. A full band played tonight. There would be dancing and more food than her stomach could handle. She adjusted the backpack on her shoulders and thought about the dinner awaiting them. Cold ambercat. Again.

At least they had been able to enjoy the warm roast for lunch. It was the last of the food they had in their supplies, and though Cal promised to deliver more before they returned to the cabin, what he brought would pale in comparison to the offerings at the festival. She sighed and turned back around. She had learned her lesson tenfold this time.

Nick's hand sought hers. "There'll be other festivals," he said, and though she knew he had intended his words to make her feel better, they did not help. She squeezed his hand and let it go.

"My mother once told me the castle threw a huge festival," he continued. "Probably five times the size of this one. The King and Queen brought in food from every area of the kingdom and invited the best entertainers to perform. People talked about it for weeks after."

"I'm sure they did."

"We should revive the tradition once we return to the castle. Maybe we could even make it bigger than your parents did."

That suggestion made her feel better. The thought of watching the people of Ærenden at the biggest festival they had ever seen warmed her. She could picture them dancing, the weariness on their faces and the grief in their eyes erased with the joy of celebration. It would be the perfect time to honor their survival and their sacrifice, to remind them they had held the kingdom together despite Garon's attempts to tear it apart.

"I'd really like that," she responded.

"Good." Nick smiled, and then focused his eyes on the horizon. Her gaze trailed after his. The field stretched before them, a deep ocean of grass under a river of stars, and she watched it dissolve into the eclipsing black. When Nick spoke again, his voice had turned into a near whisper and she realized he did not want their conversation to travel ahead of them. "It's odd," he said. "I never expected to be doing this. I never thought I'd have to worry about morale or decisions that could potentially destroy their lives."

"What do you mean?" Meaghan asked. She stopped and laid a hand on his arm, prompting him to halt beside her.

"There are a lot of decisions we'll be making as King and Queen.

Decisions that affect everyone, that could help us succeed. Or fail."

"Like our plan for tomorrow," she guessed.

"Yes," he agreed. "That's one. Another is appointing our advisor. It's a position that's second to ours. Whomever we choose will have access to everything we do, including secrets no one else will know. He or she will make decisions for us when we're not around, and give advice."

"It's a lot of responsibility for one person," Meaghan said. Nick continued walking. She followed. "And a lot of power," she added, realizing the root of his worry. "Do you think we'll make the same mistake my mother did?"

He slid his hands into his pockets. "Before we left, Cal asked me to consider him for the role. It's our decision to make together, of course, but," he shrugged.

"He's a good choice," she offered. "I'd agree if you wanted him. You've known him your whole life. He's trustworthy."

"Everyone thought Garon was, too. Your mother chose him when she took the throne because the Elders recommended him. She chose him because he grew up with Cal, Sam, and my mother. They vouched for him. None of them thought him capable of murder."

"So we need to second guess everyone now?" Meaghan asked. When Nick did not respond, she released her control over her power and cast it toward him. Although Nick took care to hide his fear, it flowed as a dark undercurrent within him. "Nick," she said and waited for his feet to still before speaking again. "Don't do this. I know we have to be careful in our positions, but we can't live by distrust."

He turned to look at her, his face now as shadowed as his emotions. "What other choice do we have?" he asked. "This decision is too important, and I don't have the luxury of your power to know if someone is deceiving me. I have no way of knowing whom to trust. I have no way of knowing what Cal's motives are for wanting the position."

"My power doesn't tell me who to trust," she corrected him. "It doesn't allow me to see into the future or to know if someone will betray us. It only lets me feel other people's emotions. While I'm good at guessing what those emotions mean, I'm wrong at times. It would be foolish of me to trust people based on those guesses. Only three things can determine trust—time, knowledge, and intuition."

She covered the distance between them so she stood in front of him, and then brought her fingers to his temple. "What does your mind tell you? You've known Cal a long time. What memories do you have of him? How has he treated you? These things will tell you the makeup of his character. But most importantly," she dropped her hand to his chest, "they trigger your intuition. Your heart can understand the depth of a soul better than your brain can, and it's faster about it. So what does your heart say?"

"It says I'm betraying him by thinking this way. He's always been there for me. Even now, he's the only one who knows where we're hiding and he risks his life to keep that secret. He's a good man." Nick turned his eyes toward the distant village. "But so was Angus. Or so I thought."

His sorrow washed over Meaghan. She brought her arms around his neck. "I'm sorry," she whispered. "I know how much you've lost because of Garon, but don't let him take Cal from you, too. Cal loves you. You don't need a power to see that. And you don't need a power to know his motive for wanting the position. It's the same reason he brings us supplies, and the same reason he led us through the wilderness when we first arrived in Ærenden. Think about it. Would he even want the position if you weren't the King? He isn't exactly the political type."

Nick pulled her closer. "I hadn't thought of it that way. Cal isn't a fan of following protocol or diplomacy. I'm sure he would do a great job, but," he hesitated.

"But it'll be a little like watching a walrus learn to walk a tightrope," Meaghan offered and grinned. "He definitely won't relish the position, so why do you think he wants it?"

"Because he's as worried about history repeating itself as I am," Nick said. "The only way he can know for certain our advisor is trustworthy is by filling the position himself. He's trying to protect me."

"I believe so. It's certainly easier for him to do that at your side."

"You're right," he said and relaxed his hold, shifting back to look at her. "Maybe we don't need an advisor after all. You seem to have the wisdom part down."

"Sure I do, which is why we're making our way through the dark instead of enjoying a party in the village."

He started laughing, and for a moment, life seemed as carefree as it had on Earth. She lifted her lips to his, relishing in his stiff surprise at first, and then in the urgency following it. He seemed hungry, devouring her in his warmth and need, and she drew their kiss deeper. Heat raged within her. Her fingers found his hair. She closed her eyes, then the sound of a cannon echoed in the distance and she remembered where they stood—vulnerable in an open field, exposed despite the cover of dark. She broke their connection, whipping around when a second cannon exploded behind them. A ball of blue light burst over the distant village and she realized it had not been a cannon, but something else.

The brightly colored balls following the first brought a smile to her face. "Are those fireworks?" she asked.

Nick's grin served as his answer. Slipping his arms around her waist, he turned her so she could see more of them, though they took on shapes she had never seen displayed in the skies of Earth. Flowers and stars morphed into animals, then faded as more orbs filled the sky, lighting up the night with elaborate scenes. Trailing blue painted the outline of a castle. Red men rode by on yellow horses. Two figures appeared, and then streams of color emanated from them and joined to represent a wedding.

"Your ancestors," Nick said.

The images disappeared, replaced by more orbs and pictures. Some depicted scenes from history—the construction of the first village, the anointing of the first Elder council, the signing of the Zeiihbu treaty—while others leapt into the sky as streaks of color or simple designs. When twenty orbs launched upward, higher and faster than the ones before them, Meaghan realized the finale had come. The orbs exploded into flashes of green, red, and blue, and then showered the night with sparkling gold.

"It's so beautiful," she said. "I'm glad we didn't miss it."

"It's not quite done," Nick told her and no sooner had he spoken than the last of the gold joined together, forming words in the sky. The words held steady for a moment before dissolving, then reappearing as new words. Three times more it happened until a message became clear.

"Long life. Peaceful journeys," Nick read aloud. "Our allegiance to the Queen. Welcome home."

Meaghan tensed. "They knew I was there?"

"Not at all. The first three lines are tradition. The last is for you, for this year."

"That's incredible." She relaxed again. "We're pretty far from the village. The fireworks must look huge there."

"Massive," Nick said. "And they're launched high so the whole sky lights up. It's awe inspiring."

"Incredible," she repeated and then frowned as a thought occurred to her. "How is that safe?"

"We've been making fireworks for hundreds of years, Meg. There are safety protocols."

"That's not what I meant." She stepped back, scanning the field for movement. "On a clear night like tonight, the fireworks would've been visible for miles. There must be Mardróch around."

"Only the people who've been invited into the village can see it," Nick told her. "The protection spell is still in effect."

"The invisibility spell stretches into the sky? How far up does it go?"

"It's not an invisibility spell. Invisibility doesn't offer enough protection."

"Then how does it work?"

"It changes a person's perception. Everyone under the influence of the spell can see the village. They just don't realize they can."

Meaghan mulled over his words, trying to fit them into her own knowledge. "Are you saying the spell essentially hypnotizes a person into seeing nothing?"

"In a way. The spell also covers anything that comes from the village, like the light and sound fireworks emit."

"That makes sense," Meaghan decided. "But I don't see how people don't stumble into the village. They might be convinced they don't see anything, but they'd know if they ran into a wall."

"They can't get close enough for that to happen," Nick said. "The spell convinces them to avoid the area. The crystals protecting our cabin work the same way."

"You mean people alter their intended course without realizing it? How is that possible? I'd think they'd notice."

Nick shrugged. "You haven't."

"I haven't what?"

"Noticed we've deviated from our course. When we started walking tonight, the village was directly behind us. Now it's to our left." He pointed to a plot of land shadowed from the moonlight by several large oak trees. "You've already started avoiding that area. You did it last time we traveled this route, too."

She concentrated on the spot Nick had indicated, trying to see anything unusual hidden among the patches of brown dirt and brittle yellow grass, but found nothing but weeds. She never would have guessed anything was there. Yet Nick had known.

"You can see it," she realized.

"Guardians don't just protect people," he told her. "What's hidden behind the spell here is an ancient residence. Cal guards it, and he welcomed me to see it last night while you slept."

"Welcomed you?"

"Like I welcomed you when we arrived at my village, and like Neiszhe did when we arrived at hers the first time. Taking your hand and saying the words of welcome lifts the spell. The spell then recognizes you as a resident, and as such, you can welcome others to see the unseen."

"Which leaves the villages vulnerable," she said. Her mind flashed back to the night of the attack on Nick's village, to the screams of pain she had heard and felt. If Abbott had been the traitor, the single act of allowing him into the village in the effort to save his life had cost the lives of many. It would be a tough decision to make, but each villager would have to bear the weight of it. They had to decide between welcoming others or turning from them, letting wanderers starve in the wilderness and strangers die from their wounds, or risking the lives of neighbors and friends in an act of kindness. And if they made the wrong call, they would live with the guilt of that for the rest of their lives.

Meaghan understood why trust would be hard to come by on this world, even for those who did not rule the kingdom. Sadness washed through her with the realization, but fear replaced it when a darker thought embraced her.

"Angus must have access to most of the villages," she said.

"He had access to some, but those have already been destroyed,"

Nick said and his grief brought tears to her eyes. She refocused her power on the doll to prevent the emotion from overwhelming her. "The Guardians were able to evacuate the majority of them in time."

"How many were lost?"

"Seven villages," he responded. "Thirty lives. Fortunately, Angus didn't travel much after your parents were killed. If he had, we would've lost more."

"And what about Garon?" she asked. "What's taken him so long to attack the villages? As the King and Queen's advisor, he must have learned all of their locations."

"I'm sure he did," Nick said, and surprised her by grinning. "But he's never been welcomed into any of them."

Meaghan frowned at the field again where Nick had pointed. "I'm confused. If he knows where they are, how can he not see them?"

"You know there's something in the field, but you can't see it. The spell has to recognize you in order for you to see what it's hiding."

"I still don't understand."

"We didn't start using the protection spell until after he came into power, at least not for villages." He took Meaghan's hand and started walking across the field, toward the location of the ancient residence. "When the kingdom was formed, the first King and Queen had the spell written to give them time to establish peace. There are several variations of the spell. The simplest one protects important structures like this. The one offering the highest protection takes a large amount of power to enact and restricts the villagers' movement too much to allow for regular living."

"You mean the variation the Elders use for the caves," Meaghan said.

"Yes. It's the only version of the spell that won't allow people back into the barrier once they leave, and only those who are greeted with a special welcome can invite others beyond the barrier."

Meaghan nodded, though her head almost seemed too heavy to move and her thoughts grew fuzzier with each step. Panic set in as she fought the urge to move in another direction.

"The spell variations in between extend the protective barrier for the villages, from several yards to a quarter mile. The largest boundary is used for the villages most likely to be attacked, like Guardian villages."

"You've led me past the boundary now," Meaghan guessed, forcing the words past her lips. "It's nearly impossible to move."

Nick nodded and she planted her feet, wrenching her hand from his grasp. She could not stand the thought of taking another step. "I understand now how others don't get close," she said. "I wouldn't have if you hadn't forced me to, but what I don't understand is what prevents Garon from camping his monsters by the villages until someone leaves. The Mardróch would have no qualms about torturing someone into inviting them in."

"True," Nick agreed. "But it would take a lot of manpower for him to camp in front of every one of them. His army's not big enough to do that. Instead, he sends his Mardróch to wander in the areas where he once saw the villages or where the maps say they're supposed to be. The odds are in our favor that he won't find them without inside help."

"That sounds too much like you're gambling with people's lives," Meaghan responded. "Even if the odds are low, they aren't zero. Garon might still find the villages."

"That's why previously established villages like Neiszhe's are given the quarter mile protection."

"We were closer than that the first time we visited Neiszhe's village," Meaghan pointed out. "If the spell is supposed to prevent that, how did we get so close?"

"The same way you're currently standing within a protective boundary," Nick told her. "I can see it, so I can lead you to it. Cal led us to Neiszhe's village. Even with his guidance, breaking the barrier wasn't easy. You were too drugged to feel it, but every step I took felt like fighting a strong current."

She nodded. "How close am I to the residence?"

"Practically next to it." He smiled. "You are welcome here."

With those words, the outline of a building shimmered into view.

CHAPTER SIXTEEN

IN THE pale stream of moonlight, the single-room home appeared almost black, its broken walls rising into the sky like craggy hands welcoming the stars. One small window faced east. Another faced west, though it had lost its support and now gaped open, a wide mouth swallowing the night air. And a fireplace sought refuge to the south, its chimney a haphazard column, bent and twisted on the ground. Beyond the main structure, a low stone wall indicated another residence had not survived, and behind that, scattered stone seemed to be all that remained of a third. Weather and vandals had taken what they could over time, and Meaghan doubted anything would remain now had the protection spell not been cast.

She stepped over a pile of broken slate, the apparent remnants of a roof, to examine the bricks forming the moss-covered walls. Instead of having the uniform appearance of the stone she had seen in the villages, they were cobbled together from varying sizes of river rock and coquina, a limestone and shell mixture she recognized from a trip to Florida she had taken as a child.

"Is there an ocean nearby?" she asked Nick in surprise.

Nick shook his head. "No, but an inlet used to cover most of this area. It receded so fast we assume some form of magic caused it."

"Why would anyone do that?"

"It's possible the southern tribes wanted more land. Moving the ocean allowed them to push north." He picked up a small shell and examined it. "Unfortunately, it also created the Barren Lands, and it had a cultural impact. Before then, the tribes in the north and south were separated."

"And after?"

He cast the shell aside. "They fought. At first over the land, and then because hate became a tradition. The skirmishes didn't stop until the kingdom was formed."

"So this house pre-dates the kingdom?" Meaghan asked. "How old is it?"

"Thousands of years. It's the oldest known residence in Ærenden."

"Amazing," she said, and trailed her hand along the stone, tracing the dry grit of too many years of dirt before stopping at a beam of petrified timber, one of three outlining the residence's doorway. She curled her fingers around it, and then yanked her hand back when a vibration snaked up her arm.

"It's," she narrowed her eyes at the stone as she sought the right word. "Moving."

Nick took her hand in his and placed it back on the wall. The vibration grew stronger, nearly pulsing against her skin. "It's magic," he said. "It's responding to your power. Close your eyes."

She did as he told her, smiling when the vibrations eased along her arm and joined the warmth residing beside her heart. Soon she could focus on little else but the heat emanating into her and returning from her power in response.

"The power comes from nature," Nick spoke against her ear. "Over the years, it's made the house a conduit." Gently, he pried her hand from the wall, breaking the connection. "Being tapped into the core of our power feels amazing, but it's easy to get lost in it. The first time I visited one of these structures, I stood transfixed by it for an hour. We don't have time for that tonight."

"I guess not." Meaghan curled her fingers over her palm, savoring the humming still vibrating along her skin. "Could the power be protecting the building?"

"I believe so. Not every building can funnel power, and the ones that do often survive longer than they should."

"What makes them so special?"

"Their history," he said, taking her hand and pulling her through the door. "Each of them has come in contact with a Spellmaster."

Bracketing her shoulders, he turned her in a slow circle so she could see the walls along the interior of the house. Lines covered every inch of available space. She did not recognize the markings, but she had no doubt they represented letters and words. She approached the closest wall and traced her fingers along what she guessed was a sentence. Bumps and knife indentations pushed against her skin.

"Are you sure this place is thousands of years old?" she asked, dropping her arm when the vibration started again.

"Give or take a century," Nick responded.

"How long has the roof been gone?"

"At least a few hundred years, by Cal's estimation."

Meaghan frowned and traced her index finger over the sentence once more, certain the deep grooves had been her imagination. "This shouldn't be here," she said. "Wind, rain, snow—all of it should have erased this long before now."

"I know. Yet it is. There are dozens of structures like this across the kingdom. Original spells cover all of them. My mother and I used to guard a granite pillar that remained exposed to the elements for a thousand years. The carvings looked to be no more than a few months old."

"Used to?" Meaghan asked, glancing back at him.

"Angus was its third Guardian."

"He destroyed it?" she asked. Nick nodded. "Why?"

"He wanted to make a point. The pillar had the original protective spell on it."

"So he's saying we're not safe from him?"

"Yes," Nick said. "And he's making another point only Guardians would understand. Many of the spells on these ancient structures are dangerous. That's why the Elders decided to hide them, but before they did, they copied the spells down and divided them into two books. The Elders took one. Angus is saying the book isn't safe either."

Meaghan crossed her arms over her chest to ward off a sudden chill. "Who protects the Elders' spell book now?"

"Sam was its Guardian for over thirty years," Nick said. "But now the Elders alternate possession of it."

"And the other book?"

"Your mother and father had it last."

A chill seeped into her, building into a ball of ice at her heart. "You mean Garon has it."

"No, I don't. We're not sure where it went." Nick slipped the backpack from Meaghan's shoulders and set it on the ground, then wrapped his arms around her. "You're shivering. Are you okay?"

"I'm just cold. Once we start walking again, I'll warm up." Drawing her hands between their bodies, she allowed his warmth to encase her. "What spells are in my parents' book?"

"Spells the royal family commissioned and dangerous spells that can only be performed by a Guardian. The Elders worried temptation would be too great if a Guardian had possession of them. That's how we know Garon doesn't have the book. He hasn't used it yet."

"How can you be certain of that? Is there a spy in the castle?"

"No, but one of the spells kills Guardians. If Garon had the book, he would be able to wipe out the strongest powers in Ærenden in a matter of days."

Meaghan's stomach rolled with the thought. "Why would anyone write a spell like that, let alone keep it?"

"It's hard to know, but the good news is wherever the royal family's book is hidden, it's hidden well. Do you want to learn how to use a spell?"

The question caught Meaghan's breath in her throat for a moment. Her eyes locked on Nick's. "Can I?" she asked. "I thought…"

"Thought what?"

"Only Guardians could do spells," she said. Nick chuckled and her cheeks warmed. "You never mentioned it before."

"You didn't have enough control before," he said and let go of her to approach the closest wall. He pointed to few lines at eye level. "This spell would be good for your first try."

Meaghan scanned the words he had indicated and raised an eyebrow. "If I could read it. What language is that?"

"Ancient Æren."

"You know it?"

"Sort of. No one knows how to speak it anymore, but I know how to translate it. It was a requirement for graduation."

"Is it complicated?"

"It can be. Translation isn't as simple as just knowing the words. To harness a spell's power, I have to maintain both rhyme and structure. I failed the final exam twice before I passed."

Meaghan grimaced. "I'm glad I didn't grow up here then. I had to hire a tutor to get through my high school Latin class. I'd probably still be in school if I had to learn Æren."

"I know a few people who would have kept you company, but the requirement is only for Guardians, so you're safe. Are you ready to try something?"

She nodded. "What do I do?"

"Repeat after me," he said, and traced the words with his fingers as he spoke. "Into the darkness shed a light, an orb to shine me through the night. A wish I gather, I do command, as power descends from these hands."

She repeated his words, but nothing happened. "Okay, now what?"

"Capture your warmth as you do when you're using your power, and then focus on it as you say the words."

She closed her eyes. Since she already held her empath power on the corn husk doll, she reached for it first and then grabbed her revival power.

"Into the darkness, shed a light," she recited. Her palms felt warm, so she held them out in front of her. "An orb to shine me through the night."

The heat moved from her palms to her fingers. She flexed them. "A wish I gather, I do command."

Her fingers burned as if they had caught fire. The air sizzled and she opened her eyes, gasping when she realized her hands had dissolved into a white light. The light emanated from her, pushing a beacon several inches into the air. Surprise removed both the breath from her lungs, and the last of the spell from her mind.

"Finish it or you'll lose control," Nick told her, and then gave her the words that had escaped her. "As power descends from these hands."

"As power descends from these hands," she whispered. The light leapt from her fingers, forming a sphere above her palms. It emanated a glow several feet in front of her, bringing daylight to everything it touched. She shook her head in amazement. The orb tightened, then dulled and disappeared. "Where did it go?"

"You lost focus on your power," he said. "Some spells are designed to stay in place after they're infused with power, like the protection spells. Others need a constant infusion of power to work. Try it again."

She focused on her power and then on her hands. The second sphere floated between her fingers, larger and brighter than the first.

"Good," Nick said. "Now send it across the room."

She lifted her head to look at Nick, but did not remove her focus from her power. "What do you mean?"

"It's in the shape of a ball for a reason," he explained. "You can throw it so you can see what's ahead of you or surrounding you in the dark."

She dropped her head again, locking her eyes on the orb. "How?"

"Send it in the direction you want it to go like you do with your power. It works the same."

She yanked on her power, imagined the orb shooting across the room, and almost jumped when it followed her direction. It flew faster and harder than she had expected, then crashed into the wall and exploded, breaking into small stars before disappearing in darkness.

"Crap," she muttered. "I didn't mean to do that."

Nick laughed. "Try again. You'll get the hang of it."

This time, she moved it with more care, dancing it around the room and into the sky above the broken roofline. She grinned as she drove it into aerial loops, giggled when Nick swore as she buzzed it over his head, and then lost control when something else caught her attention. The orb imploded into nothingness.

"That was perfect," Nick said. His wide smile forgave her for the prank, but she ignored it and the pride emanating from him.

She found it impossible to focus on anything but the monstrous stench assaulting her from every direction.

CHAPTER SEVENTEEN

NICK WATCHED Meaghan's face turn white and knew she had finally sensed the danger surrounding them. The Mardróch had been closing in for the past half hour, skirting around the house at a comfortable distance and he had hoped they would pass without incident. His choice to show Meaghan the house had served several purposes—not the least of which had been to hide her without causing her concern. Now the monsters had drawn close enough to trigger her power and erase any hope of avoiding them from his mind. The Mardróch's presence would not be short-lived.

He sensed at least a dozen of them dotted across the field, too many for this to be a casual search of the area. Nick walked to the closest window and leaned out to scan the field. Three Mardróch stood sixty yards to the left of the house. Another half-dozen had already passed and seemed to be making their way toward the village. He crossed the room to peer out the other window. On that side, a cluster of four Mardróch searched the field a hundred yards away. But they did not concern him as much as the last creature he spotted.

The Mardróch had begun piling wood in the field in preparation for a campfire. The hunting party had chosen the spot as their base.

"We're trapped for the night," Nick told Meaghan as he refocused his attention on the inside of the house. She stood in the doorway, surveying the scene, but turned when he spoke.

"They don't realize we're here," she responded. "I don't smell sulfur."

"Sulfur?" Nick raised an eyebrow. "That's an odd smell, even coming from them."

"It might not be sulfur exactly, but it's the closest description I have. It's like burnt matches or spoiled eggs, instead of their usual rotting scent. They emit the smell when they're excited."

"So they didn't see us," he said, "which means they're hunting for the village again."

"Because we were there?" she asked.

"Because they know it's the festival, and they know Cal won't miss it."

Meaghan frowned. "We have to warn him."

"I don't see how. We can't get out without the Mardróch seeing us. There's no wind to alert him, and even if there was, we don't have his power to send a message."

"I guess not," she said. A high-pitched squeal echoed along the air, followed by another, and then a third. Meaghan lifted a hand to cover her nose. "What are they doing?" she whispered. "Their emotions smell rotten, like putrid flesh."

"They're killing their supper," Nick told her and though the sound turned his stomach, whatever Meaghan smelled had to be much worse. "Wild pig, I believe."

She shuddered. "They're enjoying it. I can't believe they used to be human."

"That's debatable," Nick said and joined her in the doorway. He circled his arm around her waist. "I have a hard time calling anyone human who chooses to become one of those monsters."

A single pig gave its last, dying scream, leaving the night to eerie silence. Meaghan shook under Nick's touch and he sighed.

"You're not going to make it until morning if you don't mute your power," he told her. "Focus on my blocking power. I'll keep it on until they're gone."

"I can use the doll."

"I know, but you've been focusing on it all day. You don't have the technique down well enough to hold your focus until morning. Let me help you, okay?"

She nodded and the tension eased from her body. He stepped back. "There isn't much we can do until they leave. I'd say we eat, but…"

"Not after that." She grimaced. "Maybe never again."

"I didn't think so. We could practice some of these spells. They might take our minds off the visitors."

"How many spells do you think there are?"

"It's hard to tell," he replied, scanning the thousands of lines and tiny letters etched over the flat surfaces. Even the petrified wood bordering the windows had been covered in writing. "Maybe a few hundred. Some of them are shorter, like the one you learned. Others are longer, like," he focused on the wall next to the door, looking for an example, and then approached the section, "this one." He pointed below where the roof would have attached. "It's complicated. It would probably require three or four people to recite."

Meaghan joined him. He watched her eyes dart over the lines, still trying to make sense of them, and the effort made him smile. Even if she could decipher some of the words, their order seldom made sense to modern speakers. It had taken him almost twelve months of intense study to memorize all the rules, then years of field practice to translate while reading as he did now.

Meaghan blew out a frustrated breath. "What does it say?"

"Heat to rise above the trees," Nick read. "A column sought in upward breeze. Cost not life amid this strife. A call to four, now hear our plea. Water born to flow and freeze. Air that swirls we cannot see. Earth that shakes, stills, and quakes. Heat to sear as it will please." He stopped to wipe a small patch of moss from the wall where it covered some of the words, then continued, "Flames cast high above the ground. A column lit to bring help 'round. In this try, a desperate cry. Master of the four be found. Power born for great renown. The air, the earth, the water bound. This heat we share," he paused, frowning. "No, that's not quite right." Reaching out to touch the last two lines, he narrowed his eyes. When he settled on the word for the translation, his eyes grew wide. "It's not heat," he said, dropping his hand. "It's fire. This is unbelievable."

"What is?" Meaghan asked.

"The spell. Heat and fire use the same word in ancient Æren, but context matters." He pointed to the last two lines. "This fire we share into the air. To hear the great Elementus' sound. Meg," he said, looking back at her. "Do you realize what this is?"

She shook her head. "What's an Elementus?"

"Not what. Who," he corrected. "It's the archaic name for a Guide. The title we use now evolved when the royal family enlisted the Elementi to guide the army through the wilderness while they were scouting sites to establish permanent villages."

Meaghan's brow wrinkled. "Is fire meant instead of heat each time?"

"I believe so."

"Fire, water, air, and earth," she said. "The four elements. So it's a spell for the Guides."

"Not quite, but close," Nick said. "It's a spell to call them."

"You mean we can reach Cal?"

"If we had enough power."

Meaghan turned a slow circle in place, darting her gaze around the room. "If we're calling the elements, we'll need plenty of space. Maybe if we—"

"Not so fast." Nick placed his hands on her shoulders, pulling her focus back to him. "As I said before, this spell would take the power of several people at least."

"Several people with average powers," she countered and crossed her arms. "My revival power is stronger than most people's, and your Guardian powers have been enhanced to equal my power. Maybe it's enough."

"Maybe," he said, and frowned. "But I don't think—"

"It can't hurt. The worst that can happen is the spell fails, right?"

"Not quite. We don't know how the spell works. If it creates a tornado, for instance, we'd destroy the house and our protection against the Mardróch."

She dropped her arms. "Why would someone call a tornado to reach a Guide?"

Nick shrugged. "Who knows? It's impossible to guess what happened a thousand years ago. It's possible this Spellmaster had a malevolent streak, like the guy who wrote the famine curse."

"I guess," Meaghan conceded. Turning from him, she walked to the eastern window and leaned against the wall. Nick joined her. Two Mardróch remained on this side. They drew their arms to their faces and lowered them several times before he realized they tore bites from food they held between their hands. Red rivers coursed stains over their gray skin before dripping off their hands to pool on the ground. They feasted on raw meat. Sickness filled his throat. He pried his eyes from the scene to watch Meaghan instead. Her cheeks had lost their color and he guessed she had reached the same conclusion he had.

She turned from the window. "Can you write the spell down for me? I'd like to study it."

"Of course." He retrieved a pen and paper from the backpack, copied down the spell, then handed it to her with a warning, "Don't try to focus your power on it, just in case you're right and your power is a lot stronger than we realize."

She nodded and turned to the window again. Instead of looking outside, she glanced down at the paper gripped in her hand. He roamed the room, scanning random lines in an effort to translate spells, but found his focus too scattered to comprehend much of what he read. The Spellmaster did not seem to favor any pattern amid the hodgepodge of mad scribbling.

"It's a column of fire."

Meaghan's words drifted on the air as no more than a murmur and he could not be certain if she had meant them for him. He turned to face her.

"It's a column of fire," she repeated. "Without a roof, we have nothing to worry about."

"I don't understand. What are you talking about?"

"This." She stabbed her finger into the paper. "I'm talking about the spell. There's one place where the Spellmaster mentions 'flame' instead of 'fire'. That's not a translation error, is it?"

"No, it's not."

"I didn't think so. The Spellmaster said fire every other time but this one, and I think he did it on purpose. The spell creates a column of flames."

Nick stared at her, trying to find a reason to argue with her logic, but when he could think of nothing, he snatched the paper from her hand. "It fits," he decided. "Column and fire are mentioned together twice, one of those times using the word flame. And the last two lines hint at your interpretation."

"So we can try the spell?"

He frowned. "I'd like to say yes, but we can't be certain of your interpretation. If you're wrong, we could get hurt."

"I see." She took the paper back from him, and then chewed on her lower lip as she stared at it. "Do all spells start the same? Will this one build until it's fully recited like the orb one did?"

"Most do."

"So if we started reciting it, we'd know what it could do before it went too far, right?"

"I suppose."

"Then we have to try. Please. I care about the villagers and if there's even the slightest chance I can warn them about the Mardróch, I need to."

Nick pressed his lips together, prepared to say no again, but the worry lines carved into her brow and creasing the corners of her eyes stopped the instant reaction. When she set the paper on the window sill, her shoulders stiff with the movement, he gave in to her request. He doubted their combined power would be strong enough to work the spell, so it seemed callous to increase her misery over a moot point.

"I'll take the lead," he told her. Her gaze snapped to his, and relief brightened her eyes. "If I don't like the way it's going, we stop. Understood? And you have to promise you'll listen." She nodded in agreement and he narrowed his eyes. "Say it. I'm not in the most trusting mood after yesterday."

"I promise."

"All right." He blew out a breath and hoped he would not regret his decision. He pointed to the center of the floor. "We'll stand there. If the fire goes higher than the trees, as the spell indicates, I don't want to scorch the walls."

Meaghan picked up the paper and followed him to the center of the room. "Should we be touching for our powers to work together?" she asked.

Nick shook his head. "It's not necessary. And if a column of fire is going to erupt between us, I don't want to be embracing it. Stand here," he said, gesturing toward a spot on the ground. "Don't move."

He walked two feet away from her and marked an X on the dirt floor with his finger. Then he moved two feet further away and faced her. "We need to say this together. Read it aloud for me, please."

She read it to him, and then peered over the paper in curiosity. "Can you memorize it that fast?"

"It comes with practice. This isn't my first complex spell." He nodded toward the spot he had marked. "Focus your power there and start reciting."

She glanced at the paper in her hand, and then stared at the X on the floor. "Fire to rise above the trees. A column sought in upward breeze. Cost not life amid this strife. A call to four, now hear our plea."

Nick recited with her, focusing on the warmth of his power. It surged, but nothing else happened.

"Nick," Meaghan started, worry lining her face once more, but stopped when he nodded toward the paper, indicating for her to continue. "Water born to flow and freeze. Air that swirls we cannot see. Earth that shakes, stills, and quakes. Fire to sear as it will please."

To his surprise, this time he saw something. The warmth in him turned to an almost unbearable heat. It jumped to the X, igniting a fire on the ground no bigger than half the size of their backpack. He nodded at her again. She glanced down and recited. He focused harder on the flames they had created. "Flames cast high above the ground. A column lit to bring help 'round. In this try, a desperate cry.

Master of the four be found."

The small bonfire began spinning. Faster and faster, it turned until the orange and red of the flames separated into two columns dancing together in the moonlight. For a heartbeat, he wondered if he had been right about the tornado. A tornado of fire could still be a possibility, but his instincts told him to keep going. If their combined powers had grown this strong—stronger than he had ever anticipated—he felt certain he could control the flame enough to dissolve it in short order. He nodded one last time at Meaghan, and she dropped her eyes back to the paper.

"Power born for great renown. The air, the earth, the water bound. This fire we share into the air. To hear the great Elementus' sound."

Their voices recited in perfect unison, growing louder as the fire responded to their surging power. The column thickened, swirling faster as it cast off heat, singeing the hair on Nick's arms. When it began to pulse, he stepped back, nearly severing his connection to it, but then it pushed into the sky, a beacon searching for companionship with the moon overhead.

The column spun faster, and out of the flames boomed the voice of a groggy and somewhat drunken man, "Didn't I just get rid of you two?"

CHAPTER EIGHTEEN

"WE'D BE happy to go away again if you'd like," Nick remarked, barely covering the amusement flickering the corners of his mouth. "Or you could use the fire to see why we called you. It's your choice."

"Like I really have a choice," Cal grumbled. "One moment I'm sitting beside my wife, the next I'm yanked outdoors to," he hesitated, "where am I?"

"You can't see?" Nick asked. "Aren't you using the fire the same way you always do?"

"I can see, but this isn't the same." The fire slowed, and Nick realized Cal controlled it now. "If I didn't know any better, I'd say you're in the ancient residence."

"We are," Nick confirmed. "What do you mean when you say it isn't the same?"

"I mean my power splits my awareness. I can usually see both where I am physically and what the elements are showing me. At the moment, I'm only here. Neiszhe probably thinks I passed out."

"Would it be the first time?"

"Hardly." Cal chuckled, and then turned serious again. "You used a spell. My guess is the one by the door. Not only is that one risky, but you shouldn't be able to pull it off with just two people."

"It seems our powers are stronger than we initially thought," Nick told him. "And we took the risk because—"

"Meaghan shouldn't know this building exists," Cal interrupted. "Why did you show it to her? It's against the law."

"I wanted to give her a lesson on the protection spell," Nick answered, matching the annoyance in Cal's voice with irritation of his own. "I didn't think the law should apply to the Queen."

"That's not for you to decide. The Elders made these laws for a reason."

"I see." Nick narrowed his eyes. "That's the second time in recent memory you've deferred to the Elders' wisdom. It's not like you, and I'm beginning to suspect you're hiding something."

"It's nothing sinister," Cal responded. "Now that Meaghan's home, I'm starting to see things from a different perspective, that's all. These laws protect her, too. Just having knowledge of some of the ancient sites could put her in danger."

"I'm aware of that, but as you pointed out, it's her right as our ruler to have all the information. The Elders shouldn't be keeping anything from her any more than I should, so what's the real reason for the change of heart?"

"I meant you shouldn't as the King and as her husb..." his words grew muffled and then faded. The fire waned, dimming to pale amber before blazing into a thick column again.

"What was that?" Cal asked, his voice returning with full strength.

"I don't know," Nick responded. "The column—"

"That was me confirming you're lying," Meaghan interrupted. "I wasn't sure if my empath power would work without you physically standing in the room with me, but it does. Sorry," she said to Nick. "I didn't realize it would weaken the spell."

Nick shrugged. "Now you know. I'm guessing the spell actually transports Cal's presence to the fire, instead of only calling his power. That would explain why you can sense him."

"It's a possibility. He's definitely hiding something, though he's unhappy with whatever it is, and ashamed of it."

"Ashamed?" Nick frowned as he studied the flames and then he understood. "They made him an Elder."

The swear echoing from the fire confirmed Nick's suspicion.

"Why would they do that?" Meaghan asked. "I thought they didn't get along with him."

"They're running out of options," Nick said. "There are supposed to be five Elders on the council. Four is better than three in terms of ensuring there's at least one Elder alive when the war is over."

"And they may fight with Cal," Meaghan reasoned, "but they trust him."

"Exactly. Plus, giving him the responsibility seems to have mellowed him some. It's a good political move on their part."

"I'm still in the room," Cal reminded them. "I'd appreciate it if you'd talk to me instead of around me."

"Why? So you can lie to us again?" Nick glared into the fire. "How long has it been? How long have I trusted you with my secrets while you hid yours?"

"I didn't—"

"Answer me."

"Since shortly after you moved to the cabin, once they found out I knew where you were."

"They wanted you to spy on us," Nick realized. "You weren't trying to help us as much as you were reporting our progress back to the Elders."

"That's not quite—" Cal started to protest, but his remaining words disappeared when the column of fire dissolved, leaving only silence and darkness.

Meaghan opened her mouth, but before she could speak, Nick stormed from the house. He wanted to keep walking, into the field and into the night with nothing but the grass and small rodents to keep him company, but the protective boundary only extended so far. He halted at its border, mindful of the warning shimmer it emitted, and paced, wearing grooves into the soft dirt.

He ignored the Mardróch dotting the horizon, but Meaghan did not seem to have the same ability when she joined him outside. Her eyes locked on a pack of them and she stepped backward, giving distance to the boundary. It suited him fine. His anger did not allow him patience for company.

"I think you're overreacting," she said and his anger spiked. He tossed it in her direction.

"What would you know about it?" he asked, and stopped pacing to stare at her. "You said yourself you can't always determine who to trust. He's been spying. That isn't a small thing."

"You don't know for certain he's spying on us."

"He didn't deny it."

"You didn't give him the chance. We didn't even have enough time to warn him about the Mardróch."

"He betrayed us," Nick replied. "I didn't feel he deserved the courtesy."

"Courtesy," Meaghan echoed and frowned. "Warning him, and the rest of the village, isn't about courtesy. It's about protecting them. It's our duty, even if you don't feel Cal deserves it."

Nick shook his head and started pacing again. "They'll be fine. They're under stronger protection than we are, and we're the ones standing in the middle of danger."

"You can't be certain of that," Meaghan challenged. "Too many villages under strong protection have already been destroyed."

"Maybe," he said and her words melted some of his anger. His eyes found the horizon, and the Mardróch he had ignored earlier. He pushed his hands into his pockets and faced her again. "There's nothing we can do about it now."

"We can recite the spell again."

"You're not strong enough to do it twice."

"*I'm* not?" she asked. Her arms tightened against her sides. "Last I checked, our powers balanced when we were wed. Or did you forget I'm no longer weaker than you?"

"That's not what I meant."

"Forget it," she snapped. "I'm done wasting time on your excuses. I'll try it by myself."

"Meg," he started, and then sighed when she turned from him to reenter the house. He followed her.

"I'm not interested," she said and pulled the spell from her pocket. She held it in front of her. "Fire to rise above the trees."

"You can't—"

She raised her voice to speak over him. "A column sought in upward breeze. Cost not life amid this strife." A flame began to flicker on the ground, and then disappeared as fast as it had formed. "A call to four, now hear our plea."

"Damn it, Meaghan, stop!" Nick commanded, using her full name in the hope it would startle her into breaking her concentration. Her fingers trembled, but her eyes remained fixed on the X in the ground. She lifted the paper higher.

"Water born to flow and freeze." A flame flickered again, and this time it remained. "Air that swirls—"

"Enough," he snapped. His hand shot out, latching onto her wrist. He tightened his fingers, twisting her arm so she let go of the paper. It fluttered to the ground, landing where the flame had formed seconds before. "You'll hurt yourself."

Her eyes widened in shock and he released her arm. "Let me finish explaining."

"Like you let Cal explain?" she asked and bent down to retrieve the paper. "You deserve no better treatment than you gave him."

"That's not fair. I only meant your powers are new to you. It's easy to get exhausted with these spells. Cal intentionally—"

"I wasn't talking about what you just said. He kept one thing from you. One," she raised her finger to punctuate her point. "And you cut him off like some sort of traitor. How many secrets have you kept from me since I came to this world? How many are you still keeping from me?"

"I'm not—"

"You've given me plenty of reason not to trust you," she continued, charging through his protest. "Yet I still do. I have to because we won't get far if I don't."

"That's not the same—"

She stepped forward, forcing him against a wall. "Right. You were trying to protect me while he was obviously trying to betray you by taking a promotion, by stepping up to lead in the same way your mother did. You seemed to be happy about her promotion, so why not Cal?"

"Cal can't be our advisor if he's an Elder," Nick answered. He tucked his hands behind him and slouched against the wall. "It's a law the royal family enacted to keep one person from having too much authority. Cal knows that, which means he lied to me about wanting to be our advisor."

"It wouldn't be the first law we've bent," she pointed out.

He shook his head. "It's not one I want to bend. We can't have an advisor who reports everything we do to the Elders."

She studied him for a moment, and then stepped back. Her anger had been tempered by fear. "Are the Elders our enemies now?"

"They could be," Nick responded, and straightened. "After what we're planning to do, they may consider us to be theirs, and if Cal is reporting back what we tell him..."

"They already know," Meaghan finished when he hesitated. Her eyes trailed to the X on the floor. "We shouldn't assume he's told them. We need to let him explain."

"There's no time." He brought a hand to her cheek, his eyes scanning her face for the anger that had held it rigid only moments before. It did not return. "If we do the spell again, we won't have time to talk to him. We'll only have enough time to show him the danger. You won't be able to hold the spell longer than that."

She frowned. "I'm not as weak as I used to be. I'm not even tired after performing the spell."

"You've never been weak," he corrected. He drew his other hand up to frame her face. "You're the strongest person I've ever known, but this isn't about strength. It's about training."

"I don't understand. I've been training. I'm faster, stronger, and I have more endurance than when we started. I also have better control over my powers."

"And if that was all you needed to perform the spell, you'd be fine. But spells are mentally and physically taxing, and when they take too much from you, the decline is quick. One moment you're fine, and the next, you're suffering from exhaustion so deep you can't lift your head. Trust me," he said and pressed his lips to the bridge of her nose. "I learned that lesson the hard way and wound up sick for two days. If you really want to test your limits, I won't stop you. But I'd prefer you did it someplace safer than here."

"Two days," she muttered. "I've been sidelined enough already. I think I'll just take your word for it."

He chuckled. "In the meantime, if you want to try the spell again, I'll agree to it, but only if you stop when you feel faint."

"Okay." She focused her attention on the X. "I think we should stand farther back this time, though. I felt like I stood inside an oven before. Shall we start?"

"In a minute," he said, and placed a hand on her shoulder. With a gentle touch, he brought her attention back to him. "I'm sorry. I truly am."

She shrugged. "I misunderstood what you said. I didn't realize spells were—"

"No," he interrupted. Dropping his hand, he looked away from her. "I'm sorry for keeping things from you. I didn't realize how it felt to be on the receiving end of that until now. I feel betrayed by what Cal did, and I can't imagine you feel any differently."

"You were trying to protect me," she said, and laid a palm against his chest. "You may have gone about it the wrong way, but I understand why you did it. I don't feel betrayed because I know your intentions were good. And I think until you know why Cal did what he did, you should hold off on judging him. You had your reasons. They weren't entirely wrong, and I suspect his may not be either."

"You say you understand, but you're still mad at me."

She lowered her hand. "I guess I am, although I didn't recognize it until today. Understanding what you did is a lot easier than accepting it. I need time to sort through it."

"And to trust me again," he said.

"I trust you."

"Because you feel you have to, not because you want to. I didn't realize how much damage I'd done to our relationship. Can it be fixed?"

She held his gaze for a long minute. For the duration of that time, fear gripped him. He could not bear the thought of a lifetime of distance between them. She looked away from him, and his fear turned to ice around his heart.

"I'm angry because I'm hurt," she said. "I trusted you with my life. I gave up my entire world and followed you here, and you couldn't trust me enough to share the truth with me."

He wanted to protest, to convince her he had always trusted her, but any words of denial would be another lie. When he had brought her home, he thought protecting her meant sheltering her. And in doing so, he had seeded distrust. She had been capable, but his own fears of losing her had prevented him from seeing it.

"I don't know what to say," he told her. "Except I'd do it differently if I could."

"But you can't," she replied. "The past is done. It's not what you say, but your actions that matter now. You started sharing the truth with me last week. And tonight, you trusted me enough to show me this house. If you continue to trust me, we'll be okay."

He nodded and hoped she was right.

"We should get to the spell," she said. "Where do you want me?"

"By the east window," he instructed. "I'll stand by the one on the west wall. Are you ready?"

She took her place. He mirrored her, and then gestured for her to start. They recited the spell once more. The column of fire shot into the sky between them and a moment later, Cal's worry broadcast from the flame.

"Took you long enough. I thought something happened to you."

"I cut you off," Nick said. "I wasn't in the mood to listen to lies."

"I see," Cal muttered. "Listen, Nick. I didn't mean to—"

"Save it for later," Nick interrupted. Meaghan shot him a warning look and he checked his renewed anger, softening his words. "Meaghan won't be able to hold the spell for long and we need to warn you about the danger you're facing."

"What danger?" Cal asked, and then continued without waiting for an answer. "You called me for a reason. It wasn't just to teach Meaghan how to do a spell."

"It's a risky spell," Nick reminded him. "You know me better than that."

"You didn't have any other choice but to use it to call me," Cal realized. "You need me to see something." His voice trailed up the column, growing distant as it moved into the sky. Then it returned to the center of the room. "Mardróch," he hissed. "How many?"

"Fourteen," Nick said. "Most of them are hunting now."

"Too many. The villagers have dropped their guard because of the festival. I'll make sure no one leaves."

"Good," Nick responded. "That's all we needed to hear."

"Thank you for taking the risk," Cal said. "It means a lot that you would think of us while you're in the midst of," he paused, and then cursed. "You're trapped there."

"Probably until morning. Once they clear out, we'll start travelling again."

"It'll be longer than morning. Last time they set up camp, they stayed for ten days. You have no food or water. Hold on. Let me check on something." Cal's voice shot up the flames again, returning seconds later. "I have a plan," he told them. "I think I can jump from the column to their campfire. If it works, you'll have a way out."

"How?" Meaghan asked.

"You'll know what to do when the time comes. Just hold the spell as long as you can so I have time to make the switch. Then be prepared to run."

Nick raised an eyebrow at Meaghan, questioning whether extending the spell would be possible. She nodded, and he responded to Cal. "We're ready when you are."

"On my way. Be safe."

Nick locked his eyes on the column of fire. By his count, a minute passed, and then another. Meaghan's hands trembled, and he started to break his concentration, but she shook her head when the column waned. A third minute passed. Meaghan's breathing heaved in her chest, hard and fast, and this time he severed the connection. The column disappeared and he rushed to her side.

"Are you all right?" he asked. She swayed, so he wrapped his arms around her for support. "Meg, do you need to sit?"

She shook her head, and then pressed it against his chest. Her breathing steadied. She drew in air and exhaled it with control, then looked up at him.

"We should get ready," she said.

"Will you be able to run?"

"I think so." She stepped back from him and offered a steady smile. "Definitely."

Guttural screams of frustration bounded into the house from outside, followed by the acrid smell of smoke. Meaghan rushed for the door. Nick picked up the backpack and crossed the threshold only a step behind her.

If there had been any question in either of their minds that the time had come to run, the inferno greeting them erased all doubt.

CHAPTER NINETEEN

THE FIELD was on fire. It took Meaghan a moment to realize the flames surrounding the house on every side were not a fluke of carelessness. Although a trail shot from the campfire the Mardróch had constructed, consuming the dried grasslands with swift tongues of anger, the flames did not have the all-consuming traits of a common wildfire. They approached the protective barrier, stopping at the border in an even line that spoke of control. Cal had created a wall between the Mardróch and the invisible house. The wall stretched long, cutting off the passage of the Mardróch searching the fields to the north. Mardróch to the south and east scurried to reach their comrades, but soon found their paths blocked by offshoots of fire. Howls of frustration erupted through the flames with each failed attempt to get through.

Meaghan tried to take in a breath. Her lungs constricted from the building smoke, and she pulled her cloak over her nose to filter the air. Nick did the same.

"We don't have much time," he told her, yelling through the thick wool material. She glanced toward the only path still untouched by fire, their original route to the west. Although two Mardróch remained on that side of the house, the smoke had begun to thicken. Soon it would not only destroy what little fresh air remained, but it would prevent them from seeing. She suspected Cal also controlled the smoke for this purpose, and heeded the instruction he had given before leaving the column of fire. She began running. Nick started out a step behind her, but soon pushed past, taking the lead.

As they approached the edge of the protection spell, Meaghan dropped her hold on his power. Odors of soured milk and brine slammed into her, and she almost gagged from the overwhelming wave of it.

The wall of flames shot higher, thickening, and the odors increased, followed by another series of howls. She and Nick broke through the barrier. The heat decreased. The smoke thinned. And then the smell she feared most washed over her. Sulfur. A quick look over her shoulder confirmed her fear. Two Mardróch tore across the field toward her and Nick, their feet barely touching the ground.

"We've been spotted," she warned Nick.

He turned his head to glance at the Mardróch, swore, and then increased his speed. Despite Meaghan's intensive training over the past few months, Nick's pace pushed her limits. Her legs ached. Her lungs hurt. Her ribs burned.

She cleared her mind of panic, focused on the field in front of them, and forced her body to move even faster. They could not allow the Mardróch to get close. At best, if the creatures caught up to them, they would freeze Nick. She could no more fight a pack of

Mardróch than she could leave Nick behind. At worst, she would never have the chance to fight. If the Mardróch chose, they could kill their prey faster with lightning. And the closer they got, the better their aim would be.

The sound of sizzling filled the air, followed by a loud crack as a lightning bolt blew a chunk of ground into the sky. Meaghan cast a look over her shoulder, her heart lurching when she realized it would only be a matter of minutes before the Mardróch gained too much ground for her and Nick to escape, and then froze when another movement caught her attention.

A few feet behind the Mardróch, a wall of fire sped across the grass. Consumed with their chase, the monsters did not see the danger. They raised their hands to cast a second lightning bolt and Cal's flames overcame them. Their squeals of pain ended moments after starting, but their agony lasted longer. The smell of rotting flesh assaulted Meaghan's power and the intensity of it drove her to her knees.

Nick yanked her back to her feet. When she could not think to move, he gripped her shoulders and shook her. She gasped a new breath, choked on smoke, and then tried again with a shallower attempt. Nick grabbed her hand, and she followed him into the night.

They ran, pushing beyond any speed Meaghan's muscles had ever known. When the fire faded into a red glow on the horizon, they kept moving. When the rasping of their breath and the muted pounding of their footfalls on the grassy earth were the only sounds greeting them, they maintained their speed. And when the night chilled, turning their exhales into white ice on the winter wind, they refused to slow down. Only when the voice came did they finally stop.

"You can rest now. They're gone," it said.

The voice could only be Cal's, but Meaghan did not recognize it. He sounded faint and lost. Exhaustion had weakened him. She had suffered it too many times not to recognize it.

"You don't sound right," she said, though her own voice came out as no more than a whisper. She pressed her hands to her knees, working to catch her breath. Every cell in her body screamed.

"The fire's out," Cal told her. "I had to fight the wind for control of it. There are no Mardróch left in the search party."

The wind died down and with it, their connection to Cal. Meaghan straightened up and turned to Nick. The worry lining his face echoed within her empath power.

"He'll be okay," she said. "I'm sure Neiszhe is already forcing jicab tea down his throat."

A smile flickered across Nick's face, but disappeared as quickly as it had come. "What he did took a lot of strength, and too much energy. He won't be well for days."

"He protected us," she responded, "as he always has. Do you still doubt his motives?"

"I don't know. I still have too many questions."

"The most important of which affects our plans," Meaghan said, and then yanked her hair out of her face when the wind picked up again. She wondered if Cal had ridden across the field with it, or if exhaustion had put him to bed for the night. "What do you want to do now?" she asked Nick. "Do we continue our plan even though he may have reported it to the Elders?"

"I'm not sure. If the Elders know, they could already be there."

"They don't know," Cal's voice broke into the conversation. "I'm too tired to explain everything now, but please believe me. Your plan is too important to abandon."

Nick raised an eyebrow at Meaghan. She dropped her gaze to the ground and to the blades of dried grass as they swirled in the wind, their movements matching the vortex of Cal's words in her mind. Finally, she nodded.

"All right," Nick said. "We'll trust you on this, but you'll learn nothing more of our plan until we get your explanation."

"I'll come see you," Cal promised. "A week after you return to the cabin."

The wind died again, and Meaghan knew Cal would not return this time. Nick started walking again, leading in silence until the sun rose over the field, outlining three huts in the distance. Gray smoke snaked into the sky from the largest of them and Meaghan focused on it. The door flew open, and Faillen's wife, Ree, greeted them with a smile before engulfing them both in a welcoming hug.

CHAPTER TWENTY

"**IT'S NICE** to have company. Cal comes by every now and again, of course, but he's not one to sit and talk. He usually gets right to business training the boys and then heads back out."

Ree stopped rolling her pie crust long enough to tuck a strand of red hair behind her ear. She cast a smile at Meaghan and Nick. "I can't blame him, of course. He's afraid to stay in one place too long. There have been so many Mardróch around since your return and, uh," she paused, looked up again and blushed. "Not that it's your fault."

"I didn't take it that way," Meaghan responded. She set her sandwich down and smiled. Faillen's wife had been chattering nonstop since Meaghan and Nick had woken from their nap and joined her in the main hut. She had made them sandwiches with thick slices of fresh bread, cold venison and cheese, and ordered them to the kitchen table to eat. While they followed her command, she made dinner. Aldin played with a set of colorful wood building blocks in front of the fireplace. Handmade toys, Meaghan had no doubt, and folded her hands in front of her, enjoying the warmth the blazing fire and homey environment brought.

"Good," Ree said. Setting aside her rolling pin, she peeled the crust from the counter, and then arranged it in a tin. "We'll have meat and potato pie for dinner tonight, but not much more than that, I'm afraid. Faillen's had luck with hunting, and we have root vegetables left from the harvest, but winter's always a tough time for food."

"It's plenty," Nick told her. "Your hospitality is appreciated. Besides, I'm not sure we'll even be hungry by dinner after what you just fed us."

"You won't starve in my presence," she said, grinning when he laughed. "Dinner will be a few hours yet. Faillen and Caide won't return until dusk. And travelling has a way of working up an appetite. I'm sure you'll eat your fair share when the time comes."

"The food won't go to waste," he promised. Pushing his empty plate aside, he stood. "Is there anything I can do to help?"

"Not with the cooking," she told him. "But Aldin needs to spend time with his studies. Are you familiar with ancient Æren?"

"All Guardians are. Is he learning it?"

"He is. Cal feels they should know how to read spells in order to learn from them. Haven't they all been translated by now?"

"The ones we know about," Nick told her. "But every once in a while we find new ones."

"Like in caves?" Ree asked, glancing up at him.

"It's a popular location. Are you aware of any?"

She nodded and returned to her task. "At least three. I used to play in caves by my village as a child that were covered with ancient writing. After the war is over, you'll have to come translate them."

"I'd like that," Nick said. "Though it'll be even better to have your sons do it. Their powers will allow them to sense what the spells are meant to do. I can only guess."

"Once they learn enough, I'll show them where to go," Ree agreed and pointed at a shelf across the room. "Aldin's school book is up there."

Nick found the book and brought it to Aldin. The young boy looked up and frowned, then continued adding blocks to the tower he had been building. Nick sat down next to him. "I take it he doesn't like studying."

"He prefers reciting spells," Ree said. "He thinks it's more fun. He doesn't understand the weight of his power."

Aldin cast a large grin at Nick, then scattered his tower with a sweep of one hand. Ree raised an eyebrow at him. The boy ducked his head and began collecting his blocks.

"He's young," Nick said.

"He's more carefree," Ree told him. "Unlike his brother. Sometimes I think Caide takes his studies too seriously. He wants to prove to our people his powers aren't shameful. Zeiihbu is resistant to change, as was I when we first came here. But we all must grow."

She leaned down to pick up a block that had skittered to a stop at her feet and brought it back to her son before pressing a hand to Nick's shoulder. "I understand a lot has changed for you, too, since we last saw each other."

"Cal told you about the wedding," he guessed. "How much has

he said?"

"Just that you're our King now, although what's between you two wasn't well-hidden." Ree turned her eyes to Meaghan. "You chose well. I'm glad to see the Elders accepted your decision."

"There was no choice to it," Meaghan said. "Our powers joined us."

"I see." Ree squeezed Nick's shoulder before letting go. She smiled at him. "Why don't you and Aldin work at the table? I'll bring tea. I'd like to sit in on the lesson, if you don't mind. We have some time still before Caide and Faillen return from hunting."

"Of course."

Nick brought the boy and the book to the table. Once Ree placed mugs in front of each of them, Nick opened the book. To Meaghan's surprise, its pages contained elaborate pictures, drawn and colored by hand.

"Guardian children start studying the language around the age of five, just like Aldin is," Nick explained. "Since most of them are still learning to read anyway, and no one knows how to pronounce anything in ancient Æren, the Elders found it best to stick to simple words and associate them with pictures. He'll learn more complex words as he grows older, since his reading skills will be more advanced." He pointed to the picture of a dog, and then the word next to it, *cáen`i*. "What does that mean?" he asked Aldin.

"Dog," the boy answered.

"Right. And this one?" Nick asked, pointing to the word *y~ncy~ndí*. Aldin looked at the picture next to it and grinned. Meaghan recognized the word too, but not from the picture of the flames painted on the page.

"Fire," Aldin answered.

"Correct," Nick responded. He flipped to the next page. A list of words appeared on one side. Pictures appeared on the other. "Now show me which picture goes with which word," he instructed Aldin. The young boy drew a line between each word and its corresponding picture with his index finger. When he matched the last word, the one meaning fire, he grinned again.

"I can make fire with a spell. Want to see?" he asked, staring at Nick with pleading eyes.

"It's not time for that," Nick responded. "It's time for your language lesson."

"But it's boring." Aldin crossed his arms and slouched in his seat. "I don't want to learn it. I want to do spells."

"And you will," Nick promised. "In time. Did Cal ever tell you about the fun spells? Like the one that makes fireworks?"

"What are fireworks?" Aldin asked.

"Fireworks are colorful fire balls in the sky. They explode and make loud noises."

"Really?" Aldin curled his fingers over the edge of the table. "I can do that?"

"Absolutely," Nick said. "But the spell's written in ancient Æren. Only people who know the language can do the spell." He turned a page in the book and pointed to a word opposite the picture of a lit candle. "This word is in the spell. Are you sure you don't want to learn it?"

Aldin peered at the word, *illú'my~nní*, and bit his lip. "Candle," he said.

"Close. It actually means light. That word is in the spell five times, so now you're five words closer to being able to make fireworks."

"How many words are in the spell?" Aldin asked.

"About a hundred," Nick said. "And you have to learn them all before you're allowed to perform the spell. But learning the words will also help you do other fun spells, like changing water into ice."

Aldin turned wide eyes toward his mother. "Can I really do those spells?"

"If you learn all the words," Ree answered. "But you have to promise to study hard."

A broad grin spread across Aldin's face. He bobbed his head in agreement, and then pointed to the next word on the list, *læpæx*. "Wolf," he said after he examined the picture of the shaggy gray animal. He made his way through the rest of the words on the page and then matched the words to their pictures on the following page.

Nick made him repeat the lessons twice before the front door to the hut opened. A young man with strawberry-blonde hair entered. In his hands, he grasped the tails of two silver foxes. Behind him entered an older man with a dark olive complexion and curly, dirty-blonde hair. A brown bird with gold tufts perched on a leather glove covering the older man's right hand. As soon as the man saw Meaghan and Nick, a frown flickered across his face, disappearing only a second after it showed.

"It's good to see you again," the man said, his words contradicting the hardness Meaghan saw in his eyes. She drew her mug up to cover her surprise. After Ree's warm reception, she had not expected a chilly one from Faillen. Removing her empath power from the corn husk doll, Meaghan allowed it to roam the room. Displeasure emanated from Faillen, as well as a deep sadness she had not expected.

"It's nice to see you too," Nick responded. Caution hid behind his words and Meaghan realized he had also picked up on Faillen's mood.

Faillen turned toward his eldest son. "Clean the foxes, Caide, and hang them in the third hut. Take your brother with you."

"But I'm learning to read Æren," Aldin protested. "I want to make fireworks."

"Fireworks?" Faillen asked, raising an eyebrow.

"Colorful fireballs," Aldin informed him. "Nick said I could do them once I learned all my Æren words. Can I, Dat? Mata said it was okay."

"Of course," Faillen said. "Take the book with you. Caide knows it well enough to continue your lesson once he's done with his chores. Will you go with them, Ree?"

Ree pursed her lips in response, and Meaghan sensed anger from her, but the woman did not show it. She only nodded, and stood. Aldin followed her lead. After picking up the book, he scurried outside after his brother. Ree left last, closing the door behind her.

Meaghan turned her power onto Faillen as she had Mycale in the village, hoping the concentrated focus would allow her to catch even the smallest of Faillen's cues. It only took a minute for Nick's emotions to disappear. Without the added distraction, she sensed fear in Faillen, though she had not noticed it before.

Faillen crossed the room to a standing perch in the corner and held his arm up to it. The bird stepped onto the perch and Faillen clipped an ankle bracelet to its leg. He reached into a pouch at his side, pulled out a hunk of raw meat, and then fed it to the bird.

"Good girl, Scree," he said, running the tip of his index finger over the gold feathers covering her head.

"Scree?" Meaghan asked. The bird opened its beak and released a high-pitched call reminiscent of an extended version of its name. "Oh." Meaghan laughed. "I get it."

Faillen reached into his pouch and pulled out a larger hunk of meat, giving it to the bird before returning to the table. He dropped into the seat next to Nick. "I was eight when my father gave her to me. It seemed appropriate at the time."

The discontent in him grew and Meaghan frowned. "You aren't pleased to see us," she said. "Please stop pretending otherwise."

Faillen's shoulders stiffened and he crossed his arms over the table, though guilt gripped him instead of anger. "Is there anything your power doesn't sense?" he asked.

"The truth behind the emotions. Especially when they're so conflicted."

"You sense even my torment," he said, and glanced at the bird again. Scree held the hunk of meat in her untethered claw as she tore small bits from it with the point of her beak. "Have you heard of my type of bird? Most people never get the opportunity to see one."

"She looks like a falcon," Meaghan answered. The conflicted emotions in him settled, subdued by fondness for the bird, and she followed his lead in the conversation. "She's about the size and coloring of one, except for the gold. Where I grew up, there aren't any birds like her."

"No, there wouldn't be," he said, looking back at her. "The species is only found in the mountains separating Zeiihbu from the Barren Lands." He nodded at Nick. "I trust you know what she is?"

"I do," Nick responded. His eyes remained locked on the creature. "But I thought the gildonae had gone extinct."

"They nearly have. We used to train them as hunting birds because of their abilities, but they don't breed in captivity so we've since made the practice illegal. I keep Scree because she's known no other life since she was a chick."

"Abilities?" Nick asked. "You mean they have powers?"

"They have unnatural speed and they can smell prey for miles. I can only assume those are powers." Faillen smiled at Meaghan. "Her tuft isn't the only thing that's gold."

Meaghan turned her attention back to the bird in time to see her preening her wings. The feathers on the underside of both wings gleamed bright gold. When she flicked her tail into the air, Meaghan also saw a gilded sheen.

"Beautiful," she whispered.

"She is. I use her to carry messages. My father and I have been sending her back and forth with updates since I've been here." Faillen brought his eyes to Meaghan's and the sadness returned to him. "I can't send her back this time. It's not safe."

"Why not?"

"For the same reason I can no longer uphold the promise I made to you the last time you were here. Garon has taken over Zeiihbu. He put a Mardróch by the name of Stilgan in charge." Nick hissed out a breath and Faillen raised an eyebrow at him. "You've heard of him?"

"Unfortunately," Nick responded, the heat in his voice reflecting his anger. "He was one of the best generals in the royal army. I understand Garon turned him early."

"Cal said as much, though he wouldn't talk about it. Stilgan's smarter than most Mardróch and no less cruel. He's been torturing and killing Zeiihbuans since his arrival, with the purpose of forcing my father to make a choice between the Ærenden treaty and the lives of our people. It's not much of a choice. Zeiihbu has now joined forces with Garon."

"Garon will destroy everyone," Nick warned him. "He'll use your people to win the war and then he'll dispose of them."

"He promised my father immunity," Faillen said. "Our people will become a permanent part of Garon's army after the war, but they'll be alive."

"As slaves," Nick said. "That's not a life."

Faillen cast his eyes down. "What else can we do? Mardróch overrun the country and our best warriors are under Stilgan's power. He can hypnotize people into doing his bidding."

"Your father, too?" Meaghan asked.

Faillen shook his head. "Garon needs my father to act willingly for now. Our people will follow his decision if they know it's truly his."

"So your father has made his choice," Nick said. "But you can still honor your pact with Meaghan. Your father's actions don't break that."

"I've made my choice, too," Faillen replied. His voice grew soft, but he held it strong. "Garon will not honor his promise to my father unless I return home."

"You don't want to," Meaghan said. The surge of guilt and sadness within him swelled. "Does Ree know about this? I sensed anger in her before, but not until you asked her to leave the room. I would have expected more from her if she knew what you had decided."

"She doesn't know. She won't agree with my decision, but I have to follow Garon's summons. I won't cause the deaths of my people."

"There's another option," Meaghan told him. Hope sparked within him and she realized this would be the only chance she would get to convince him of her plan. "We have the power to defeat Garon, all of us, if we work together. We want you to lead our army."

Faillen stared at her, his emotions as blank as his face. Shock had overwhelmed everything else. "Your army?" he finally mustered. "The royal army?"

"Not just the royal army," Nick said. "Our villagers have been fighting this war, though they aren't properly trained. It's time to make them part of the army, train them, and give them the chance to succeed. You can train an army, and you have the wisdom of your people, the advantage of knowing generations of strategies for combat. It's why Zeiihbu and the royal army were evenly matched in battle. Imagine how unstoppable we could be if we joined our powers with your tactics."

He could imagine it. Meaghan sensed his hope growing and knew he envisioned the same success she had seen. But as fast as the hope flourished, he killed it. "I can't," he said, and sorrow filled him at the decree. "It will take too long to train them. Garon will learn of my hand in the betrayal, and there'll be nothing left of Zeiihbu by the time the war is over."

"So you'll go home," Meaghan said. "And you'll live under Garon's rule and wonder if you could've made a difference for a better world."

He nodded. Closing his eyes, he sighed. "I wish it could be another way."

"And your sons?" Nick asked. "What will happen to them?"

"They'll be cared for," Faillen told him, opening his eyes. "Garon wants Caide to study under him, to become his second in command. I'm sure he'll also want Aldin when he realizes his power is the same."

His fear blossomed and Meaghan understood. "He's going to take them away from you," she said. "He won't let you live if he does. It'll be the only way to ensure you don't try to reclaim them."

"I know," Faillen said. "He'll kill Ree, too, if I let her come back with me. But I love her too much to allow that to happen. She'll remain here. Cal promised me he'd look after her."

Meaghan stared at him. She could not imagine being in his position, forced to sacrifice his children and his life, to abandon his wife in exchange for saving the lives of thousands. She would not have wanted to make the decision, and yet deep within her, she believed he had made the wrong choice. She was not the only one who thought so, she realized, when a flood of strong emotions broke through her focus on Faillen. Grief, horror, fear, and anger surged from outside. Meaghan's eyes shot to the door and she realized it had remained open a crack. Ree stormed into the room, her cheeks red beneath a wash of tears. Faillen stood to face her.

"How dare you!" she screamed. He caught her in his arms. Her fists found his chest and she pounded against it, her grief erasing all other emotions. "You can't do this. Take their offer. Fight him. You have to."

"I can't," Faillen whispered. Ree's pounding slowed and he drew her into his embrace, into the warmth of his body and his shared grief. "We can't let everyone die for us."

"My boys," she wailed. "Don't take them. Don't go. Please don't do this."

"You don't love me for being a selfish man," he told her, then pressed his lips to her head as her words stopped coming, lost to racking sobs. "I don't want to do this. Please believe me. I can't bear the thought of losing your love in the end."

Sorrow overwhelmed Meaghan. She focused her power back on the doll, but found much of the emotion remained within her. She stood, and Nick did the same. The time had come to leave. Without making any noise, they found their way to the door, stopping when Faillen spoke.

"My Queen." Faillen held his gaze on her. "I'm sorry. I truly am. I hope you won't remember me by this final act."

"I'll remember you as the great man you are," she replied. "And I'll remember what Garon has done. If your road ends as you fear, please know that I'll return your sons to Ree. I'll uphold my promise or I'll die trying."

"Thank you," he whispered before pressing his face into his wife's hair.

Meaghan could no longer contain her tears as she and Nick turned their backs on the couple and forged into the dark of a growing night.

CHAPTER TWENTY-ONE

IT BLED. Meaghan's enemy stood tall and regal against the dawning sky, waiting for her next strike, though its strength had begun to wane. Long gashes scarred its dark brown skin and dripped maple blood over the ground.

Lifting her sword, she swung high, surprised when the tree blocked her attack with a thick limb. The spell remained active, the tree undefeated. Another branch swung at her, pushing her away and she doubled her effort, tightening her grip on her sword and striking once more. Sun glinted off allestone as the blade met its mark, stripping a chunk of bark from the tree's advancing arm. She lunged again, stabbing a low part of the trunk, and then danced away in time to avoid the swipe of a surface root.

The frustration that had tensed her muscles over the past half hour began to ease. She parried another swipe and allowed the exercise to erase her worries from her mind. Her conversation with Faillen dissolved first, then the twenty-four near-sleepless days since, along with Cal's overdue promise to visit. Last, Vaska's unmarked grave at the edge of the field faded, relegated to distant memory by the intensity of her fight and the resilient cold of the waning winter.

She focused on only two things—the doll tucked beneath her cloak and the flurry of branches and limbs as they flew at her, driven by magic and the instinct to survive. Each blow, each thrust, each block and advance heightened her control over her power and her skill. She spun around the tree. Wind whipped her hair behind her and wiped sweat from her brow. She ducked to avoid a thick attack of budding leaves, and then she landed the killing blow, thrusting her sword into a knothole the spell had marked as the tree's heart.

The shock of the blow, the power of it, echoed down her arms and then the tree went limp. She stared at her foe, at its limbs drooping to the ground, and knew the spell had succumbed to her aggression. She pulled her sword from its mark, and then pressed her forehead against the edge of the knothole as she worked to control her breath. Closing her eyes, she focused on the heat emanating from her body and stretched it out, along her arms and into her fingers. She rested her hands against the bark and gave her foe the gift of rebirth. Her revival power surged, warming her skin and heating the bark. When she opened her eyes, all evidence of the fight had disappeared.

In its place, the healed tree bore white blossoms and the promise of spring. She headed across the field to the cabin. It would not be long before her skill with the sword matched Nick's. The next time she challenged him, she intended to win. Perhaps today, after he returned from his hunt.

She entered the cabin and deposited her sword with the other weapons in a corner of the room, then added a log to the remnants of the breakfast fire. The morning chill eased from her skin as she moved on to practicing spells, reciting the one that formed a ball of light first. It blossomed between her palms as she focused on it, expanding it to the size of a basketball before flicking her hand to throw it across the room. She drew it back a fraction of an inch from the wall, and then tossed it away once more. A chuckle echoed from the fire. Following it, a familiar voice filled the room with joy.

"I saw Scree toy with a mouse in exactly the same way once," it said.

"Cal." Meaghan turned to look at the fire, though she could not see him. "You're all right."

"I haven't met a Mardróch smart enough to catch me yet," he responded. "I'd say it's good to see you, but frankly, you look terrible."

She laughed. "Thanks. I thought it was time to increase my training. Our trip to Faillen's didn't go well."

"He told me. I saw him yesterday."

"He's still in Ærenden? I thought he'd be gone by now."

"He isn't anxious to meet his death," Cal said. "And he doesn't want to leave Ree yet. He's planning on leaving soon though. I won't welcome that day."

Meaghan frowned. "Neither will I. I wish I could help him."

"Fight the war. Defeat Garon. That's the best you can do."

"While sequestered here?" She locked her hands together behind her back, and started pacing the room. "I'm ready to fight, Cal. It's just a matter of convincing Nick. I can't do anything productive until we rejoin the others."

"Where is he?" Cal asked.

"Hunting. Will you speak with him?"

"When the time is right," he agreed. "But I'm not sure you're ready either."

She whirled around to face the fire. "I'm strong," she insisted. "I'm fast. I can fight."

"No doubt," he said. "But it's a matter of your empath power. The doll works for now, but it won't work indefinitely. There are thousands of people in the caves now. They're set up in different areas, but you'll come in contact with most of them in time. Holding your focus on the doll takes energy. How long can you do that without wearing yourself out? Days, maybe? It's not enough."

She shook her head in disagreement, intending to argue, but she could not find a rebuttal against his logic. The doll was a Band-Aid for a wound needing sutures. She had yet to figure out how to transition Nick's technique into a more permanent solution. "So what do I do in the meantime?" she asked. "I can't stand the thought of continuing to do nothing."

"A time will come when you'll wish for these days of inactivity," he warned her, "when you'll long for the peace of the cabin."

"Perhaps. But that time isn't now."

"I understand," he said, and the sadness in his voice told her he meant it. "After talking with Faillen, you're grieving, and you're feeling helpless. But more than that, you're angry. When you go into battle, though, you can't fight with your emotions. You need to clear your head. You need to follow your training and your training alone.

Promise me you'll heed that advice."

"I will," she promised, and pushed the emotions away with a controlled exhale.

"Also, when you fight, don't bother using the doll to control your power. The safest thing to do is focus on Nick's blocking power. You can do that without having to think about it, right?"

"Of course," she said and then narrowed her eyes at the fire. "Why are you telling me this now?"

Cal sighed, and Meaghan could almost feel the weight he carried with the sound. "Because it's time for your first battle. The Mardróch have attacked a village a few miles north of you. The villagers need your help to survive. Go to them. But Meaghan," he commanded when she spun on her heels and started for the door. "Do everything Nick says, *exactly* as he says. If you get killed because I told you about the battle, he'll never forgive me. I need your word on that."

"You have it," she said, then grabbed her knife belt and ran out the door.

She did not have to go far to find Nick. He had just started up the steps to the porch when she skidded to a stop in front of him.

"What's the rush?" he asked.

"There's a battle not far from here," she answered. "Cal says they need our help."

Nick raised an eyebrow. Moving around her, he hung the wild turkey in his hand on the hook in the porch ceiling, then tied it with a piece of rope. His movements seemed too slow, too calculated, and she knew his answer as soon as he faced her again.

"The villagers are losing," she said. "We have to help them."

He slid a quiver of arrows from his back and rested it against the door. "Two people aren't going to make a difference in a losing battle. We'll only add to the casualty count."

"You don't know that," she insisted, crossing her arms in front of her. "We have stronger powers than most people. We have better training."

"We don't have active powers," he reminded her, setting his bow next to his quiver. "And you have no battle experience. The people already fighting are probably more qualified than you."

She pressed her lips together and glared at him. "How am I supposed to get battle experience if you won't let me fight? I'm ready."

"You aren't or you wouldn't be so excited to go. You'd want to avoid it."

She blew out a hot breath and trailed her eyes north. "They're my people. If they're fighting, I should be, too."

"You do the most good to them here," he told her.

"Living as a coward?" she countered, turning from him. "I'm tired of hiding, Nick."

"Meg, you don't—"

"Understand," she finished a sentence all too familiar to her. She wheeled on him. Her eyes shot fire. Her tone blasted him with heat. "I don't understand what I'm getting into. I don't understand what it's like. I never will. Not if I don't go. Not if I don't help."

Nick sighed. "You are helping. By staying here and finishing your training. By staying alive so you can rule."

"Rule *what*? Every battle Garon takes more land, more lives.

Every day he steals what matters, and he destroys the people I care about." She closed her eyes, squeezing them tight over tears that wanted to fall. "I can't let him keep doing this, not when I might have a chance to stop it."

Nick said nothing. He put his arms around her and drew her close. The comfort he offered nearly unleashed her tears, but she fought to hold them back. She pulled away from his embrace enough to look at him, for him to see her face and gauge the sincerity in it. "We agreed we would do these things together. I don't want to break that promise. I don't want to fight alone, but I will if I must."

"Where's the battle?"

"Three miles from here, to the north. Nick, I'm ready. You have to trust me. I need to do this."

He nodded and let her go. "I'll get my sword," he said, then reclaimed his bow and quiver and brought them inside. When he returned, he had his sword strapped to his back. "I have a few rules you'll need to follow if we're going to do this. If you can't agree to them, we won't go. Do you understand?"

"Yes."

He pinned her with a withering look she had never seen from him before. The command in his eyes surprised her. It was effortless, practiced, and she realized that from this moment, she would no longer be his wife. She would no longer be his trainee. She would be a soldier, and he would not allow her the grace for disobedience she had received in the past.

"Our plan is to survey the battle," he told her. "Nothing more. If I don't like what we see, we return to the cabin."

She frowned at his decree, but he silenced her urge to protest with a single, steely gaze. "*If* it looks like we have a chance of survival, we fight under two conditions. One, you don't leave my side. You use my power to block yours and under no condition will you attempt to read anyone's emotions without my permission."

He paused. She nodded in confirmation. "And two?"

"You do exactly as I tell you, when I tell you to do it. No objections, no arguments, no questions. Every second counts, Meg. You break this rule and you end up dead. This isn't training. It's not a game. It's real."

"I never thought differently," she protested. "I understand the risk involved—"

"It's real," he repeated. The hardness in his eyes dissolved. He brought a hand to her shoulder and gripped it. "And losing you would be too real for me."

She swallowed the lump forming in her throat, and finally understood the true risk. It did not belong to her. It belonged to him. She had no doubt he would get through the battle. Even if Abbott had not foreseen Nick at his public coronation, his skill as a fighter, his experience, and his intelligence increased his chances of survival. He did not have the same assurance with her. Added to that, the fear of her death had been tangible for both of them since the Dreamer had predicted she would not be around for the same coronation.

She pressed into his arms, and turned her face against his neck. "Every word," she promised. "I'll follow your every word. I'm not leaving you today."

"You'd better not," he whispered, and held her for a moment

longer before letting her go. "We should leave. We'll run as far as we can, then slow down to maintain quiet. There's no reason to call attention to our presence."

With those words, steel returned to him. He charged into the forest and she followed his lead.

CHAPTER TWENTY-TWO

THEY RAN with the speed of those accustomed to the woods. Fleet-footed and nimble, they flew over rocks and roots, past dips, and over hills without hesitation. They remained as silent as they could while listening for every sound they could capture. Woodland animals fled, rustling the underbrush as they scurried deeper into the forest. Birds launched into the sky overhead, the flutter of their wings accompanying their warning trills to their own kind. Each noise heightened Meaghan's senses and tensed her muscles, but nothing slowed them until they heard the first evidence of human activity. The whistling started first, followed by the boom of a magical bomb. It echoed from their left, and Nick deviated in that direction.

When the sounds of yelling and the clash of metal on metal joined the bombs, they stopped. Nick cocked his head to the side, listening, and then gestured for Meaghan to move in a different direction. Soon the trees gave way to the edge of a field. Nick threw out his arm to block her, preventing her from leaving the protection of the trees.

They remained in the shadows as they studied the battle before them. Several hundred people and Mardróch fought using swords and bows, knives and powers to slay their opponents. As Meaghan had witnessed before in the battle at the ravine, the powers displayed were vast. Mardróch felled men and women with lightning, turning them to ash. Telepaths tossed arrows out of the air with sweeps of their hands. A man levitated out of reach of a sword. A Firestarter fought a woman who doused his efforts with waterfalls formed from a stream. And here, too, someone had the ability to change people into stone. The man dashed across the field, tagging his enemies in a seemingly childish game. But his power held no innocence, and neither did the grin stretched across his face. Meaghan could not forget it. Nor could she forget the patch of stark white hair twisted through his long, black locks. It commanded her attention as he touched a woman with a red ribbon on her wrist, solidifying her into solid granite. Sun glinted off the woman's sparkling stone eyes, and Meaghan looked away before the grotesqueness of it turned her stomach.

Further down the field, some of the fighters disappeared, only to reappear a few minutes later, and then disappear again.

"What's happening there?" she asked Nick, pointing at them.

"They're stepping into the protected boundary for the village," he responded. He took her hand in his. "You are welcome here."

A village appeared. This one stood as big as the Guardian village had been. And like that village in the end, many of the houses burned or had already collapsed to the ground. More people fought Mardróch in the streets and alleys between the buildings.

"Someone must have invited them in," Nick said.

Meaghan nodded, feeling sick at the thought of the betrayal, and then allowed her eyes to trail to the ground, to the bodies she had not wanted to see before. Almost as many people lay dead or dying as she had seen fighting on the field.

"Can we help?" she asked.

"There aren't many Mardróch," Nick assessed, scanning the field again. "Maybe a dozen or so, which means the majority of Garon's soldiers look like our allies. I've been to this village once before, but I don't know the villagers well enough to recognize who to kill and who to save."

"And I know none of them," she realized and frowned. "Still, there must be something we can—"

"Turn slowly," a voice commanded from behind them. "And don't try to use your powers or it will be the last thing you do. I'm armed."

Meaghan held up her hands and followed the instructions she had been given. Nick turned toward the voice as well, but instead of raising his hands, he moved so that his hand rest against Meaghan's side, positioned to grab one of her knives.

The man studied them both with a calm face accustomed to battle and to enemies. His black hair hung at the nape of his neck in a tight ponytail. His dark green eyes glinted with hatred, but held no fear. Two days of stubble dotted his jawline, hinting at his endurance in battle. And his hands held the reason why he had survived so long. A blue orb crackled between his fingers. He lifted the orb, the gesture a clear threat. "Tell me who you are and why you're here. And keep in mind, I'm not a patient man for lies."

"We're here to help," Nick told him.

"No one comes to help. Not without an army of their own. Not when there are Mardróch around."

"We do," Meaghan said. "We weren't far from here and—"

"Enough!" the man barked. He spread his hands and the ball of electricity expanded. So did the hatred in his eyes. His focus moved from Nick to her. "Tell me who the traitor is," he hissed. "Tell me so I can kill him after I finish you."

"We aren't with Garon," Meaghan tried again. "We came—"

"Artair," Nick interrupted. "That's your name, isn't it? It's been a few years, so I'm having difficulty remembering, but you're Malcon's son, aren't you?"

The man's attention snapped back to Nick, and with a flick of his wrist, the orb covered half the distance between them. "Garon's trained you well. How long has our spy been feeding you information?"

"He hasn't," Nick responded. "I've met you. Try to remember. You don't want to kill your allies. You have too few of them right now."

Artair's eyes narrowed into slits. "I'm sure we haven't met."

"We have," Nick insisted. "Your father had a broken leg. My mother healed him. She brought her apprentice, Sal, with her so your village would have a Healer."

"You're Nick," Artair said, recognition dawning over his face. The orb quivered and then floated back into his hands. "Sal is dead. So is my father."

"I'm sorry. We didn't know about the battle until today."

"What would it matter if you had?" Artair asked. "You're only two people. You don't have an active power, do you?" Nick shook his head. "You?" he asked Meaghan.

"No," she said. "Not really. I can make plants grow. I can sense emotions. That's all."

"Emotions," he scoffed, and the orb disappeared with a soft pop. "Go home. There's no reason for you to die with the rest of us." He turned from them, took a step, and then stopped. A second later, his head came back around. He stared at Meaghan. "Emotions," he said again, and this time his voice held wonder. He faced her. "My father was the Head Guardian of this village, which I guess makes me the Head Guardian now. I've been trying to keep the villagers fighting. Sal made potions, but we ran out of them. Garon's soldiers still have a steady supply. And, of course, the Mardróch don't sleep." His eyes trailed to Nick. "Can you do what your mother does?"

"I can't heal anyone," Nick told him. "I don't have my mother's powers, but I know how to make potions for energy, and ones to keep everyone awake. Do you have the right herbs?"

"I have Sal's kit," Artair said. "If you can make the potions, our people can keep fighting. Exhaustion has made them weak, but we have greater numbers. And if we can use her power to dispose of the Mardróch, we actually stand a chance of winning."

Nick raised an eyebrow. "Her power?"

"The empath power," Artair clarified. "The rumor's true isn't it? Please tell me it is."

"What rumor?" Meaghan asked.

"The one that you," he hesitated, then licked his lips. "The one that the person with the empath power can't be frozen. That the Queen can't be," he stopped. His eyes grew wide as he realized what he had said. It had taken him too long to put the information together and she realized what it meant. She approached him, and placed a hand on his forearm.

"Where's Sal's kit?" she asked.

"That way," he gestured behind him. "I needed to keep it safe, so I hid it in a tree."

"Show us," Nick told him. They followed him into the forest. Nick retrieved the kit from the tree Artair indicated and set it on the ground, crouching over it as he began to work. Meaghan brought Artair to a tree stump. It did not take much coaxing to convince him to sit down.

"How long have you been awake?" she asked.

"Three days. Three," he repeated. He pressed his hands to his eyes, and then dragged them down his face. "Please forgive me, my Queen. I'm not thinking well. I never should have recommended you fight." His eyes drew up to hers and then his face paled. "I threatened you. I didn't—"

"You did what you needed to do," she interrupted and brought a hand to his shoulder. "Please call me Meaghan."

"Whatever you wish, Queen Meaghan."

"No, just Meaghan." She smiled. "Your plan is good. I came to fight and I think if I'm most suited to battle Mardróch, that's what I should be doing."

"His plan is good, except for one thing," Nick corrected her. He portioned herbs from separate vials into a small, ceramic container. After adding liquid from a glass jar, he capped the container. "I can't mix potions and stay by your side at the same time, which means you won't be able to fight."

She pressed her lips together in frustration, but remembered her promise to him and nodded. "How long will it take you to make enough potions for everyone?"

"A few hours at least."

"The Mardróch could kill dozens by then," she said and turned her attention back to Artair. "Do you think it's possible to lure them to me? Do you have people who'd be able to do that without getting close enough to be frozen?"

"I could do it," Artair said. "And we have two other people with active powers who could possibly help."

Nick delivered the container to Artair to drink, then addressed Meaghan. "Do you have a plan?"

"If you agree to it. Your power works for me from a distance. If I stand on the edge of the field, I can fight Mardróch while you mix potions in the woods."

"It didn't work that well from a distance in my village," he reminded her. "I know you were overwhelmed there, but this is your first battle. You might be here, too."

"I'm stronger than I was then," she reminded him. "As is my focus."

Nick shook his head. "I'm sorry, but I can't let you fight without someone at your side. His plan can wait until I'm done. And if you help me, the task will go faster."

"I can fight with her," Artair offered. His voice sounded stronger and Nick and Meaghan turned to look at him. He stood. His eyes shone brighter than they had before, and color had returned to his cheeks. "I may not be her personal Guardian like you are, but I am a Guardian. I can protect her well enough so that she could get the job done."

"I'm sure you have the ability," Nick said. "But she's my charge. I'd feel more comfortable if she stayed with me."

"I understand," Artair responded. "I'd probably feel the same way in your position, but several hours could cost us the battle. The people who receive your potions might survive. The others won't. They need something to galvanize them."

"They need to be reminded the Mardróch aren't invincible, that Garon's army can be defeated," Nick said. "It would revive their hope. I've seen it work before."

"It could change the course of the battle."

Nick inhaled a long breath, then nodded, and turned to Meaghan. "What will you do if you lose focus on my power?"

"I'll retreat," she promised.

"All right." He picked up the medical kit from the ground. "Let's get to this."

§

NICK SET up the kit on the edge of the forest as Meaghan had asked. Before she began fighting, he insisted they establish every piece of their plan in advance. Artair found the two people with active powers he thought might help and brought them back. He introduced the first as Millice. Milli, by her nickname. She stood no taller than five feet, and her blonde hair hung down her back in an elaborate braid for half that length. She greeted Meaghan with gray eyes still filled with hope, even below the exhaustion hazing them. Artair explained that she had the ability to shake the ground in any direction she chose. She had developed her power to the point where she could focus it on a specific area, knocking whoever stood in the area to their knees, while those surrounding her target remained standing. The second person Artair introduced looked more like a beanpole than a man. He grinned at her from below a shock of bright white hair.

"Call me Iza," he told Meaghan after accepting a potion from Nick. "My power draws people toward me, essentially lassoing them. My wife hated it, but I always enjoyed getting kisses when I felt like it. Of course, I can't say I ever thought I'd be dragging a Mardróch toward me."

"It's a first for everyone," Artair told him. "But Adara has a special power. The Mardróch can't freeze her, which means she can get close enough to kill them. At least, she can kill them more easily than we can."

"Is that so?" Iza asked. "I thought only one person had that power, but it seems we were wrong. It's a good thing *Adara* came along."

Milli laughed so hard she choked on her potion. Artair frowned at Nick. "I told you a fake name wouldn't keep her identity a secret."

"Sure it will," Milli said once her sputtering stopped. "We're certainly not going to say anything, and no one else will come close enough to the Mardróch to see she isn't freezing. They'll just think she's able to kill them more easily for another reason." She handed her container back to Nick. "I have to get closer to the Mardróch to get them to follow me. Their intelligence means I need to make it obvious I'm the one shaking them. While I'm out there, I'll tell people to come see you."

Nick nodded. "Sounds good. I guess we're ready then."

"Not quite," Artair said and pulled two red ribbons from his pocket. He handed one to Nick and the other to Meaghan. "Put these on your right wrists. If anyone comes around who doesn't have one on, or who has one on their left wrist, don't trust them."

Meaghan tied her ribbon, and then they all set to work. Milli found her way onto the field, knocking down enemies as she went with a tap of her foot on the ground. Artair took his place next to Meaghan on the edge of the field, and Iza ran to help a friend who appeared to be losing to an opponent not far away.

"There's a Mardróch over there," Artair told her and pointed to their left. "If I start lobbing orbs at him, he'll come running. Are you ready?"

She nodded, though the gesture was a lie. Standing on the field, this close to the action, the reality of the situation struck her. Not fifteen feet away, she watched a young woman about her age fall from a knife wound to the neck. The middle-aged man who had murdered her raised crazed eyes in Meaghan's direction before taking an electric orb from Artair. The burn mark the orb left behind seared through clothing and flesh, leaving an unmistakable stench she would always associate with death. The man toppled over his victim.

Behind the piled bodies, another person fell. This man, his wrists free of ribbons, became a symbol of victory for her allies. But he looked no different to Meaghan. She did not see an enemy. She only saw the lifeless form of a human being, the soulless eyes of someone's father or son. And in that man's vacant stare, she understood the truth Nick had been trying to tell her. To survive the battle, she would have to take a life. She had trouble killing the fake Mardróch in her field test and he had been a grotesque creature with no hint of humanity left within him. How could she kill someone who looked like he could be her neighbor? How could she stare into the eyes of someone with a recognizable soul and dim that light?

The thought drew bile up the back of her throat. She could not kill. And if that was her answer, she would not survive. Panic overwhelmed her. Another ribbonless enemy drew close, and then fell to the ground, victim to another of Artair's orbs. She witnessed it all like a slow-motion movie, surreal and muted, before primal fear drove her into action. She turned to flee. She took no more than a single step before Artair's efforts drew the closest Mardróch toward them. The monster came too fast, and his red eyes caught Artair off guard. Artair froze, an orb still sizzling between his fingers, and Meaghan lost her only protection.

The Mardróch raised his hands. Lightning arced between his fingers. His laugh echoed his sinister intent as he eyed his frozen prey. He pushed his hands forward, preparing to strike, and Meaghan did what her training had taught her to do. She found a knife, slipped it from her belt and threw it with the speed and accuracy her muscles had come to memorize. The knife passed between the Mardróch's hands, slicing through his lightning bolt, and sank into his exposed face. He crumpled to the ground, revealing a second enemy behind him. An arrow sat within the man's bow, ready to fly. He pointed it at her, drew his elbow back, and instinct drove her second knife into his heart.

Only after he fell did she see his humanity, and recognize him as more than her enemy. Though she understood she had no other choice—she had to kill him or she would be dead—she would never forget his face. And she would never forget the look of disbelief that passed over it when his life slipped from his grasp.

CHAPTER TWENTY-THREE

"**INCOMING!**" **ARTAIR'S** voice boomed beside Meaghan. He gripped her arm. "To your right," he shouted and she tore her eyes from the dead man. The Mardróch had begun to find their way across the field, joined by some of their comrades. Meaghan retrieved her spent knives, hastily wiped them clean on the dried grass, and continued to fight.

The first woman who raised her sword to strike found a swift end when Meaghan's blade sliced through her neck. She bled out within seconds. Before Meaghan could retrieve her knife, two more people attacked. A man came from the left, his hand clutching what looked to be a smaller version of a scythe. A woman charged from the right, weaponless at first glance, but Meaghan soon realized the woman held a far greater tool. She narrowed her eyes. Her lips upturned into a knowing smile, and pain seared through Meaghan's head, a fire that burned all thought from existence. She crumpled to her knees, and then forced her legs to sustain her weight once more.

The pain surged again. Even with her best efforts to ignore it, it distracted her, blinded the edges of her vision, and filled her ears with high-pitched ringing. It would not take long before the enemies overcame her. The sharp blade of the man's scythe glinted in the sun as he raised it. Meaghan blocked his strike, and then shoved him away. He tripped over a body and landed flat on his back.

Meaghan turned in time to see the woman remove a small knife from her belt. Though Meaghan's arms hung heavy like lead, she forced them up, using her knives to deflect the woman's first attack. She missed the second. The woman flicked her wrist, twisting the knife so the blade bit the flesh of Meaghan's forearm, drawing blood.

Meaghan barely registered the injury. The throbbing in her head blocked out all else. She tried to lift her knife to deflect another attack, but failed. This one sliced her upper arm. Pain charged through her shoulder, hot and swift. It commanded her attention, stealing the focus from her head.

Adrenaline coursed through her. She lifted both of her hands, deflecting another blow and pushed against her attacker. The woman staggered backward. Meaghan did the same, putting more distance between them, and then turned in time to block a scythe blade from slicing her head. The man locked eyes with Meaghan, growled, and then reached for a knife at his belt. He made a move for her stomach. She jumped back, barely avoiding the tip of his blade, and then became the aggressor. Her knife met its target, though it did not embed in his chest as she had hoped. It sliced through cloth and skin, bringing enough blood to the surface to soak through his shirt. The wound would not be fatal, but it would slow him down.

As Meaghan's injuries had done to her.

She struggled to move her stiff shoulder. Warm blood coursed a path down her arm and over her hand, making her grip on the knife slick. She crossed her blades, deflecting another blow. The pain in her shoulder surged with the impact. The pain in her head swelled, too. A glance behind her confirmed the woman had rebounded. She charged at the same time the man took another swing with his scythe. Meaghan blocked it, but could not turn in time to stop the knife the woman threw in her direction.

Meaghan saw it coming. She understood its accuracy and its fatality. She raised her own blade to deflect it, understanding, too, that the effort would be useless, and then the knife froze. It trembled in the air, then reversed direction and flew into the head of its owner. The woman collapsed to the ground. Meaghan saw it all happen, and though confusion replaced the pain that no longer gripped her head, she could not dwell on it. She heard a grunt beside her, and spun around in time to halt the scythe's descent. The man raised his blade again, but before he could bring it down a second time, he backed away from her.

Not backed away, she realized, but slid backward across the grass. His eyes grew wide. His face stiffened in panic. He dropped his scythe to the ground. Then he turned in time for a sword to pierce his stomach.

Iza smiled at her before pulling his weapon from the body of her attacker. Then he raised an eyebrow and pointed into the field. The battle had grown too noisy for him to speak so she could hear him, but she understood what he meant. A Mardróch had frozen a woman a hundred yards away and had begun advancing on her. Instead of using electricity to dispense of her, he held a blade in his hand and Meaghan realized he intended to take his time killing his prey. Iza wanted to know if she felt prepared for the monster. Meaghan nodded, and he yanked the Mardróch away from the woman.

The creature wailed as Iza dragged him across the field. Meaghan recognized the sound of frustration and relished in it. Her satisfaction did not last long. When Iza released the Mardróch, the creature advanced on her. He raised his hands. Lightning shot from finger to finger. Then he grinned and stared her straight in the eyes. She pretended to freeze, and when he moved to strike, she dove out of the way. She hit the ground and rolled to the left. The lightning bolt shot over her head. It struck the earth behind her, kicking up a shower of grass and dirt.

The Mardróch swore. "You," he hissed. "You're foolish to come here. This will be your last day."

"If it is, you won't see it," she responded. She drew a knife and struck, but the blade only bounced off the Mardróch's impenetrable cloak. She debated throwing her weapon, but the thought fled as fast as it had come. She stood too close to him, and from this angle, she would never be able to throw the blade with enough force to kill.

She rolled to avoid another bolt of lightning and her back hit something hard. Launching to her knees, she grasped behind her for the object, and then pitched forward to avoid another lightning strike. The bolt created a small crater in the ground where she had been kneeling.

Jumping to her feet, she tore across the field. Sun glinted off the scythe blade in her hand. She tightened her grip on it. She could hear the Mardróch's rasping breath as he chased her, smell his joy in the odor that assaulted her nostrils, and when his laughter rattled close to her ear, she spun around to face him. Holding the scythe between both hands, she swung it. He tried to block her, but the blade broke past his arms, finding purchase within the opening of his hood. His joy ended as he fell.

Meaghan stared down at him, and then looked around for another impending threat. Grief and fear came from her right. Agony and excitement flowed from her left. And though no one fought close by, she realized the danger confronting her. She had run too far. She could no longer sense Nick's power. The emotions washed over her and through her, paralyzing her to her spot. Terror, anxiety, and hatred joined the fray in her head. Exhaustion drew on her muscles. Anticipation accelerated her heart. Pain almost brought her to the ground. And the overwhelming mix of everything returned bile to her throat.

She willed her body to find its way back to Nick's power, but it refused to obey. Something hit her shoulder. She expected to feel the warmth of her own blood coursing down her back, the bite of steel or the swift heat of a piercing arrow, but only numbness greeted her. The sensation emanated from the point of impact, creeping along her skin like dozens of tiny spiders.

She reached for a knife, prepared to turn around and face her attacker, but her legs would not budge. She struggled to gulp another breath, drawing it in moments before the numbing sensation spread across her chest. Then she saw him.

He advanced around her, slow and taunting, as a crooked smile crept over his face. He held no weapons in his hands. None hung from his belt, and she realized as soon as her eyes fell on the white streak painted through his black hair that he did not need them. His touch alone guaranteed her death. He lifted a hand to wave, the good-bye gesture not lost on her, and then she turned to stone.

The clang of metal on metal, the explosions, whistles and screams, the commands and yells—they all disappeared, lost to cavernous silence. Her eyes remained open though she could not see. She could not blink. She held her right index finger at an odd angle. She wanted to straighten it, but it refused to twitch. Her feet sunk into the ground, useless. Her arms hung heavy, glued to her sides. And her lungs ached as if a hundred rocks had been piled on top of them. They burned with the need to release her last breath.

Nothing of her body obeyed her command. Yet by some cruel design, her power still forced its way through her prison, bringing with it hundreds of emotions. It tortured her, pulling on every fiber of her consciousness, and it left her with no relief—no tears to ease the sorrow, no screams to erase the torment. Not even the ability to throw up to release the poison filtering into her. She remained trapped, connected to every emotion in a way she had never experienced before.

She would have preferred the pain of death at a Mardróch's hand to this. She thought of the doll, of the technique Nick had taught her, and wondered if it could quiet her last moments. She needed to focus her power on something, *anything*. The rough hilt of her knife pushed back against the palm of her hand, so she cast her empath power toward it. The power moved some, but it did not shift enough. She brought her focus to the stone encasing her, but could not grab hold of it. Then, in a last desperate attempt, she turned her power to the only thing she had left—her own emotions. They echoed back to her. She felt fear, and then sensed it before the two blended into one. Panic came next, then sadness, though she held that emotion not for her death, but for Nick. Then those, too, reverberated, and quieted. Pain came last, searing her lungs and signaling the end.

Her power overlapped her emotions, driving the world out, and soon she felt nothing but relief.

CHAPTER TWENTY-FOUR

"BRING THEM here," Nick commanded from a distance. "Lay them down."

Meaghan floated through the air. Something hard pressed against her back. Fingers touched the base of her neck.

"She's breathing." Nick's voice came from above her this time before moving away. "He's not though. I need to get his heart going. Felix, grab the syringe from the kit, the one with the red end. Let's hope this works," he said after a brief pause. Silence elapsed, and then Meaghan heard a raspy gasp. "That's it," Nick said. "Stay down, Artair. Rest for a while, all right?"

"Okay," Artair agreed. His voice sounded weak and ragged, and she doubted he even had the strength to rise. "What happened?"

"You were turned to stone," Nick told him.

"Yes, that's right," Artair whispered. "I remember now. Adara ran off. I tried to catch her."

"It's kind of a habit with her. She's fine though. She's just a little slow waking up."

"Your concern is touching," Meaghan muttered. Opening her eyes, she sat up. Wounded lay on the ground around her. Some slept. Others drank potions. All of them showed bruises, dried blood, and bandages. Nick crouched over Artair, but when she spoke, he turned toward her. His smile of relief broadcast the truth of his concern.

"Don't worry," he responded. "You'll know my feelings soon enough. You broke your promise."

"I'm sorry," she said. Her sadness for him still seemed raw and real so she stood and went to him. Kneeling beside him, she took his hand in hers. "It wasn't intentional. I had to run from the Mardróch. It was the only way I could survive."

Nick's face remained controlled, but she could see the fear in his eyes. She focused her empath power on him. "You can stop blocking me," she said. "Use your energy for other things."

"If I do, you'll—"

She shook her head, cutting off his protest. "I found another way to use your technique. I think it's how the power's meant to be controlled. It feels natural." Relief and then curiosity blossomed within him before pride overshadowed his other emotions. He smiled, and she returned the gesture. Then she focused her power back on her own emotions, silencing it.

"How are we no longer stone?" she asked, shifting her mind back to the battle.

"Dahlia killed the man who attacked you," a voice behind her answered. She turned to see Iza standing a few feet away. Tears coursed down his cheeks, mixing with splattered blood. In his hands, he held a cream, knit cap saturated red in places. The blood on the cap still looked fresh.

"My daughter killed him," he whispered. "She has a telepathic power. Had," he corrected and closed his eyes. "She had that power. She was helping us protect you, but a Mardróch, he," Iza's voice broke. His fingers tightened around the cap, and his shoulders shook.

"I'm sorry," Meaghan whispered.

She remembered the knife, which had reversed direction in mid-air and understood what had happened. Dahlia had saved her life. Twice. And in exchange, she had become a sacrifice. It did not seem right. Meaghan shook, too, but not from grief.

"How many Mardróch remain?" she asked.

"Six," Nick responded. "Iza got the one who killed his daughter."

"Then I have work to do."

"You need to rest. You haven't had time to—"

Rather than argue, she ignored him. Standing, she turned toward the field, but found her way blocked by a man who looked more like a mountain of muscle than a human being. If she had been on Earth, she would have pegged him as a professional wrestler. Here, his mass served the better purpose of a wall. He raised a bushy eyebrow over a storm blue eye, and crossed thick arms over his chest. His bald head only added to his imposing demeanor.

"I believe the Healer is talking to you," he said.

She crossed her arms, mimicking his posture. "He's not a Healer, and I don't know who you are, but I'd appreciate it if you'd get out of my way."

"He's the closest thing we have to one right now," the man replied. "And he's due the same respect. He's saving lives, and from what I can tell, you're only costing them."

Meaghan's cheeks heated. She pressed her lips together to cover the sting his words had caused. "I'm not—"

"Felix," Nick warned from beside her. "That wasn't necessary."

The man's eyes snapped to Nick and he frowned. "She needs to learn proper respect for Guardians," he said. "It's obvious from your discussion that her disobedience caused Dahlia's death. If she'd had more respect for what you told her to do, Iza's daughter would still be alive."

"No," Meaghan protested, but the truth in his words melted her anger and dragged down her shoulders. Nick's arm came around her waist. He stiffened with the anger she had lost, but he did not get the chance to lash out against Felix's accusation. Iza beat him to it.

"Adara didn't do anything wrong," he said, the fury in his voice erasing the shaking that had weakened him previously. "I saw the whole thing. She had no other choice but to run, and she fought well. Dahlia died because of this battle. She died because of whoever let Garon's soldiers into the village. And if I know anything about my daughter, I know one thing," he stepped forward, stabbing his finger into the air to punctuate his point. "She gladly gave her life to save this woman and to save Artair. She was a good person who valued others, and I will not let you sully her memory."

Felix cast his eyes down. "I just thought," he shook his head. "I don't know what I was thinking."

"You're tired," Nick offered. "You've been helping me with these potions the whole time, but you haven't had any yourself. Sit and drink one. Take a break. In the meantime," he turned to Meaghan.

"You want revenge. I get that, and I'm not going to stop you."

"Good," she said, and brushed past him. He gripped her arm.

"I'm not going to stop you, *but*," he stressed. "I'm also not going to let Dahlia's sacrifice be in vain. You're bleeding. You won't last long if you don't let me tend to your wounds."

She stared at him, and then dropped her eyes to her arm. The blood had lessened, but still streaked down her sleeve. She had been ignoring the ache so long that she had forgotten about it.

"Oh," she said. "I didn't realize."

"Sit down," Nick told her. "This won't take long. Once Felix is done with his potion, he can find Milli so you can finish what you started. Agreed?"

She nodded, and followed Nick back to Sal's kit, sitting down next to it when he did the same. He removed a familiar green powder from inside and mixed a small portion into a bowl with water. When the poultice had reached the desired consistency, he parted the slice in her sleeve.

"The wound's not bad," he said. "Not as deep as I expected. It won't need stitches."

He lifted a small amount of the green poultice with his fingers and spread it over the wound, then covered it with a slip of white gauze. The cut on her forearm received the same treatment.

"How does that feel?" he asked.

"Better, but the poultice isn't as cold as it was in the cabin."

"Snow activates that part of the medicine," he said. "It'll still work the same. Once we're able, we'll head to Neiszhe's village and have her heal you. Try not to add to her work, all right?"

"I'll do my best," she said, and smiled when he pulled her to her feet, but did not let go of her hand. His eyes met hers, the sincerity in them demanding her attention.

"I understand your need for revenge," he said. "Dahlia saved your life. I would do the same. But don't let that need overtake you. Don't let it blind you."

She remembered the promise she had made to Cal, to not let her emotions drive her in battle, and nodded. She wanted revenge, but she had to focus. She had to follow her training. She needed to survive.

"I won't. You've taught me better than that."

"Good," Nick said, and by the time Felix returned with Milli, Meaghan had calmed enough to honor her promise. Felix also had another person in tow, a young man with a baby face who had Felix's eyes and height, but a lankier frame, and a thick head of curly blonde hair.

"Garon's soldiers are failing," Felix told Nick. "I'm going back out to fight. My son, Origio, will help you with the potions in my stead. Nearly everyone has had one, but in case this battle stretches longer, I think it'll be wise to keep a stock on hand."

"I agree," Nick said. "Thank you for your help, Origio."

Rather than respond, Origio shoved his hands into his pockets and scowled. Felix shot him a look of censure, and nudged him.

"You're welcome," Origio grumbled, then addressed his father. "I can keep fighting. I'm not tired."

"He's fighting?" Meaghan asked in disbelief. "He doesn't look old enough."

Origio's scowl deepened. "I'm trained to fight. I'm a Guardian."

"And you're a fine one," Felix said. "But as such, you'll obey orders. If I hear you abandoned Nick, I'll feed you to the Mardróch myself."

Origio dropped his arms, the look on his face making it clear his father instilled a healthy fear in him. He nodded, and Felix turned and found his way back to the field. Milli and Meaghan followed close behind.

"I tracked two of the Mardróch to the village before Felix came to get me," Milli informed Meaghan. "They killed a friend of mine today, so if you don't mind, I'd like to start there."

"Of course," Meaghan agreed.

The two women skirted around the edge of the field, making their way toward what remained of the village. Some houses still burned, but most stood as shells or black bones stretching into the backdrop of a late afternoon sky.

Only one enemy spotted them before they reached the village streets. She swung a sword in her hand as she charged. Meaghan lifted a knife from her belt, ready to cast it, but did not get the chance. An orb of electricity knocked the woman to the ground first. Meaghan and Milli spun around.

"Artair," Milli said with a grin. "I didn't think Nick would let you return to the fight."

"What he doesn't know won't hurt him," Artair responded, returning the grin. He formed another orb in his hands and nodded toward the village. "It feels nice to be hunting the Mardróch for once, instead of the other way around. I'd hate to miss it."

"Then by all means," Milli said and gestured for him to lead the way. He nodded and took the opportunity she gave him. The mood settled into the seriousness their hunt deserved, and they found their way to the main street of the village, crossing onto it with silence and caution.

Bodies lay strewn in their path. Most of them had red ribbons attached to their wrists. Many of the ones who did not had been burnt beyond recognition. Meaghan caught her breath when she saw the small form of a child, his black hands reaching toward the sky. She could imagine the chaos. She could feel the heat from the fire as it must have raged through the wood-framed houses. She could smell the smoke as it barreled down the streets, suffocating those in its path. She could hear the screams, sense the panic and the agony of death as it came in the form of flame or blade. She felt it as if she had lived it. And how could she not? It had only been a handful of months since she had stood in the center of similar destruction, since she had heard the screams of death as they surrounded her, and experienced every emotional moment of the dying.

She paused, and then closed her eyes to collect her thoughts. The emotions swelled within her, so she tamped them down, ignoring them as best she could to ensure she remained focused when the moment came to fight.

They walked the length of the main road. No one remained within the shadows of the skeletal buildings. Only the souls of the dead resided in the alleys. She could not figure out why the Mardróch would come to a place with no victims, and then they found the pair of monsters Milli had tracked. They rooted through the remains of a burnt out building, tossing support beams like twigs.

"It's here," one of the creatures growled to the other. "It has to be. He said we had to bring it back."

"Bah," came the response. "He must have been mistaken. I don't see why it would be."

"Mistaken?" the first asked. "You dare question King Garon? He'll have your tongue for it."

"Only if you tell him. And if you get the notion, yours will be cut out of your mouth along with mine. You called him an imbecile only last week."

The first Mardróch chuckled. The gravelly laugh sent chills down Meaghan's spine. "A term of affection, I assure you. You may be right, though. Why would he be here? He's supposed to be with her."

"Do you think it's true that they're wed? He's more concerned about the boy being a ruler than he is about her."

"It must be true. Why else would he care? He believes what the Dreamer said. The truth potion brings out even the deepest secrets. Ah, here it is," he said. He lifted a skull from the fire. A thick film of soot clung to the bone in place of flesh. The Mardróch's fingers cleared white streaks through the black. "Do you think it's him? Garon will know won't he?"

"Most likely," the other Mardróch said. "And if it isn't him, he'll take our own heads in place of it."

The first Mardróch tossed the skull aside. "Maybe it's best if we don't bring anything back. Garon doesn't know for certain the Guardian was here."

"If he didn't, why would he send us? We had a spy here. We

know the village wasn't worth attacking otherwise. They had no spell books, no major powers."

"There's the electrical orb guy."

"True, but he doesn't matter. He'll be dead soon enough. They'll all be."

"Including the spy. Garon said he's done with him."

Laughter erupted from both Mardróch, but the noise soon faded when they turned, spotting the party flanking them. Meaghan had a knife ready in each hand. Artair held a well-formed orb of electricity at his fingertips. And Milli had armed herself with only a grin.

In desperation, the Mardróch tried to pin their attackers with red-eyed stares. The first Mardróch succeeded in freezing Artair. The second tried to catch Milli, but she looked away. He attempted again with Meaghan and she met his gaze.

"Got her," the Mardróch crowed to his comrade. "Blow up the short one. I'll take care of Mr. Orb."

Meaghan sent the knife in her right hand flying through the air. It found its mark before the Mardróch realized she had thrown it. His partner's gaze broke from Artair as he turned shocked eyes toward Meaghan.

"You!" he exclaimed, only to have his next words cut off as he joined his friend on the ground, his face disintegrated by the orb that Artair had held in his hand.

Artair grinned. "That was too easy."

"So says the guy who got himself frozen," Milli pointed out.

"And what's your body count?" Artair countered. "You might as well have been the one frozen for the amount of good you did."

Milli crossed her arms over her chest. "I thought I'd let our Queen do the honors first, then I'd take my turn. You didn't give me the chance."

"Move faster next time." He chuckled, but turned serious as Meaghan retrieved her knife. She wiped the blade on one of the Mardróch's cloaks and then sheathed it.

"Let's go find the last four," she said, and began walking. Milli and Artair did not follow.

"Is it Nick?" Artair asked.

Meaghan stopped, turning to face him. "Is what Nick?"

"The person they were talking about. The Mardróch may be borderline dumb, but I'm not. I don't know why they thought he was here. As Nick said, he hasn't visited in years. But they seemed to be pretty confident about the wedding of our ruler. As far as I know, the only person set to rule is you."

"So?"

"So… is the person you wed Nick?" he prompted. "They said he was a Guardian. By the way you two behaved after you were turned to stone, it seems to be the only logical explanation."

"We're wasting time," she told him and continued walking.

"Deflection is as good as confirmation," he said, quickening his step to catch up to her. Milli kept pace on Meaghan's other side.

"Do me a favor?" Artair continued. "Convince him not to throw me into the dungeon once you reclaim the castle. I've heard of that place and I'd rather not confirm the rumors in person. I didn't realize I was giving the King the slip back there or I might not have done it."

Meaghan grunted and slid her eyes in his direction. "If you don't stop talking about this, I'll throw you in the Pit myself."

His face went pale as Milli's laughter echoed around them.

They found another Mardróch not far from the village. His attempts at freezing them proved futile as soon as Milli set the ground trembling. He lost his footing and hit the earth with a resounding thud. Meaghan drew a knife, but Milli beat her to the kill. She slipped a small blade from the waistband of her pants and drove it home before the Mardróch could regain his footing.

The last three monsters proved to be more difficult to manage. They fought with a guard of fifteen of Garon's soldiers, and though Meaghan never would have attacked a crowd so large, the Mardróch left her no choice. They found Meaghan's hunting party first.

Milli shook the ground. Some of the soldiers lost their footing, but others levitated above the effects of her power, lifted into the air by the power of one of their own. She tried again and again with the same result, and then froze when a Mardróch managed to look her in the eye.

Artair had greater success. His orbs took down four men, but soon he also succumbed to the monsters' freezing power, leaving Meaghan alone. She backed away from an advancing Mardróch, retreating until her back pressed against the unyielding bodies of her two frozen friends. Unable to move any longer, she threw the knife in her left hand at the Mardróch's face. Her aim hit its mark, and she grabbed the last knife from her belt, clutching it in her hand.

Two knives remained at her disposal against eleven men and two Mardróch—one woman versus thirteen enemies. She swallowed hard and suddenly wished she knew nothing of math.

CHAPTER TWENTY-FIVE

MEAGHAN'S HEART drummed. The rhythm of it set a beat for the shifting feet of the soldiers as they waited for their command to attack. She could take out three, maybe four. On her best day, with luck on her side, she might fell five. But the remaining eight would be upon her before she could do more. They would tear her apart, save her head for Garon's prize, and her amulet for Angus.

The amulet.

Terror gripped her with crushing hands. The cold metal of her mother's necklace still hung against her skin. Why had she not thought to leave it in the cabin? No one could have found it there. But here, once her life had been taken, it would be stripped from her neck and used to end the war. The people of Ærenden would become powerless slaves because of her thoughtlessness.

She could not allow that to happen. At least, she would not let it happen without her best fight. She tightened her grip on the hilts of her knives, and prepared to make the first move. Her only hope was to take out as many of the soldiers as she could, then launch at the

Mardróch. If she could get them to blow her up, there would be nothing left of the amulet or the Reaper Stone to use.

She set her jaw, and eyed her first target—a small man close to her height and weight. He seemed an easy mark. She took a step forward, and then paused when one of the Mardróch screamed. The noise seemed unnatural, even for the monstrous creature. His high pitch mimicked the whistle of a tea kettle. He clutched his hands to his ears, sank to his knees, and then spewed blood from his eyes and mouth before collapsing face first onto the ground. Artair unfroze, and tossed an orb at the remaining Mardróch, freeing Milli from his spell. She shook the ground. As before, one of the men levitated the soldiers, but then he, too, fell to his knees screaming in pain. He bled and died as fast as the Mardróch.

Milli shook the ground once more. This time she knocked down most of the ten remaining soldiers. She continued moving the earth so the men could not keep their feet under them when they tried to rise. Between Artair's orbs and Meaghan's knives, the men soon found punishment for their attack.

Meaghan tried not to look into their eyes. She tried not to see their faces, but the battle had taken its toll. She had grown sick with the bodies piling around her, and weary from the weight of her mounting crimes. *Kill or be killed,* she reminded herself. It did not help, but the face greeting her after she turned from her last victim did. Nick parried the sword of an enemy trying to lunge for her, and then countered with his own move. He had better skill with the sword and soon felled the last man who attacked them. Nick cleaned his blade and sheathed it before coming to her.

"Hold strong," he said. "This is almost finished."

Her eyes trailed over the battlefield. Although Garon's army no longer overran the area, bodies littered the grass, contributing a river of red to the ground. In the distance, the fighting continued, the figures in combat turning to dark shadows as night overtook them.

"It doesn't look like it," she whispered.

"It is," he promised and then wrapped his arms around her. "I can sense your sorrow," he said. "It's a lot stronger than you realize."

And he had come to her as soon as he had felt it. She had not known he could sense that emotion. She buried her head in his chest and held tight. She had to set her sorrow aside to keep fighting. It would be as distracting and detrimental as her anger, but despite her efforts to subdue it, it grew stronger with each life she took.

"What you've had to do today steals a piece of you," he continued. "It changes you, but in time, you'll come to terms with it."

She had her doubts. She pulled back so she could look up at him. "Why do we have to kill them?" she asked. "Why can't we take them as hostages? So many are dead. So many lives are wasted already."

"We can only take them hostage if they surrender," he answered. "Garon's soldiers don't do that. They'd rather fight until the death. And we'd rather live. There isn't much choice. Don't convince yourself otherwise. That guilt doesn't belong to you."

She closed her eyes. "Then why do I feel it?"

"Because you're a good person," he said and pressed his lips to her forehead. "Because you value life. And Meg," he whispered so her name belonged only to their ears, "your life is worth defending. Remember that always."

She nodded and opened her mouth to speak again, but Artair interrupted, the urgency in his voice commanding her full attention.

"I hate to disrupt this beautiful moment," he said. "But we have enemies heading our way. You may want to be prepared."

Meaghan grabbed her knives and spun around. Milli stood at the ready, her arms crossed, her eyes pointed toward the two people who approached. Artair drew up beside her. The air sizzled and a ball of electricity appeared between his hands.

"Another few steps and I can attack," he said, then narrowed his eyes as the man and woman sauntered closer. "They're unconcerned for two people facing death."

"They're unconcerned because they're not our enemies," Nick said, stepping in front of Artair. His sword remained sheathed. His posture stayed relaxed. "They're with me."

"With you?" Milli asked. "How's that possible?"

"They're Guardians," Nick responded, then moved forward to greet the man and woman. Milli, Meaghan, and Artair followed.

"What's the update?" Nick asked.

"We have thirty fighting," the man replied. "Or I should say, we have thirty here. There isn't much fighting left to be done. Once the remainder of Garon's minions realized the battle had been lost, they took off. We're tracking them." He grinned, then turned to Meaghan and offered her a discreet bow. "It's a pleasure to see you again, my Queen," he said. "And to hear of your success today. I understand you have a handy talent with the Mardróch. Well done."

"Thank you," Meaghan replied, smiling in response to cover her confusion. He seemed to know her, but she did not recognize him.

She studied the man, and the woman who stood next to him. They looked similar. Each had pale green eyes and curly auburn hair—his cut short, hers pulled into a ponytail. Both of them had freckles splashed across their cheeks and the bridges of their noses. Though he stood six inches taller than she did, they both had similar, lean builds. Siblings, she guessed, and then remembered. Twins. She had met them at the party in Nick's village.

"It's nice to see you again, Talis," she responded. "Talea," she nodded toward the woman. "I'm glad you were able to join us."

"We could hardly miss a get-together such as this," Talis said with a wink. "The Elders sent word to the Guardians when they heard the village had been attacked. I'm stationed in a village not far from here to the east. Talea came from the west. It's a good thing she did, too. Looks like her power saved you."

"You're the one who killed the Mardróch and the levitator?" Milli asked, her eyes widening. "I've never seen anyone with your power before. How does it work?"

Talea grimaced. "You don't want to know. I try not to think about it myself if I can help it."

"Let's just say we're all glad she's on our side," Nick told Milli before turning back to Talis. "How many Guardians did the Elders dispatch?"

"There'll be another twenty or so coming. We'll ensure the Healers have enough help before we send the others home."

Nick raised an eyebrow. "Why so many?"

"There's a rumor the King was hiding in this village," Talea responded. "Nobody wanted to take the chance the rumor might be true."

"Do you honestly think I'd hide in a village with this many people?" Nick asked. "You've known me long enough to realize I'm smarter than that."

"I would've thought so," she said. "But I wouldn't have thought you were stupid enough to wed a non-Guardian, so," she shrugged. "I guess you're not as smart as you appear."

"Nice," he grumbled. "Don't forget that I can have you arrested for saying stuff like that."

She laughed. "Let's see you try."

They shared a grin born of a friendship built on teasing and then Talea turned to Artair. "You're the Guardian of this village, right?"

Artair nodded. "One of them. Felix is the other. My father was killed in battle. He was the third."

"Felix has been lost too," she told him, her voice soft. "I'm sorry."

"What about Felix's son?" Milli asked. "Is he safe?"

"He witnessed his father's death," Talis said. "Someone said he ran into the woods soon after. We're looking for him."

"He was close to his father," Artair told them. "They hunted together. He might be hiding in one of their usual spots."

"Do you know where those are?" Talis asked.

"I do. I can lead a search party if you think it'll help."

"It's worth a try. If you go to the field hospital, you'll find a man by the name of Avil. He'll help you organize your party."

"I can help," Milli offered. Talis nodded, and both Milli and Artair headed back toward the woods.

"What can we do?" Meaghan asked.

"Leave," Talis told her.

It took her a moment to realize he had not been joking. She frowned. "Until these people are all cared for, I don't intend to go anywhere."

"You don't have much of a choice."

Meaghan raised an eyebrow. "Are you sure about that?"

"Positive," Talis said, knitting his hands together in front of him as he stared her down. "They know who you are."

"Who?"

"Everyone," Talea answered. Though Talis' voice had been strident, his posture stiff with his authority, Talea addressed Meaghan with kindness, her tone easing the tension building in the air. "Forgive Talis. He means well, but he's a bit too used to dealing with people by bullying them into doing what he wants. He seems to have forgotten who he's talking to." Her eyes slid to her brother, sending a warning that had even Meaghan squirming. "It is, of course, your decision if you want to stay, but the villagers have figured out who you are. We don't know who let the Mardróch into the village. If the traitor is still around, you may be risking your life. And since we already know the villagers will be safe, the risk makes little sense."

Though Meaghan disagreed, she nodded, accepting Talea's reasoning. "If any of Garon's people escape," Meaghan said, "they'll report back that I was here. It won't be long before more soldiers come."

"We know," Talea said. "We're organizing everyone who's healthy. They'll be led to one of the Elders' protected areas tonight.

Those who aren't healthy enough to be moved will be guarded until they're healed. No one will remain here after tomorrow is through."

"I guess it's time for us to go then," Meaghan decided. "I won't forget about this."

"It's an honor to help," Talea responded. She rested a hand on Meaghan's shoulder. "And if you don't mind me saying so, I know you aren't happy about going, but you shouldn't feel like you're leaving without finishing your job. You should be proud of your service. You've proven to be a worthy fighter today."

§

THE MOON had begun to make its decent by the time Nick and Meaghan came within range of their cabin. It played with the clouds, dancing beside and behind them, filling the woods with light and then shadows in turn. In the waxing and waning darkness, Meaghan easily recognized parts of the training course as she neared the clearing. The tree with the scarred trunk waited like an old friend. The fake hornets' nest, repaired and returned to its limb, waved at her in the breeze. Even the dormant creeper vines seemed to welcome her home. She could almost smell the fire Nick would build before they slept, and it brought her a feeling of safety she had not experienced in weeks. She counted her steps, focusing on the trees for the glimmer of the blue protection crystals. Weariness captivated her, and she allowed it to dull her usually heightened senses. When a twig snapped behind her, she realized the mistake in that decision.

She turned. Nick did the same, placing his body between her and the person who stood only a few feet in front of them. It took a moment and the reappearance of the moon for Meaghan to recognize the curly blonde hair of Felix's son.

"You shouldn't be here, Origio," Nick told him. "Go back to the village. Artair is looking for you."

"My father's dead," Origio said. He turned his head so his blue eyes shined bright by the moonlight. Meaghan saw tears in them. "Someone shot him with an arrow."

"I know," Nick responded. "I'm sorry, but you can't follow us. We're not going someplace safe for you. You need to find Artair. He'll take you to the Elders."

"I'll miss him," Origio continued as if Nick had never spoken. He sniffed, and wiped a hand across his nose. "He taught me so much. He taught me what was important." His voice shook. "He taught me the truth about our world and about your power." His eyes turned toward Meaghan. Something in them warned her and she drew her hand to the hilt of one of her knives before casting her power toward the young man. She felt his grief and an excitement that seemed out of place.

"He taught me how to fight," he said. He raised his right arm. The red ribbon tied around his wrist fluttered with the movement. "And he taught me how to defeat those who are a threat to our world." His fingers, which he had folded flat over his palm, opened, revealing a handcrafted holster. Five small blades, each no bigger than a dart, rested within it, their tips pointed forward.

Nick yanked his sword from its sheath. Meaghan pulled her knife and threw it. Neither of them proved faster than the young man. He stepped sideways to clear Nick's protection, took aim at Meaghan, and cast his hand forward. All five blades met their marks. One tore through Meaghan's side. Another sliced her pant leg, biting into her skin. A third embedded into her throwing hand. The fourth lodged in her stomach, and the fifth sunk into her neck.

She collapsed and pain hazed her vision, clouding out the sight of Origio's lifeless eyes staring at her from his resting place on the ground.

CHAPTER TWENTY-SIX

NICK DID not dare touch the blade. He kept his distance from it, though he loathed seeing the stark evidence of his failure mocking him from the side of Meaghan's neck. The other blades would be easy to manage, the wounds they created no more than a novice's challenge for a Healer. But this knife had sliced through an artery. Once removed, even the kingdom's best Healer would have trouble stopping the flow of blood in time.

Not that he had a Healer.

Panic overwhelmed Nick and he fought hard to control it. Carrying Meaghan from the woods to the cabin had been hard enough. One wrong arm position or nudge and she would be dead. He had not wanted to move her, but he did not see another option. Origio could have broadcast their position with a hidden commcrystal at any time. If he had, the forest would be crawling with Mardróch before noon.

Frustrated, Nick sunk down to the floor beside Meaghan's cot. Abbott's face flashed through Nick's mind and his words rung in

Nick's ears, as potent as they had been when first spoken. Abbott might not have said Meaghan would not live through the war, but the truth of his vision had hung in the air. And the threat of it had haunted Nick's dreams. He had seen her die a thousand times since. He had suffered through those nightmares, and formulated plans on how to stop each one. He thought he had prepared for every scenario, but he had failed to see the danger a young boy could pose.

Meaghan shuddered. Nick could still sense her, but her presence felt distant. He took her hand in his and tried not to weep when her faint pulse slowed under his touch.

It did not seem right that her life would end this way. She deserved better. She had fought valiantly. She had saved lives, and honored those who had saved hers. She had even battled to protect the people who betrayed her. Nick shook his head in disgust as he watched pain tighten her face. He could not believe it. Nor would he allow it. Not today.

He stood. He needed to call his mother. She could meet him somewhere away from the Elders' protection and heal Meaghan. If they moved quickly, they might be able to manage it before the Mardróch followed his teleportation trail.

Nick located the commcrystal on a bookshelf, but before he could activate it, a voice disturbed the somber air in the cabin. A voice he wanted to rip from its throat.

"Hello in there! Anyone home?"

Focused on reaching his mother, Nick ignored both the anger coursing through him, and Cal. Meaghan's life depended on it. The commcrystal turned blue, then dimmed back to gray when the cabin's front door flew open. Nick swore and spun around, fighting the urge to drive the crystal through Cal's skull.

The older man cast a lazy smile at him from the doorway. "You could've answered. You had me worried," he said, then knit his eyebrows together. "You okay?"

"This is your fault," Nick told him, his words exploding with pent fury. "If you hadn't told her about the battle, we wouldn't be in this mess. You're a reckless, useless—"

Cal stepped out of the doorway and Nick lost his voice. Neiszhe stood behind him. She looked confused, but as soon as her eyes found Meaghan, she flew to the cot. Cal's gaze followed his wife and he turned pale.

"She wasn't supposed to—" he started, but Neiszhe interrupted him.

"How long has she been unconscious?" she asked. Her fingers moved to the blade in Meaghan's neck. "You didn't remove it. That's a miracle. You saved her life."

"She's fading," Nick told her.

Neiszhe nodded. "How long?" she prompted again.

"It just happened."

"This will take everything I have," she told him. "I'll need to heal the wound around the blade. Then I can remove it and heal her again."

"Two rounds of accelerated healing," Nick said and understood the enormity of the endeavor. "You can't, Neiszhe."

"The baby," Cal whispered, and reached out to grip the doorway. "May said—"

"The baby should be developed enough by now," Neiszhe responded without allowing him to finish the thought. Her eyes met his and a tangible worry passed between them. "We have no other choice."

Cal nodded, and she began working. Meaghan remained unconscious. Nick hoped it would allow her to endure the healing process pain free, but instead, she seemed to hover on the edge of awareness. During the other times she had gone through this, he had held her hand or pinned her down, the tasks distracting him from his own feelings. Now he could do little to help. He pulled the other four knives from Meaghan's body when Neiszhe requested it, but otherwise, stayed a safe distance from the delicate procedure, pacing to ease his nerves.

Cal proved no better at waiting. He chewed on his fingernails, walking the floor with Nick, though he respected Nick's anger with as much distance as he could muster in the small space. They both avoided looking at each other. The tension rose. The cabin became a harbor for the repetitive noise of shuffling feet. Finally, Neiszhe had enough.

"Out," she commanded. She did not remove her eyes from her patient. Her face appeared red and streaked with sweat. Her hands shook, but her voice remained strong. As did the authority she carried within it. "You're distracting me. You need to leave."

Nick froze in his path. "I have to be here in case—"

"Now!" Neiszhe barked. She lifted her eyes to his for only a heartbeat, but it silenced him. No argument would change her mind. He had seen the same look on his mother's face during healings before. She usually reserved it for the panic- or grief-stricken, the overly anxious parents or spouses who could not cope with their loved one's suffering. Nick had escorted them out many times, always with a kind word and a feeling of empathy for their situation. But he had never expected to be one of them. He swallowed hard, nodded, and followed Neiszhe's order.

"You too," she said to Cal. "Light the fire first."

Cal did not argue. He started stacking wood in the fireplace as Nick stepped into the cold air and shut the cabin door behind him.

The sun had begun to rise over the tops of the trees, dragging a waking morning behind it. It looked like it would be a clear day. No clouds dotted the sky. Birds had begun to dance their songs through the trees. What remained of the night still sheltered a chill, but the first promises of spring had begun chasing it away. And Nick ignored it all in favor of watching the toes of his boots as he paced the length of the cabin's porch.

Today should have been a near-perfect day. He and Meaghan should have slept until lunchtime, and awoken revived. He had no doubt she would have seen the warming weather as an opportunity to train, but he would have convinced her to take a break. He had intended to roast the turkey for dinner, and then while they ate, they would have talked about her empath power. It had both surprised and horrified him to realize she had been aware the entire time she had been stone. Her suffering still tore at him, but it seemed some good had come of it. And she had survived the ordeal.

Only to have death reach for her again, greedy in its need.

Nick wanted to be in the cabin with her. He wanted to monitor

Neiszhe's progress. He could sense Meaghan out here, of course. Her pain still flowed strong while her consciousness remained weak. But sensing did not ease his mind as much as seeing her did.

Nick cast his eyes toward the closed cabin door. He would always be in debt to Neiszhe for what she did today, and if the baby could not withstand the energy Neiszhe needed to heal Meaghan, he would not forget her sacrifice. Nor would he forget Cal knew to bring her. It seemed the man held more secrets, covered more lies, than Nick thought him capable. And this last one had nearly cost everything.

Though Origio had unleashed the blades that cut Meaghan, and Garon had waged the war that placed her in the path of the young man, Cal had pushed her into harm's way. Nick harbored enough anger to share among all three enemies. And since Cal was the only one within arm's reach, as soon as he stepped onto the porch, shutting the door behind him, he received the brunt of that anger.

Two swift steps and Nick caught the older man off-guard, pinning him against the door. A well-placed forearm served as the only weapon Nick needed. He stiffened it against Cal's throat, cutting off most of his air.

"You recognize this hold?" Nick asked.

Cal nodded. He had taught Nick the technique. The right amount of pressure would crush Cal's windpipe, leaving Neiszhe no time to save him.

"You're a traitor," Nick continued, keeping his voice low so it would not carry into the cabin. "You deserve death, but out of respect for Neiszhe, I'll spare you. *If* you answer my questions. Who are you aligned with? Garon or Angus?"

"No one," Cal wheezed. "Please."

"I don't believe you. You lied to me about your Elder position. You spied on me for them, and now this." Nick tightened his arm against Cal's throat. "Are you also spying on the Elders for the other side? Was this battle your doing?"

"No," Cal managed, and shook his head, the movement slight. "I'd never—"

"Tell me! Who's your contact?"

"Vivian," Cal whispered.

"You're a liar. She'd never do that. She wouldn't sacrifice Meaghan."

"She did," Cal whispered, and the agony in his voice surprised Nick into loosening his grip. "I hate her for this. I'd never have done it if I'd known."

Nick dropped his arm and backed away from Cal. The truth lay bare in front of him—in the tears in Cal's eyes, in the sorrow on his face, and in the guilt dragging down his shoulders. Nothing remained of his usually tall and proud posture. He looked like an old man, confused by a world he no longer recognized.

"Why?" Nick asked, feeling equally as lost. "When?"

"I don't know why," Cal responded. His voice croaked and he drew a hand to his throat. "As far as when, she gave me her instructions the last time I saw her. It's how I knew you'd come to the cabin and—"

"How many of them are left?" Nick asked. "How many of the things she told you to do?"

"None."

"Don't lie to me." Nick stepped forward again to challenge Cal. "Not this time. I don't want any more surprises. If you lie to me about this, I won't forgive you."

"I'm not lying," Cal said, and sighed, dropping his hand. He walked to the steps and sat down.

Nick joined him, though he left distance between them. It may as well have been a canyon by the injured look painted over Cal's face.

"Nick, I swear to you. I never would've followed her instructions if I'd had any idea this would happen. I wouldn't even have known about the battle if it wasn't for her. The Elders hadn't reached me yet and there was no wind on the battlefield. I couldn't see how bad it was."

"She wasn't injured in battle," Nick said. "The traitor's son followed us back here."

Cal nodded and rested his elbows on his knees. He folded his hands between them. "Why would Viv do this? She'd never guided me wrong before."

"What exactly did she say to you?"

"She told me Meaghan needed to be there, that she would be injured, but the injury would be minor, and I'd know how to help her when the time came. I hadn't met Neiszhe yet, but once I did, I realized what Viv meant. If I'd known the extent of Meaghan's injuries, I wouldn't have brought Neiszhe. I would've asked May to come." Cal closed his eyes. His voice shook. "I just found out I'm having a son yesterday, Nick, and now I'm going to lose him. How could Viv not have known about the pregnancy?"

"She couldn't see everything," Nick said, but he had his doubts.

Vivian should have known. Not just about the pregnancy, but about everything that had happened during the battle and after. Her visions did not always show her every event, but when they did show her one, they left out no details. He did not want to believe it, but it seemed Vivian had chosen to put everyone in danger.

"Maybe," Cal echoed, though his words also sounded devoid of conviction. "I'm sorry, Nick. I truly am, and not just for this, for everything. But please know I've never lied to you and I've never intentionally betrayed you. I couldn't do that."

Nick's anger, which had started to soften with empathy for Cal's potential loss, blossomed again. "You asked me to consider you for my advisor," he pointed out. "You never meant that, not if you'd already accepted the Elder role. I consider that a lie."

"I omitted things," Cal said. "Things I should have told you. But I didn't lie about wanting to be your advisor. I intended to resign as an Elder if you decided to appoint me."

That had not occurred to Nick. He pressed his lips together in thought. "Why did you become an Elder if you meant to step down eventually? And why wouldn't you tell me about it?"

"I didn't tell you because I didn't want you to think I was spying on you. Being out in the wilderness can play with your mind. It can be lonely, and it's hard to tell who you can trust. I wanted you to feel like you had someone you could always turn to." He brought his knotted hands up to his chin and chuckled. The sound held no hint of humor. "That didn't work the way I intended."

Nick raised an eyebrow in doubt. "So you weren't spying on us? Why else would the Elders promote you?"

"Before I answer that," Cal said, "let me clarify one thing. I know the Elders started out on the wrong foot with you. They shouldn't have tried to replace you as Meaghan's Guardian, and you have reason to distrust them for that, but they aren't second guessing you now. They don't feel the need to spy on you. They do ask me about your progress. I keep them informed, but I haven't told them anything you wouldn't want them to know."

He paused and Nick turned his attention to the horizon again. Daylight had swept the red from the sky, replacing it with pale blue. Nick found no comfort in its beauty.

"But you're right in a way," Cal continued. "They did ask me to become an Elder because of you."

Nick brought his gaze back to Cal. "What do you mean?"

"We've never talked about what happened after your father's murder. Those first few years, you were an angry child, hurting and scared, and your mother didn't know what to do with you. She did her best to help you cope, but she had trouble finding her own way through her grief."

"I remember," Nick said and mimicked Cal's posture, using the steadiness of his fists to brace for the conversation. Facing his grief from losing his father was difficult on most days. Today, on top of his fear for Meaghan, it seemed almost impossible. But he needed the truth from Cal, even if it hurt to hear it, so he pushed the conversation forward. "That's when you started showing up."

"It is," Cal confirmed. "Traditionally, my brother should have filled the role after your father died, but he was on Earth. He made me promise I'd stand in his stead. Because of that promise, I'm still alive today. You saved my life."

"I was eight."

"You were." Cal smiled. "You were also a precocious child, curious, and affectionate. And even though you lost much of the trust you used to give freely, you trusted me. It wasn't long before I fell in love with you." He drew his hands back down. "Did your mother ever tell you why I wound up in the wilderness?"

"I always assumed it was because of the Mardróch."

"It is now. My time in the wilderness taught me how to hide in a way I can't do in the villages, so I've stuck with it. But initially, I sought out the wilderness for escape. I didn't just promise my brother I'd help you. I promised to help May, as well. I didn't see how I could be much use to her, but my brother understood how well I understood her grief."

Cal rubbed his hands together and looked down at them. His voice grew soft. "I coped with Alisen's death poorly. I ran away. I'm not proud of it, but I lost the three people I cared about most, and I didn't know how to deal with it. Ed was like a brother to me. My own brother disappeared to a world where I couldn't reach him, except through the occasional visit from his wife. And my wife," he shrugged. "I chose to escape rather than face my grief. I chose the wilderness, and when the Mardróch started hunting me, I didn't see much point in living anymore. I grew reckless. I taunted them. I wanted them to get the best of me. Then when I promised to take care of you, I realized I couldn't do that anymore. You needed a father figure. You needed me, and I couldn't let you down."

"I didn't know."

"You were young," Cal told him. "But you didn't have to know to help me. I didn't realize it at the time, but I needed you as much as you needed me. You gave me something to live for again."

Cal placed a hand on Nick's shoulder and squeezed it. "I never told you any of this before, but I should have. And maybe I should've told you the truth about how I feel about you, but I didn't want you to think I was trying to replace your father. I can't do that, but that's never stopped me from thinking of you as a son. I always will." He lowered his hand. "May knows how I feel and because of that, so do the other Elders."

"They chose you because they knew you could never betray me," Nick said and felt miserable for the realization. Meaghan had been right. Deep down, he had known the truth all along.

"The Elders are doing everything they can to make sure you stay alive. No matter what they think of me, they know I will, too." Cal paused and then swore. "I thought I was," he corrected and whatever small amount of joy the conversation had brought him dissolved from his face. "I'm sorry, Nick. I never wanted you to go through the sorrow I experienced when Alisen died, but it seems I may have caused it. I don't expect you to forgive me. And frankly, I doubt I'll ever forgive myself."

"Neither will I," Nick said and closed his eyes. He had shut off his sensing power when Cal exited the cabin, but now he turned it back on and reached for Meaghan's pain. He found nothing. Panicked, he jumped up, and then realized he had sensed something else from Meaghan, something he dared not believe.

"She's healed," he said and stared at Cal. "Her presence is strong again. I can feel it, but…"

He did not have to finish his thought for Cal to know. Even using an accelerated power, the healing had gone too fast. Meaghan's injury must have been worse than they realized, forcing Neiszhe to push her power beyond healthy limits.

Cal vaulted across the porch and into the cabin in two large steps. Nick followed close behind. As he had sensed, Meaghan slept on the cot, her face a blanket of peace. Neiszhe sat on the floor at her side, hunched over and drenched in sweat. Despite the warmth cast by the fire, she shivered.

Cal rushed to her, taking her in his arms as he dropped to the floor beside her. "Tea," he commanded, and Nick moved to the fire to put on the kettle. He hoped it would be enough.

"Neiszhe," Cal whispered to his wife. "What have you done, love?"

She buried her head in his neck. "There was too much blood," she said. "It came so fast. I had no choice."

Nick turned and spotted the red staining the white sheets and wool blanket underneath Meaghan's body. The amount of it scared him, but he locked away the emotion. She lived. And Meaghan's life may have cost Cal and Neiszhe the life they had created together. He wished the kettle would boil faster.

"You did a wonderful thing," Cal responded. His voice trembled as his arms tightened around her body. "How do you feel?"

"Weak," she answered, and though Cal did not ask the question, his hand slipped down her side, seeking her belly. "He's faint," she whispered. "He's holding on, but he's weak, too."

"You need to rest," Cal told her. He stood, supporting her against his side. Halfway across the room to the other cot, they froze when a panicked voice broadcast through the room.

"Nick, please tell me you're there," May begged.

Nick picked up the commcrystal from the table where he had left it. It emanated blue within his hands.

"I'm here," he responded. "What's wrong?"

"The battle. I know you and Meaghan fought."

"We did," he confirmed. "If you're calling to lecture me, it's not a good time."

"I'm not. I'm," her voice broke. "The battle was a ruse. Garon's army spread the rumor you were living there so we'd send our closest Guardians. They did it so we wouldn't be able to respond in time when they reached their true target."

Nick's eyes locked on Cal's. He saw the horror in them and realized they had both reached the same conclusion.

"Nick, it's gone," May continued. "Neiszhe's village has been destroyed. There are no survivors."

Cal caught Neiszhe as she crumbled to the floor. He carried her the rest of the way to the empty cot.

"No, Mom," Nick corrected. "There's one."

Now they knew why Vivian had lied to Cal. If she had not, he would have left Neiszhe in the village. Vivian had saved Neiszhe's life.

CHAPTER TWENTY-SEVEN

"Mycale?"

Meaghan watched Nick's face for any sign of hope, any sign that what she had heard could not be true. She had awoken to overwhelming grief and worry. The emotions battered her power and filled the cabin, turning the air stale and thick. Despite her pleas, Nick had refused to answer any of her questions until she had eaten and allowed him to change the bedclothes. Then he had told her about the village.

"Did he make it?" she prompted.

Nick shook his head. "No one made it."

Her throat felt raw. Her eyes burned from unshed tears, but she tried to be strong for Neiszhe. It had been her village, her friends who had been lost. Yet Meaghan could not keep their faces from running through her mind—the baker at the festival with his spiky brown hair and red-apple cheeks, the gray-haired man with equally gray eyes who had handed Nick a goblet of founder's juice, the people who had greeted Cal while he escorted Nick and Meaghan through town, their friendly waves and smiles showing their love for the husband of their Healer. Tall and short, plump and skinny, old and young, there were too many ghosts vying for Meaghan's attention, too many faces wanting her to know their stories. She swam through them, soaking in the memories until she thought she might drown. And in the center of them all, the face of a young man with eager green eyes and curly red hair haunted her most. Mycale had traveled a great distance looking for answers, but he only found death.

"No one," she echoed, forcing her voice to work. "The children, too? It wasn't that long ago we saw them playing at the festival. Garon couldn't possibly—"

Nick silenced her by bringing a palm to her cheek. "He did," he whispered, and the pain in his eyes begged her to stop asking.

She turned her head to look at the other cot. Cal stroked Neiszhe's hair as he stared at the wall, shock turning his face to stone. Neiszhe's emotions had been muted in sleep, but within her a stronger sensation came through. Despite the horrors of the past two days, it brought a smile to Meaghan's face.

"He's trying to make her feel better," she said.

Cal's eyes drew to hers. His brows knit in confusion. "Who? What are you talking about?"

"The baby," Meaghan answered. "He's trying to make Neiszhe feel better."

Cal's free hand sought his wife's stomach. He laid it flat over their unborn child. "You can sense him?"

"His emotions," Meaghan said. "He's tired, but he's also feeling determined and playful. Since the emotions are moving around, I can only assume he is too."

"He's moving?" Cal asked. "Are you sure?"

"Fairly certain," Meaghan answered. "Neiszhe can confirm, but he seems energetic right now."

"Amazing," Cal muttered. He drew his hand across Neiszhe's stomach, caressing, and then leaned down to speak where his hand had been. "That's it, son," he said. "That's a good lad. Keep playing with your mom."

Neiszhe stirred. "Don't encourage him," she said, and though her voice sounded groggy, her eyes appeared clear when she opened them. "It feels like he's doing back flips in there."

"It worked," Cal responded. A broad smile spread over his face. "The potion May and Nick came up with worked. Meaghan said he's playing to make you feel better."

"He is?" Neiszhe lifted a hand to cover Cal's. "He seems stronger."

"He's a fighter," Cal said. "He's going to make it."

Neiszhe laughed. "Did you ever have any doubt? He's your son after all."

Cal planted a kiss on her lips before leaning down to do the same to her belly. "Hang in there, son. I promise we'll make it worth the effort."

"He's moving again," Neiszhe said and linked her fingers with Cal's. "Can you feel it?"

Cal shook his head. "I can barely feel the bump in your stomach. He has to be a tiny thing. I don't know how you can feel anything at all."

"She shouldn't be able to," Meaghan said. "Quickening isn't usually felt so early. How far along are you? Twelve weeks?"

"Close," Neiszhe responded. "Fifteen. What did you feel from him?"

"Contentment," Meaghan said. "It's a basic emotion. How can you feel him move if you're only fifteen weeks along?"

"She isn't exactly feeling him. She's sensing him," Nick answered for Neiszhe. "My mom said she could sense me moving at two months. All Healers can. And it's the same reason Neiszhe already knows he's a boy. On Earth it's five months before they know the sex of a baby, isn't it?"

"Give or take. And they have to use an ultrasound. That's a machine that can see a baby inside a woman's body," Meaghan explained when Cal and Neiszhe exchanged a puzzled look. "Sometimes it's not that accurate. I'm assuming Healers always are?"

"Yes," Neiszhe said. "We can tell if a baby is a boy or a girl at three months. But we can't sense emotions. Can you sense him now? I'd like to know what he's feeling."

"Scared," Meaghan answered. "He knows you're distressed and he's reacting to it."

"Poor guy," Cal muttered. "He doesn't know what's going on." He crouched down next to the cot and spoke to Neiszhe's stomach again. "Don't be scared," he said. "We're all safe."

"That's interesting," Meaghan said. She narrowed her eyes, focusing her power solely on the baby. "I didn't expect that."

"Expect what?" Nick asked.

"He's calm. He seems to calm down each time Cal talks to him."

"He knows my voice?" Cal asked. He turned on his heels to look at Meaghan for confirmation. She nodded. "No kidding," he muttered and spoke to the baby again. "You're going to get sick of my voice, you know. The first time you break a rule, you'll really hate the sound of it."

Neiszhe laughed. Nick and Meaghan shared a smile. Cal continued to speak to his son, his ramblings a welcome change from the quiet that had previously choked the room. Meaghan snuggled under the covers of the cot and monitored the baby's calm, feeling comforted by it, but as she allowed her power to roam, another emotion added to her comfort. Hope. It grew within everyone. The knowledge that Neiszhe and Cal's son would be okay had eased their sorrow. Meaghan sought Nick's hand, threaded her fingers through his, and drifted to sleep.

§

THE SMELLS of Christmas and Meaghan's growling stomach woke her from a nightmare she could not quite remember. Her fingernails cut into her palms, so she forced her fists to uncoil. Her heart raced, so she took controlled breaths to calm it. The adrenaline coursing through her blood ebbed away. In its place, scents of cinnamon and rosemary revived her, chasing away the last of the shadows clinging to her mind. It was Christmas. It had to be. She could smell a turkey roasting in the oven. Baking apples and nutmeg wafted on the air, and if she was not mistaken, so did the faint hint of sweet potatoes. She must have fallen asleep after eating the big breakfast she and Nick had prepared. Dinner would be done soon, and then they would all open their presents. She had purchased a beautiful blue sweater for Nick. It cost a little more than she could afford, but the color had been perfect, and when she touched the delicate cashmere, she had to get it for him. He would love it.

And he had. Well over a year ago. Her sleep-filled mind had confused the past with the present, though she remembered it clearly. The smile on his face had touched her. And when he had thanked her, she could see the joy in his eyes. He had seemed almost childlike that day.

It had been his first Christmas. His first, and her last, though she did not know it at the time. Just like she did not know she had sensed his joy, rather than reading it on his face. Christmas had come and gone, and now she lived in a place that did not celebrate the holiday. Although the heavenly aromas surrounded her, she knew they had to be another part of her memory. She held onto them a moment longer, and then opened her eyes, pushing the memory away. The images dissolved, but the aromas remained.

She turned on her side to scan the room. In front of the fireplace, Nick, Cal, and Neiszhe played with a deck of cards. Cal smiled at her.

"Welcome back," he said. "I trust you feel better?"

"I do," she responded. Sitting up, she wrapped her arms around her knees and tucked them under her chin. "Did I sleep long?"

"I'd say so," Cal answered. "Unless you're a bear. You've napped away the last of yesterday and nearly all of today." He turned his attention back to the cards in his hand. He laid them down face up, and then chuckled when Neiszhe scowled at him. "Did I go out on you again?" he asked. "Sorry."

"Somehow I doubt it," Neiszhe muttered. "That's the last time I play Palidane with you."

"You make that threat every time," Cal said and collected the cards. Neiszhe crossed her arms over her chest, her face stormy with anger, and a grin spread over his face. "I'll throw the next game if it'll make you feel better."

Neiszhe huffed and Meaghan could no longer control her laughter. "I can't believe I slept so long," she said when Cal started dealing cards for another round. "Did I miss anything?"

"Not really. We have a nice feast cooking. I've been drooling over that bird Nick caught since you fell asleep, but he didn't want you to miss it, so last night and most of today we've been eating silten."

"Don't complain," Nick said. "You're the one who stocked our supply of it."

"A decision I heartily regret," Cal grumbled. "I still don't see why she couldn't make do with cold turkey. It's not our fault she decided to sleep the day away."

"It's not her fault either," Neiszhe told him. "Her body needed time to recover from the healing." She glanced toward Meaghan, her intense focus indicating she did more than study her patient. "I sense you're almost back to normal. How do you feel?"

"Better," Meaghan responded. "Much better. I haven't felt this refreshed in weeks."

Cal set the deck of cards down. "Maybe you needed more than recovery time."

"Maybe," she admitted. Trailing her eyes to the fireplace, she smiled at the sight of the turkey hanging from the spit. "I thought I imagined the food. I was dreaming about Christmas." She turned her attention back to the group. "That's a holiday—" she started to explain but stopped when Cal held up his hand.

"Nick told us all about it. It's why we're having the feast. Neiszhe managed to scrounge up some of the dishes he described. You had apples already. They're baking in a sugar and cinnamon mix that I can't wait to try. And we didn't have," he turned to Nick, "what did you call them?"

"Sweet potatoes," Nick answered.

"Right," Cal said. "We don't have those here, but we have something Nick said is similar. Though they're purple, not orange."

Meaghan grinned. "It smells wonderful."

"It will be," Nick told her and retrieved one of his shirts from the table. Instead of folding it neatly, as he usually did with his clothes, he had rolled it into a thick ball. "I thought it would be a nice tradition for us. Just because we don't celebrate the Earth holiday in Ærenden doesn't mean we can't have the same feast. We could make it standard for your birthday."

"My birthday?" Meaghan asked, dropping her knees in surprise. "That's not until spring."

"On Earth," Cal said. "Our calendar doesn't line up with theirs. But if you have any doubts about the date, I was there when you were born. Winter still had us under its control and proved it by dumping a foot of snow on the ground. I guess you thought it was too cold, because you took your lazy time coming into the world."

"I still don't like the cold," Meaghan said. "How long was my mother in labor?"

"From bedtime two nights before your birthday until just after the moon rose the day of. Your father wore a hole in the living room rug with his pacing." Cal laughed. "At least he did after May kicked him out of the bedroom. He was the most nervous father-to-be I've ever seen."

"Just wait," Neiszhe said, patting him on the cheek. "I suspect you'll be worse."

"No chance," Cal said. "Nothing gets me nervous. I'm a rock."

Neiszhe grinned. "They all say that. And then they turn into babbling brooks."

Nick sat next to Meaghan on the cot. He placed his shirt down between them. "We don't typically give gifts here. At least, not in the way you're used to, so we don't have wrapping paper." He nudged the shirt toward her. "It's the best I could do. You'll just have to pretend. Go ahead. Open it."

She did as he requested, unfolding the shirt layer by layer until she discovered the most exquisite pair of gloves. Deep burgundy thread contrasted grayish-tan leather, the close stitching indicating a master artisan. She slipped the gloves onto her hands and marveled at the perfect fit. They seemed to be made for her. She wiggled her fingers, relishing in their warmth, and allowed an indulgent smile to cross her face.

"I guess I don't have to ask if you like them," Nick said. He captured one of her hands in his. Flipping back the cuff of the glove, he exposed the fur lining and ran a finger over it. The fur changed color from pale olive to light tan, the new color trailing his finger like a wave. She studied the effect and then realized what he had shown her. The fur had not simply turned olive, but had matched her skin tone. And wherever Nick's finger touched, it mimicked the tan his hands held from training all day in the sun.

"The ambercat," she whispered.

Nick nodded. "Cal picked up the gloves from the tailor before he came here."

She slid them off her hands. "They're beautiful, but I can't wear them. Not when it's my fault the man who made them is dead. I'm sorry."

Nick clasped one of her hands between both of his. "I understand. But Meg—"

"You'll do no such thing," Cal interrupted.

Meaghan turned to look at him, surprised when he wiped moisture from his cheeks. "It's not your fault," he told her. "It's the traitor's fault, whoever it was that let Garon's army into the village. Or if that doesn't ease your mind, you can blame me. But you're not responsible for this. No one even knew you were there."

"I couldn't blame you," she protested. "You didn't do anything wrong."

"Neither did you. Garon could have been getting even for the fire I set to his Mardróch hunting party. Or he could have been after Mycale. Many people feel his father is protecting valuable secrets. Or it could be—"

"Me," Neiszhe whispered. Her hand shook as she combed it through her hair. "He's always targeted Guardians, and since I wed Cal, I've moved up on his list."

"That's not—" Meaghan started to protest, but stopped when Cal nodded at his wife in agreement, then raised a hand to her cheek and stroked a thumb across her skin.

"It could be any of us," he said. "That's the point. We don't know and even if we did, we can't allow Garon to push his guilt onto us. He wants that. He wants us to feel responsible for his actions because it weakens us." Cal dropped his hand to Neiszhe's leg and left it there. "But the truth is, he won't stop until we're all dead. Once he gets the most powerful of us, he'll move down to those he considers weaker. Then when he gets them, he'll keep going. It's him, Meaghan. He's the one who made the choice to kill our friends, not you."

Meaghan stared at the gloves clutched in her hand. Guilt tugged at her. While she and Nick had walked to Neiszhe's for lunch on the last day they had been in the village, the tailor had waved at her from his front porch. He had smiled when she lifted her hand and called out a hello in return, then a moment later, he resumed working on the purple velvet dress in his lap.

Cal knelt beside the cot and removed the gloves from her hand. "They fit perfectly," he told her. "Ebit only had to see your hands to know exactly how to cut these. He was an incredible man with a talent that far surpassed his power." Lifting Meaghan's hand, Cal slipped a glove over it. "Wear these with pride and remember the man who made them. Remember him for who he was and what he did, not for how he died. That's what he would have wanted."

She nodded. Tightening her hand into a fist, she stared down at the glove, burning the last image she had of Ebit into her mind.

"Good," Cal said, and turned to look at Nick. "Be sure to do the same with your pair."

"I can't," Nick told him. "They aren't mine."

Cal raised an eyebrow. "Who else would they belong to? Ebit gave me two pairs."

"They belong to the person who brought me my first ambercat," Nick replied. "It's one of my fondest memories and I thought it fitting to return the gesture."

Cal swallowed hard. "You can't give those to me. They're too rare."

"It's done already," Nick said. "Unless my hands grow, the gloves will only fit you."

"I…geez, lad." Cal choked up, and then pulled Nick into a crushing hug. "I don't know what to say. Thank you."

"It's the least I could do," Nick said and focused his attention on the fireplace. "I think we're due for that feast. Then after we've stuffed ourselves, it's time to teach Meaghan how to play Palidane."

"What's Palidane?" Meaghan asked.

"A card game. Think of it as a cross between Go Fish and Rummy with a twist."

"Sounds like fun. What's the twist?"

Nick laughed. "Cal always wins."

CHAPTER TWENTY-EIGHT

THEY SPENT several days in the cabin, taking time to recuperate and reassess their plans. Meaghan knew the break had been necessary, but she still itched to train. As soon as her feet touched the floor at first daylight, she wanted to be outside, running the course or practicing with her weapons. Instead, she controlled the urge by keeping her hands busy. She forced Nick to sit so she could cut his hair, and then cut Cal's at Neiszhe's request and against his protests. She cleaned the cabin, wiping down every surface and scraping dirt from corners that had not seen a rag in years. She prepared the rabbits Nick and Cal caught the first day, roasted the hen they captured the second, and then did her best to make silten palatable on the third day, when they returned empty-handed. Her efforts produced an herbal porridge, which could have done with a few handfuls of cheddar cheese. The missing ingredient did not stop everyone from devouring it.

After dinner, Nick, Neiszhe, and Cal played another round of Palidane while Meaghan paced the room. She could no longer tolerate being inside and the need to get outside commanded her feet to move. Nick watched her over the cards in his hand, his reflection frowning at her from a windowpane when she stopped to stare into the night.

"You look like an animal in one of Earth's zoos," he said.

"I feel like one." Clutching her hands behind her back, she faced him. "I have nothing left to do. I need to get back to training."

"You still need another day or two of rest," Neiszhe told her.

"I'm fine. It's not like I've been sitting around twiddling my thumbs anyway."

"No, you haven't," Neiszhe agreed. She set her cards down on the table. "But what you've done isn't strenuous. Your injuries were severe and you lost a lot of blood. Even though my power can fix those things, your body still needs to recover from the trauma. Running, throwing, and fighting will only tire you."

"I'd welcome being tired," Meaghan said and began pacing again. "Right now, I have more energy than I can stand." She stilled her feet to cast a glance over her shoulder at Nick. "Couldn't I at least go hunting with you tomorrow? You've been promising to teach me."

"Without the ability to throw or run?" Cal asked. "You'd guarantee another fruitless day."

She huffed and resumed her movement. Nick dropped his cards onto the table. "I wish you'd stop that," he said. "You're making me nervous. Come sit with us and play a hand."

"Sit where?" she asked. Nick and Neiszhe had already taken the two chairs at the table, and Cal sat on an upended bucket.

Nick stood from his seat. Pulling it out, he swept his hand over it in answer. Meaghan sighed and gave in to his request, sliding into his vacated chair. He found another bucket and flipped it over next to her, then sat down.

Neiszhe collected everyone's cards and reshuffled them. "You're used to being active," she said. "I know it's hard to relax, especially now with everything that's happening, but it's good for you."

"I know," Meaghan conceded, and said no more. She had no need. These were her friends, her family. They understood, and the fact calmed Meaghan more than anything else could.

Neiszhe dealt the cards, ten to each person, and Meaghan picked up her hand and sorted it, feeling a surge of hope when she realized she had a shot at beating Cal. Nick's joking had turned out to be true. Cal had not lost a single game in the past three days. His luck frustrated her, and she wondered if people hid cards up their sleeves on this world as they did on Earth.

Nick drew from the deck first and discarded. Cal did the same. On Meaghan's turn, she picked up a card from the deck and realized she needed it. Her excitement grew, as did her luck. Each turn produced something useful. Cards flew from the deck into the discard pile. Grumblings gave way to complaints and laughter. Cal traded a card with Nick. Meaghan stole one from Neiszhe, and then her heart jumped on her next turn when Nick discarded the last card she needed to win. She picked it up, but could not lay her cards down yet. If she did, she would go out, and she still needed to trade a card with Cal.

Cal raised his hand and extended it toward her. "I'll trade for that last card you picked up," he told her. She cursed and handed it over, taking a useless card from him in turn. He promptly laid down his cards, winning again.

Meaghan sighed. She had scrutinized the man's every move, and despite her suspicions, he had not cheated. He seemed to be as good at strategizing as his brother, and Meaghan had never been able to beat James at any of the games they played either.

Nick collected the cards and began shuffling. Neiszhe stood. "Does anyone want tea?" she asked.

"Sure," Cal said. "I think we could all use some."

Neiszhe crossed the room to put the kettle on the fire, and Cal turned a grin on Meaghan. "I thought for certain you'd figured me out on that play, but you looked pretty upset when I took your card, so I guess not."

"Of course I looked upset," she responded, crossing her arms over her chest. "I had the win on my next turn. And what do you mean 'figured' you out?"

"I didn't think my excitement when Nick laid his card down would be hard to sense," he said. "I'm surprised you didn't leave the card to prevent me from getting it. All you had to do was discard over it."

She shook her head. "Using my power wouldn't be fair. I don't cheat."

"I didn't think of it that way," he confessed. "Though I know you're not the type. Nick told me he hasn't been using his blocking power around you and the doll's on the shelf across the room." He shrugged. "I just figured you had no choice but to sense our emotions."

"I can focus on the doll from across the room," she informed him. "But I don't need it anymore. Didn't Nick explain what happened?"

"It's hard to explain something I don't know," Nick said. He set the deck of cards in the middle of the table without dealing them. "We haven't had the chance to talk about it yet. What happened when you were turned to stone?"

"You were turned to stone?" Cal asked. He stared at her, his eyes wide in disbelief. "I can't believe Viv told me nothing would happen to you."

"Nothing did," she reminded him. "Nothing permanent, anyway. Besides, I doubt I would have figured out how to control my empath power any other way. Every time I became overwhelmed in the past, I'd use Nick's power or escape the situation. Becoming a statue forced me to endure it."

"I don't see how that's a good thing," Neiszhe said as she returned to the table. "It sounds painful."

Meaghan knit her hands together on the table, and tried not to think about that aspect of her stone imprisonment. "It was necessary. While Nick's technique works to control my empath power, it takes a lot of energy. Because of that, I'm bound to short visits with large crowds of people. Trapped in stone, I couldn't use Nick's technique. I had nothing to focus on externally, so I focused on the only thing left."

"You focused on yourself," Nick guessed, "on your own emotions."

"Exactly," she said. "The first time I focused on myself, I felt an echo. I was afraid, and then I sensed my fear. After a while, the echo disappeared and I felt only my original emotions. I didn't feel anyone else's either."

"And now?" Cal asked.

"I'm getting better at it. It only takes a few seconds for the echo to go away."

Nick captured her hand. "Right after we revived you, you said the technique seemed natural. Is that still true? Is it still easy?"

"It's effortless," she told him. "Once I settle into it. Sometimes it takes ten minutes or so, but I think in a couple of weeks I'll have it down."

"Good." Cal nodded. "Great," he decided, and a large grin returned to his face. "It won't be long before you can rejoin the Elders then."

"I think I have enough command over it now to keep my empath power in check around other people. I was hoping we could leave when you and Neiszhe do."

"If you're using the word *think*, then it's not worth the risk," Cal told her. "When you *know* you have enough command, then you can come."

"But I could be useful to the villagers. Maybe we should ask the Elders what they think."

Cal chuckled and picked up the deck of cards. "You just did," he reminded her. "And I said no. Update May every week on your progress and we'll revisit the decision each time. Until then, you stay. Neiszhe and I leave in two days."

"So what am I supposed to do in the meantime?" Meaghan asked, crossing her arms over her chest. Her cheeks burned with her anger. "Am I supposed to just sit here and wait for more people to die?"

Cal stood. "You can train," he told her. "After nearly a week of being lazy inside the cabin, I'm sure you'll need it."

She sputtered, at a loss for words, and then laughed despite her frustration. Cal planted a kiss on the top of her head before turning to retrieve the kettle from the fire.

CHAPTER TWENTY-NINE

IT MUST be a goose. Its stark-white feathers and bright orange bill had given it away, though Caide had not seen one in years. The last time his father had caught one, Caide had helped dress it, then relished in the smile lighting his mother's face when he gave her the feast. He hoped to bring the same smile back to her today. She had seemed melancholy over the past few weeks, though she had tried to hide it from him.

Scree had delivered bad news. The silent looks his parents exchanged, tense with fear and anger, confirmed it. It bothered him that they would not share the news. They still thought of him as a child, but he had grown since they had fled their homeland. He had gained wisdom because of his power. His friends had teased him. The adults had ostracized him. And Mardróch hunted him. Some men would crumble under the guilt and pressure, but it made Caide want to become stronger, faster, and smarter than the foolish boy he had been. He had no choice. He would be leader someday, like his father, and he had to ensure his people valued him. Not just for his command, but also for what his spellmaster power could do.

It would be important to his people someday, even if they did not realize it yet. He had witnessed first-hand the threat Garon's Mardróch posed. He had overheard stories his father shared with his mother detailing what the monsters had done to Zeiihbu. And he had known when he met Queen Meaghan that he would be valuable to her, once he learned how to fight in the war. Although Cal did not think Caide would be able to control his powers in time to help, he had other plans. His alliance with the Queen would keep Zeiihbu in favor with Ærenden, a necessity both his father and grandfather had instilled in him since soon after he could understand words.

In the meantime, he had to prove his worth to his family. He had failed in protecting them when he had divulged the secret of his power to his friends and they, in turn, had shared it with the tribe. But he would make amends for his mistake by protecting them now, and providing for them.

The white bird had not yet heard Caide. He moved his feet with a light step, careful not to rustle branches or snap twigs, and he took the shallowest of breaths. He belonged to the forest. He respected it and received easy passage in turn.

The bird halted for a moment and Caide removed an arrow from his pack, his movements slow and steady. As soon as he nocked the weapon, the bird began moving again, weaving around trees and under bushes as it sought its dinner. Caide had missed his opportunity, but he did not mind. There would be another. Patience belonged to the true hunter, just as luck belonged to his prey.

He did not have to wait long before the bird stopped again to root in the dirt. Caide circled a tree, keeping his eyes locked on his target. Then, when he saw his chance for a successful shot, he drew back his elbow, aimed, and let his arrow fly.

A loud noise startled the goose. It flew into the air, disappearing among the tree branches with a loud honk. Caide's arrow lodged into the ground where the bird had been. He uttered an oath he had heard from his father on occasion, and then ducked behind a tree when the noise in the woods grew closer. Several heavy creatures lumbered in his direction, taking no care to avoid breaking branches as they passed. By the sound of their gait, he realized they could not be animals, and by their carelessness, they could not be hunters. No hunter this noisy would have lived so long into the winter.

He flattened his back against a tree, and then turned sideways so he could peer in the direction of the noise, catching his breath when he saw two Mardróch and a human companion. The latter wore a red cloak, the garb of a lead soldier in Garon's army.

"They're around here somewhere," the soldier said. "Tooley saw the boy's father last week in this area."

"Tooley's an idiot," one of the Mardróch complained. "And a drunk. We can't be certain what he saw wasn't a hallucination."

"We can," said the soldier, stopping to glare at the Mardróch who had spoken. The Mardróch cast his eyes down. "Garon put him in the stockade until he got the location right. It's amazing how fast withdrawal improved his memory."

The second Mardróch chuckled. "It's no less than he deserves. He nearly ruined our attack on that healing woman's village by sending his Mardróch guards a few weeks early. I'm surprised Garon hasn't killed him for that mistake."

"He intends to," muttered the first Mardróch. "And I'm sure he would have by now if Tooley hadn't had information to share. Once we have the Spellmaster, the fool will breathe his last."

The soldier grunted. "And so will we if we don't find the boy." Stopping short, he looked down at his feet, and then shuffled a shoe over the dried leaves remaining from autumn. "The spell should have plenty of fuel to start. Once it reaches the trees, it'll spread like," he chuckled, "wildfire."

"You're certain your shield will protect us?" the first Mardróch asked.

"Of course," the soldier replied. "I can cover four people. Garon doesn't want the rest of the family. They'll die in the blaze. No one will know we set it, and no one will know we have the boy. They'll assume he died, too."

"Good," the first Mardróch responded. "I love this part of my job. I always thought Adelina made a mistake not getting rid of those animals in Zeiihbu. It'll be nice to fix her weakness by killing the ruler's family."

"All but the older boy," the second Mardróch said. "It's a shame he'll live. It's more than the filth deserves. Maybe he can suffer an accident—"

The soldier whirled on him, his movements so fast Caide barely saw his sword leave its sheath. He hovered the tip of the blade between the Mardróch's eyes. "Enough. The boy's protected. If you dare consider otherwise, I'll have your life. Do you understand?"

"Yes," the Mardróch choked out.

Instead of lowering his sword, the soldier slashed it through the air, bringing the Mardróch to the ground. He turned to the other monster and brandished his sword again. "The threat was for your understanding," he said. "I don't believe in second chances. Do you fall in line with his thinking?"

"I follow orders," the Mardróch answered. "Garon ordered us not to harm the boy. It doesn't matter what I think."

"Good," the soldier said, and this time, he put his sword away. "Let's get this done. I want to be home for dinner."

He turned toward the spot where the goose had been standing and frowned. Caide hoped his arrow would blend into the forest, but his luck did not hold.

"What's this?" the soldier asked, freeing the arrow from the ground. He ran a thumb along the feather quill, and then traced his fingers down to the stone arrow. "Nice craftsmanship. It's Zeiihbuan without question."

"The boy's?" the Mardróch asked.

"Or his father's. Can you sense anyone?"

The Mardróch lowered his head and then a moment later, lifted a hand to point in Caide's direction. Caide swallowed hard. Panic rose in his throat, and he did the only thing he could. He ran.

Although he knew the woods better and could find swift footing among the roots and bushes without looking, his skill could not match the Mardróch's speed. The chase only lasted a quarter mile before the monster grabbed Caide and spun him around. Caide remembered what his brother had told him about the Mardróch freezing power, but he remembered it too late.

He stared into the monster's red eyes and found a form of torture he had never known before. Free from physical constraint, his mind wanted to flee, but his body refused to follow the command. Terror constricted his muscles, shortened his breath, and rolled his stomach. Despite his strong will, he could not break its grip over him.

"Nicely done," he heard the soldier say. A red cape drifted across the bottom of Caide's sight and then disappeared.

"It's him, isn't it?" the Mardróch asked. Caide could see the monster's lips move, but his eyes remained unblinking.

"No question about it," the soldier said. "He's practically his father's twin. I met Faillen once you know. He was a boy at the time, and he walked through the castle with his father like they owned the place. I'm sure they intended to overthrow the Queen eventually, but King Garon beat them to it. And now the King will use one of their own against them."

"That's justice," the Mardróch said. "It's just too bad we won't get to smoke the boy's family out."

"Who says we can't?" the soldier asked. "Garon won't know we caught the boy before we had a chance to set the fire. Before, after," he shrugged. "All he cares about is the end result."

The Mardróch's laughter chilled Caide, as did the realization of what the soldier intended to do. Caide's family would not stand a chance against a fast-moving fire, especially one started by a spell. They would not be able to outrun or stop it. Caide could, if he could speak, but his lips refused to move. Tears welled in his eyes.

"We have a crybaby here," the Mardróch said and ground a bony finger into Caide's cheek.

"Imagine that," the soldier replied. "Animals have feelings after all."

Caide heard the soldier walk away. Soon, the sound of rustling leaves and breaking twigs followed. Muttering came next, though Caide could not make out all of the words, and then he smelled smoke. They had cast the spell. The soldier stepped back into view. He pulled a roll of tape from his pocket, tore off a piece, and then secured it over Caide's mouth.

"Insurance." He grinned. "We're not interested in being turned to stone like the last Mardróch you met."

Caide's younger brother had done that. His father had told him about it, but Garon did not know Aldin also had the spellmaster power. He considered telling them, divulging Aldin's secret to save his brother's life, but he could not consign Aldin to a life of horror as Garon's slave. Caide had a feeling he would wish he was dead soon, too.

The Mardróch threw Caide over his shoulder. Unfrozen, Caide struggled, kicking and punching to get free, but his efforts proved useless. The Mardróch's grip only tightened. Black smoke began to choke the air as the fire fed with a ravenous hunger. A force field drew up around them, creating a bubble of clean air. He thought he saw the shadow of a man through the smoke, a man of his father's height and build, but no sooner had he seen the ghost than the soldier began talking.

Another spell, Caide realized, and lost consciousness as a black curtain descended over him.

CHAPTER THIRTY

MEAGHAN STUFFED her mother's book into the backpack, then wrapped the corn husk doll in one of her shirts and placed it on top of the book. They had buried the leftover food in the woods. Their supplies, except for their weapons, would remain behind. Cal had come earlier in the week to collect Nick's bow and arrows, their extra clothes, and the medical kit. He had left a few emergency items behind, in case someone needed them, but he had made Meaghan promise to avoid anything that might cause injury during her remaining days in seclusion. For the most part, she kept her promise, with the exception of one last training run the morning of their departure. The course had become a daily companion for her. She needed to say good-bye.

She reached for her mother's amulet, ensuring it still hung around her neck, and then zipped the backpack closed and set it next to their weapons beside the door. They would meet Cal soon in the crystal cave so he could show them their new home.

The door opened and Nick stepped inside. "Ready?" he asked.

She nodded and scanned the room one last time. Although she intended to look for items they had missed, she only saw what they would leave behind—the kettle that had brewed far too many batches of jicab tea, the fireplace that roasted ambercat, turkey, and a number of other meals throughout the winter, and the spot in front of the fireplace where they had wed. She could still see him standing there, the torment on his face as clear as the day it had happened. And she could see the colors pouring from them both, binding them together forever.

It had been the first time she realized she had no control over her life, and the first time she had truly understood how much she had lost.

She turned from the memory, and caught Nick staring at the same spot on the floor.

"It seems so long ago," he said. Sadness washed over her, an emotion that belonged to both of them, and she reached for Nick's hand. A lot had happened in this place and Cal had been right to say she would long for the comfort of it someday. She had already started feeling as if she had lost something else important.

"Maybe we can make it a vacation home," she offered. "Once all of this is over."

He laughed. "I can see it now, the King and Queen traipsing through the woods, spending time in a rustic cabin, hunting their own food and ignoring the protests of their Guardians. I don't think it'll go over well with the Elders, do you?"

"Maybe not," she conceded, and then grinned. "But at least I can guarantee my Guardian won't be protesting."

Nick chuckled and leaned down to pick up his sword. Swinging it over his shoulder, he fixed it to his back. "Are you still using your power?" he asked.

"Yes, until we meet up with Cal. I suspect it'll be some time before I'm able to use it again, so I thought it'd be best to let it roam free."

"It's not a horse. It doesn't need to be exercised regularly."

"Then why have I spent so much time training with it?" She strapped her knives to her waist, and then turned the conversation serious again. "I'm going to miss it. I feel like I'm shutting off a part of me."

"You are," he said and cupped her cheek. "Do you remember the first days you spent in Ærenden? Back then, you saw your powers as separate from you. Now you've found your connection with them."

"I guess I'm making progress," she decided. Bringing a hand up to cover his, she squeezed it, and then drew both of their hands down and released him. She picked up the backpack and slung it over her shoulders, then followed him from the cabin.

Nick led the way into the woods, but allowed Meaghan to set the pace. She chose to stroll toward the cave, meandering in an effort to absorb the last of the forest's solitude. Cal would not arrive for some time, and despite her desire to return to the protection of the Elders, she did not wish to rush the reunion. Quiet would be nonexistent within the overpopulated caves.

Less than a quarter of a mile from their destination, the air took on the distinct smell of smoke. Although it started out faint, within a matter of minutes, Meaghan could see a heavy black cloud rolling toward them, chased by an unmistakable orange glow.

"Fire," she started to warn Nick, but choked on the word before she could complete it. Nick glanced toward the advancing fury, grabbed her hand and pulled her along behind him, hastening their pace toward the cave.

It all seemed too familiar, like she had returned to the fire Cal had set in the field. But this time, though the sense of déjà vu made it seem surreal, she realized Cal's power did not control it. They had no protection from the flames.

Her eyes stung. Her nose burned. She pulled the neck of her sweater over her mouth and breathed through it. It helped, but it would not keep her alive for long. They would only be safe when they reached the cave. Even if Cal had not yet arrived, they could teleport somewhere else. She did not care where, so long as they escaped the inferno chasing them.

She moved faster, watching Nick's feet as the smoke grew thick, clouding her eyes. She recognized a boulder with a red vein running through it, and a stump shaped like a chair. They crossed the frozen stream, now trickling with new melt. A hundred yards remained. She could almost taste the clean air that would greet them when they found their way to the deeper caverns. The need drove her, and then something tugged at her awareness and she froze mid-stride.

"Meg, move!" Nick commanded. "What are you doing?"

"Fear," she said, dropping her sweater. She took in a mouth of smoke and gagged on it. "People." She pointed into the woods away from the cave. The smoke hung so thick she could not see the trees where she pointed.

Nick's eyes tracked the direction of her finger and he nodded. He dove into the deepening black, and she followed. She could see an arm's length in front of her, but nothing more. She pulled her sweater over her nose again. It did little to help. She held her last breath in her lungs, but the ache came quick. They would not last long in this direction.

Nick pressed his lips to her ear. "Where?" he asked.

She focused her power, found the fear she sensed, and ran toward it. The shape of a man emerged from the smoke. He stumbled and fell to his knees in front of them. Nick slipped his hands under the man's arms, lifting him back to his feet, and Meaghan saw his face. Faillen, she realized with horror. In his arms, Aldin stared at her. The boy clutched a book to his chest, clinging to it like a life raft as tears streaked paths through the smoke blackening his face.

Nick tried to pull Faillen in the direction of the cave, but the Zeiihbuan would not budge.

"Ree," Faillen choked out. "I need to find her."

Meaghan stretched her power again, but sensed only Faillen and Aldin. She shook her head at Nick.

"No," Faillen protested, but did not seem to have the strength to resist again when Nick urged him forward. He fell and Meaghan removed Aldin from his arms. The cave entrance stood only a few yards away. She could see the outline of it, but her feet refused to move toward it. Her head began to spin. Her lungs convulsed, forcing her to draw a breath, and she paid for it with a mouth of smoke. Coughs racked her body. She pitched forward, twisted to avoid landing on Aldin, and then stopped falling when hands caught her—hands too big to be Nick's.

"Cal," she said, though the word came out as a rasp.

"That's it, lass, just a little farther," he told her. The smoke parted for him, leaving a path of clean air. She gulped it in and by the time he pushed her into the cave, she felt steady again.

Smoke filled the first room. They found their way to the crystal cave, which had started to haze, and then the world turned to white. The air cleared as the new cave materialized around them. Cal let her go before turning to Nick, who still supported Faillen.

"Ree?" he asked both men. "Caide?"

"They took Caide," Faillen wheezed. He closed his eyes. "I couldn't stop them. We escaped. Aldin said a spell to make us faster than the fire, but," tears flooded his cheeks, turning gray as they coursed their way down his skin. "The smoke came too thick. I lost her. I lost Ree."

Cal teleported as soon as Faillen spoke the words. Faillen collapsed onto a nearby rock. His face sought his hands. Nick stared at Meaghan, his grief matching hers. In a matter of minutes, the world had turned from clear and hopeful to dark and despairing. Even inside a cave flooded with bright light, shadows squeezed around her heart.

Aldin began to weep again, shaking in Meaghan's arms and she sat down on another rock, holding him against her. Only then did she realize the strength of her own fear. It tensed her muscles, instilling an urge to flee. She scanned the walls for escape, but found none. Crystals filled every surface in an endless circle.

She turned to Nick to ask what they should do, but a shimmering on the other side of the room caught her attention. May walked through the wall. The Elder scanned the room and then panic blossomed within her, reminding Meaghan to refocus her power. She turned it inward and everyone else's emotions dissolved.

May bent down to take Faillen's hand. She whispered to him before turning to Nick and doing the same. After crossing the room to Meaghan, she held her hand and spoke the words that made the door appear. "You are welcome here," she said, then repeated the greeting to Aldin. Neiszhe walked through the door a moment later, followed by the other two Elders, Sam and Miles.

"What happened?" Neiszhe asked. Her eyes fell on Faillen and she frowned. "Where's Cal?"

"There's a fire," Nick responded. His voice sounded detached, hollow. "The forest is consumed. Cal went to find Ree."

Sam's eyes widened. He turned and disappeared through the door.

"Who's Ree?" Miles asked. He tugged a hand through his salt and pepper hair and nodded toward Faillen. "And who's he? We can't invite people in here we don't know."

"I know him," May said, then held up her hand when Miles moved to speak again. "There's no time to explain. These people need care. Neiszhe, heal the boy's lungs, please. I'll manage his father's."

Neiszhe nodded and took May's place in front of Meaghan as May studied Faillen. She placed a hand on his chest and then knelt in front of him.

"This won't hurt much," she told him. "It's one of the few things

I'm capable of doing that doesn't. Breathe out when I tell you to, all right?"

Faillen nodded.

"Breathe," she said. He exhaled and a cloud of smoke puffed out with the effort. "Again," she said, and the same happened. Neiszhe mimicked the procedure with Aldin and soon, the young boy stopped wheezing.

May stood and turned to Miles, but did no more than open her mouth before Cal appeared in front of her, a woman cradled in his arms. His eyes connected with May's. A look passed between them Meaghan could not read, and then he laid the woman down on the ground.

Both May and Neiszhe flew to her. Meaghan realized the woman had to be Ree, but she did not recognize her. Ree's red hair had been singed black. Her beautiful, pale skin had ugly welts and blisters where the fire had licked it, and soot caked her clothes so dark they looked like tar.

"Mata!" Aldin cried. He dropped his book, and tried to push out of Meaghan's arms. She held tight.

May and Neiszhe laid their hands on their patient. Within minutes, sweat soaked their clothes and their faces turned red from the energy they forced into Ree's body. They closed their eyes. They muttered quiet commands to each other. They pressed their hands harder against Ree's body. Then finally, they let go.

"I'm sorry," May said and turned to Faillen. "The fire took too much. She's gone."

Meaghan went limp from shock. With a wail, Aldin broke from

her grasp and flew into his mother's lifeless arms.

CHAPTER THIRTY-ONE

ALDIN'S SOBBING swelled, bouncing off the crystals and enveloping those who grieved in a blanket of sound. Though Faillen had wept at first, his eyes now remained dry. He stared at the floor while everyone else stared at the walls, at each other—anything to avoid looking at the woman who lay in death before them.

The boy continued to cry, begging for his mother's attention, and when no one else tried to comfort him, Meaghan went to him. She laid a hand on his back and Faillen sprang to his feet.

"Don't you dare!" he yelled.

Miles stepped in between them. He extended a hand, throwing up a magical force field to block Faillen's advance. Faillen narrowed his eyes. He toed the force field and Miles extended his hand, pushing him back a foot.

"It's you," Faillen said, slamming a fist into the shield. "You're the one who took my son. Where is he?"

Cal moved toward Faillen, stopping when the man pulled a knife from his belt. Cal raised his hands. "It wasn't him," he said. "Many people have his power."

Faillen swung the knife toward Miles. "You're all the same. You only want my family for what my sons can do. You don't care about us."

"We care," Meaghan told him. She moved around Miles, but refrained from exiting his protection when he placed a hand on her shoulder. "I saved Aldin, remember? Even before I realized what he could do."

"You lie. You knew. You've always known. This is your fault!" He stabbed his knife through the air, gesturing toward Ree's body. "If you hadn't come, if you hadn't made your request, I wouldn't have doubted what needed to be done. I would have gone to Garon and she would still be alive."

Miles punched his hand forward, casting his shield with enough force to throw Faillen backwards. Faillen stumbled, but caught his balance in time to swing his knife toward Cal who had reached out to catch him.

"Get back," Faillen commanded.

Cal remained rooted to his spot. "I'm trying to help you."

"You aim to take me out. You protect her."

"I do, and I protect you, too, in case you forgot. This isn't Meaghan's fault."

"It is. If she hadn't come to my hut, we wouldn't be here. If she'd never returned to this world—"

"Aldin would be dead," Cal reminded him, and took a step forward. "Garon sought your sons long before Meaghan came along. She's always had your best interests in mind. Always."

"Because of my sons."

"Because she cares. Because she values your help. What she asked of you has nothing to do with them. She isn't Garon. She knows your boys are children. She doesn't want them to fight in this war."

Faillen's knife wavered. Tears escaped the corners of his eyes. "Ree," he whispered. "She—"

"Never wanted you to accept Garon's offer. That's the real reason you didn't go sooner."

Faillen trembled. He shook his head. "I didn't do this to her. I didn't."

"No, you didn't." Cal took another step forward. His hand closed over Faillen's wrist and the knife fell to the ground. "I've been where you are. Garon took my first wife from me. I know your anger. I know your pain and the depth of your sorrow. And I know your guilt. It makes you want to blame the world, but you can't, Faillen. And you can't turn against the people who care about you. We can help you."

"No," Faillen said. "You can't help me anymore."

He glanced at Meaghan one last time, the anger in his eyes slicing through her better than any weapon could, and then he turned and left the cave.

"Dat," Aldin screeched and raced after his father. Nick caught him, lifting the boy up before he could exit the cave.

"Should we go after him?" May asked Cal.

Cal shook his head. "Give him time. He needs to grieve in peace."

"He needs to be confined," Miles argued. He lowered his hand, dropping the force field. "If he's aligned with Garon, he's a danger to all of us."

"He's not dangerous," Meaghan said.

"He tried to attack you. I'd consider that dangerous."

"He wouldn't have done her any harm," Cal said. "He's not aligned with Garon. Garon has threatened to kill everyone in Zeiihbu if Faillen doesn't return."

"So Faillen turned against us?" Miles frowned. "I recognize him by his name, and I understand the position he's in, but choosing to align with Garon is unacceptable under any circumstance. Especially since Zeiihbu has never been Garon's target. It's an empty threat wrought for the purpose of increasing Garon's ranks."

"It's not an empty threat," Nick told him. "Faillen's sons are Spellmasters. Garon isn't aware of Aldin's power, but he knows Caide's. And now he has him."

"Spellmasters," he echoed. His eyes widened. "That's not possible. They're from Zeiihbu. They couldn't—"

"They could and they are," Cal said. "Faillen didn't feel he had a choice. His delay in returning to Zeiihbu has already cost dozens of lives."

"And you've been protecting his family," Miles said, his voice bitter with anger. "You protected them without a ruling from the Elders, which is against the law. On top of that, you kept it from us even after we promoted you."

"I gave him permission," May said, then crossed her arms when Miles turned his anger on her. She scowled. "Don't be so egotistical to believe the Elders are impenetrable. Cal has been protecting them for well over a year. If he'd informed the Elder council, Angus would have divulged their location to Garon. These things are best kept between as few people as possible."

"I should have been one of those people," Miles responded. He held her gaze a moment longer before turning his attention toward the boy in Nick's arms. "You're certain he's a Spellmaster? He's young."

"We watched him turn two Mardróch to stone," Nick told him. "Though Cal's seen more than we have. He's been training both of Faillen's boys."

Miles nodded. He turned to address Cal. "How long will it take for Garon to convert the older boy?"

"Caide will stand his ground," Cal said. "But we all know what Garon can do. Once he realizes Caide can't be swayed, he'll do whatever he can to force him. Caide's power isn't strong enough to do mass damage yet, but he can make the war more difficult."

"Then we need to put together a plan," Miles decided. "After Nick and Meaghan are settled, we'll convene again tonight."

"In the meantime, we have a more pressing problem to manage," a voice said from the doorway. Sam stepped into the cave and then swept his arm in a gesture of invitation. The move puzzled Meaghan until a group of people filed into the room behind him. Three women and five men stood at attention, their eyes fixed on Cal.

Cal scanned the line before nodding. "This will do nicely. You all know the danger?"

"We do," said a young woman with short blonde hair. She looked to be no older than Nick. "We can manage it."

"A spell created this fire," Cal warned them. "It will fight against your powers."

"We'll fight back," said a man with spiky blue hair. He grinned at Cal. "It beats hanging around in the cave all day."

Cal laughed. "That it does, Zellíd. Nice color choice this week."

Zellíd ran a hand across the top of his head, his grin broadening. "I thought so."

Cal's eyes fell on the youngest in the group, a thin waif, near-starved to bone, with long, mousy hair and a nervous shake to her hands. She clutched them in front of her, swallowing hard when Cal approached. "What's your name?" he asked. "Where are you from?"

"Kadel," she squeaked out, then swallowed and tried again. "From the village at Vallem Valley."

"That was destroyed months ago," he said. "I thought no one survived."

"A group of survivors showed up last week," Sam told him and placed a hand on the girl's shoulder. "She's thin because none of them were good at hunting, but she's strong. They survived in the wilderness because of her."

"Did they?" Cal raised an eyebrow at the girl. "You're not a Firestarter or a Waterhelm like the rest of this lot, are you?"

She shook her head. "I'm a Guide."

"Fantastic." Cal lifted the girl's chin with his fingers and she met his eyes for the first time since they began talking. Her nervous swallowing doubled. "To keep your people alive for that long in the wilderness is no small task, even for a Guide. Have confidence in yourself." He drew his hand to her arm and squeezed. "Stay by my side today. After we put out this fire, you'll train under me going forward."

The girl's eyes turned to saucers, and then a grin jumped over her face. "You'd do that?" she asked. "But you're Cal."

"Ah, so you've heard of me," he said, and chuckled. "If I'm special, then so are you. Don't forget that."

He turned to address the group. "The forest is burning at a rate unnatural for a fire, even with the dry winter. Our best bet is to contain it, and then weaken it with water. Which of you are Firestarters?"

Four of them raised their hands.

"Stand there." He pointed to the center of the cave. "I'll teleport you to a separate area from everyone else. Push the fire east. We'll be waiting for it. Once we start dousing it with water, follow its trail and help us contain it."

As the four volunteers moved to the area Cal indicated, Meaghan turned to Nick. "How can they contain the fire if they're only Firestarters?"

"They can control fires," he answered. "Just like Cal can. The difference between his power over fire and theirs is why they have the name. They can start one from nothing. Cal needs some sort of ember or spark to make a fire blaze. That's why he never extinguishes a torch fully and why he has to strike a flint to start a fire."

"That makes sense. What's a Waterhelm?"

"Someone who controls water. Their power does everything Cal's does."

"Not exactly," Cal corrected. "Neither power can use its element to see. Only a Guide has that ability. And for a Waterhelm, a more important difference is he or she is almost always a Rainmaker, too. Although the powers are considered separate, it's rare that someone isn't born with both. The only time I've ever heard of it happening is with identical twins. In those cases, each twin has one of the powers."

"I see," Meaghan said. "So should I assume a Rainmaker's power does as it sounds?"

In answer, a small raincloud formed in front of Meaghan and poured water on her feet. A short man with a pointed beard flicked his hand and the cloud dissolved as fast as it had arrived.

"Nice first impression, Dillon," Cal muttered. "You've just soaked our Queen's feet."

Dillon shrugged. "She asked."

"Come on," Cal said, and waved to the remainder of the group. "You're with me. Are you ready?"

The response came unanimously, their nervous energy contagious. Cal disappeared with one group, and then reappeared. A moment later, he left again.

Only then did the reality of Cal's task hit Meaghan. Neiszhe reached down to close Ree's eyes with a shaking hand, and Meaghan prayed Faillen's wife would be the only person they had to grieve today.

CHAPTER THIRTY-TWO

"WE'VE DONE the best we can under these circumstances," Sam said as he led Meaghan and Nick through the maze of underground caves housing the temporary camp. May had left to speak with Miles, no doubt continuing the argument they had curbed in the crystal cave. Neiszhe had taken Aldin to her tent for a nap. And Sam had offered to guide Meaghan and Nick on a tour of their new home.

He seemed to have aged a decade since Meaghan last saw him. His white hair and beard had thinned. His portly size had decreased, making him almost underweight. Weariness shadowed his once jovial steel blue eyes. And a ghostly pale complexion made the fine veins streaking his nose and cheeks stand out like red rivers. His physical decline served as a grim reminder that he had lost his daughter in the village attack. Grief left no one unscathed.

Meaghan followed him around a short alcove, ducking to avoid hitting her head on the deep gray rock, and entered into one of the main living areas. The cavern stretched long in front of her, then banked to the left, continuing until Meaghan could only see shadows in the distance. Along the walls, torches burned with white fire.

"There are several caverns like this throughout the kingdom," Sam told them. "They've allowed us to create habitable living arrangements. It's not ideal, but…"

"The people seem happy," Nick finished, smiling as a woman waved at him. She had not been the first to recognize the King. Many had waved in recognition since the tour began. Meaghan accepted the woman's broad grin with a nod, but did not stop as Sam led them between several evenly spaced rows of boulders.

"They're safe," Sam said. "It's what matters most. This section serves as our gathering hall. We use it to hold weekly meetings and school sessions. At the end of the cavern, there's a separate area for the children to play. Some of the parents carved a playground in the rock with their powers."

He turned to his right, taking a passageway Meaghan had not seen before and led them into a smaller, rectangular cave. Families gathered in front of tents, talking or cooking small meals over carefully managed fires. These, too, glowed white. She trailed her eyes from the flames to the roof of the cavern, surprised to see no smoke collecting over their heads. When she glanced back at Sam, he smiled.

"You're wondering about the fires," he said.

"I've never seen anything like it before."

"They're smokeless. We found a spell in one of the first caves we inhabited. It seems the ancient people of this world had already discovered the hazards of living in caves without enough ventilation. Shall we continue?"

She nodded and he wove his way among the tents, leading them toward the back of the cave. "We organize hunting and gathering parties every day to ensure we have enough food. Everyone old enough takes a shift at least twice a week. We've had good luck with it so far, but as our numbers grow, that will change. If we aren't able to win this war soon, we may have a starvation issue."

Meaghan frowned, and then chased the reaction away when a woman who had been watching them shook her husband's shoulder and pointed in their direction. Meaghan kept her voice low as she spoke. "What plan do we have in place to battle Garon?"

"We don't have one," Sam responded. "We've been waiting for the right time."

"The right time for what? It seems the need is now."

"We're not ready yet."

She halted in the back of the cave. Miles and Nick stopped alongside her. A few people watched, but none sat close enough to overhear.

"How can you not be?" she asked. "You've had over fifteen years to prepare. Garon destroys more villages and depletes our numbers every week. If you wait any longer, we might not have enough people left to fight him."

Sam tucked his hands into his pockets, and then rocked back on his heels as he studied her. When he frowned, she felt both judged and dismissed. "You haven't been in Ærenden long enough to understand," he said. "It's more complicated than it seems."

"Then explain it to me."

"We're waiting for a sign an ancient prophecy predicted."

She stared at him, uncertain she had heard him correctly at first, but then her cheeks burned with anger when she realized he had meant what he had said. "A sign?" she asked. "You're basing your entire campaign on some sort of mystical prediction?"

"As I said, you don't know this kingdom well enough to understand."

She took a step closer to him, finding it difficult to care if the people around them saw her reaction. "Don't tell me I don't understand. I understand plenty. I understand you and the other Elders are hiding behind a prophecy because you don't have enough courage to take control. And I understand that by not fighting, you've given Garon all the leverage he needs."

Sam's eyes locked on hers and he met her attack with one of his own. "I find it convenient that you choose to dismiss the prophecies you don't want to follow, and then wield the ones you do as a noble shield. Do you think I'm a fool? Do you think I don't remember you used a prophecy to protect Nick from being punished for your wedding?"

"The wedding happened without our permission. It's not like we chose to break the law."

"Then I guess you should have taken more *control*," he spat back. His attention turned to Nick, who stood in silence beside her. "And what do you think? You grew up here. Do you agree with her? Are we cowards?"

"Her word choice is unfortunate," Nick responded. She stiffened, but he took her hand in his and squeezed it. She heeded his request to remain silent. "She knows you aren't cowards, but she can also feel our people's suffering more than we can."

"And we see them suffer every day," Sam countered. "We heal them. We guide them. And we counsel them after Garon subjects them to the deaths of their loved ones and horrors beyond their worst nightmares. All while she's done what? Hid from the war in safety and comfort?"

This time Nick stiffened. He grabbed Sam's arm, but did no more than urge him into an alcove, away from any prying eyes. "You know better than that, Sam. Meaghan has done exactly what the Elders requested of her. She's trained and she's ready. She wants to help and I think you do, too. Waiting is bothering you as much as it's bothering her, isn't it?"

Sam glared at him for moment and then sighed. He shoved his hands into his pockets. "We've discussed it, but we can't do anything until the sign comes."

"Why?" Nick asked. "I know how important prophecies are, now more than I ever did before, but I also know we have to prepare for them. If the sign comes, are we ready to fight? If not, we have work to do, and we need to start doing it. That's all Meaghan is saying."

Sam nodded and brought a hand to Nick's shoulder. "I've watched you since you were a small boy," he said. "But somehow, I didn't realize how much you'd grown up. You have a lot of wisdom and a good way with words. We're lucky to have you as our King."

The compliment brought a smile to Nick's face, but as they continued walking, it weighed on Meaghan's mind. Nick would make a great King, but she had her doubts about whether she would make a good Queen. More so now, after Nick had smoothed over her argument. Sam was supposed to be her ally, not her enemy. Her mind flashed to Abbott's prediction, and though she usually tried not to think about it, today she held on to it. She needed to ensure Nick fulfilled the Dreamer's vision, even if she died doing it.

§

MEAGHAN WISHED she had her mother's power. Making her way across a city of tents in the darkness seemed like a fool's journey. Adelina could have done it without even stubbing a toe, but Meaghan had not fared so well. Bruises dotted her calves and knees, evidence of her inability to navigate rocks without more than the gentle glow of a few dimmed torches. She had held in her curses and suffered the pain without the aid of a single moan, all to avoid detection. She trailed a hand along the cave wall and hoped the villagers remained frozen in sleep. It would not take much, just an errant leg or arm extending into her path and her mission would fail.

Nick still slept in their tent. The Elders had retired hours ago after granting Nick and Meaghan full permission over the protective barrier to the caves. She could now exit and enter as she pleased, unlike most everyone else who lived within its boundaries. Miles had also lectured her on the responsibility of her new freedom. She must be careful about the people she let inside, and she must be wise about when she left. The wrong choice could cost lives.

She suspected her willingness to test both warnings would not meet the Elders' satisfaction, but she had little choice. Not after the decision that had been made tonight.

She bit back a curse when her knee found a boulder, and kept moving. Based on her memory of today's tour, she should be close to the back entrance of the sleeping cave. The next cave offered enough light through a hole in the roof to allow her to dash through it to the exit. Then it was only a matter of hunting the hunter.

A faint glow greeted her from the right and she followed it into the larger cave beyond. Focusing on the moonlit forest framed in the entrance, she broke into a run. She had almost reached the outside when a man stepped out of the shadows to block her path.

"Where do you think you're going?" he asked.

The teasing in his voice bothered her only because her heart still galloped from the surprise. She huffed out a breath and glared at Nick's oldest friend. "You almost gave me a heart attack."

"I have a hard time believing you're so easily scared. I've heard stories about your first battle. They said you were a rock." Max chuckled. "Literally."

"Funny." She planted her hands on her hips, narrowing her eyes into slits. The feigned anger only increased his laughter. "Quiet," she hissed, afraid his noise would travel. She had not punished her legs sneaking out of the caves to have him wake everyone while she stood feet from escape.

"Why?" He cocked his head to the side. "You're not sneaking off to somewhere, are you? Meeting a lover, perhaps?"

This time, real anger turned her body rigid. She dropped her arms. He had not stopped joking since he had come to greet her and Nick earlier in the afternoon. Given how few months had passed since Max had lost his wife, Meaghan had forgiven the often inappropriate comments as a defense mechanism, but this time he had crossed the line.

Max seemed to understand his mistake almost as soon as he made it. He ran a hand through his hair, following the blonde strands until they ended at his shoulders, and then offered her a meek smile. "Sorry."

"Forget about it," she said, letting her anger go with a forced exhale. "We all cope differently."

He nodded and looked away. "I'm glad Nick figured out the trick with the doll. It's nice having him around again."

She smiled, but said nothing. Nick had told everyone she controlled her power by transferring it to the doll. If his suspicions were true about Abbott, and a traitor still resided in their midst, he hoped the lie would draw the person out of hiding. Stealing the doll, and her power, would be too much for any of Garon's minions to resist.

"Can I see it?" Max asked, his joking tone returning. "It must be an ugly thing. Nick was always terrible in crafts class."

"It's hidden," she told him, crossing her arms over her stomach. "I'll show you tomorrow. I have somewhere I need to be."

She stepped around him and continued toward the forest.

"You shouldn't go out there alone," Max called after her.

"I'll be fine," she said, turning around to look at him. "Go back to sleep."

He tucked his hands into his back pockets. "I don't sleep much anymore. I tend to wander the caves at night. I'd prefer to walk outside, but I can't get back in. Can you?"

"Yes."

"I figured as much. It makes sense to give the Queen free rein over the castle, even if the castle is a dump inside the earth." He smiled again, but this time the gesture held no levity. "You're lucky to have your King, you know."

"I know."

"Good. Then don't forget what it'll do to him if you get in trouble. You're looking for the Zeiihbuan, right?"

Surprised he had guessed, she could not find the words to respond. He stepped forward, closing the gap between them.

"I'll take that as a confession. You were asking about him today. I heard you. And you stopped asking when the old woman said she saw him run into the forest. He's dangerous."

Meaghan held her ground, though Max took another step forward. "He's not dangerous," she said. "He's a good man."

"Then why are you looking for him without your Guardian? Is it because Nick doesn't approve?"

She shook her head, but could not think of a plausible reason to object. She could not tell Max the truth. She and Nick had never discussed looking for Faillen.

"You're not going," Max continued. "As Nick's fellow Guardian, I'll stand in his stead. I won't allow it."

He closed the last of the distance separating them, but before he could grab her, she turned and ran. He did not pursue. If he exited the cave, he would never be able to return for help. But that would not stop him from sounding an alert. At most, she had twenty minutes to accomplish her goal.

They would need to be the twenty luckiest minutes of her life.

CHAPTER THIRTY-THREE

AN OWL hooted in the distance. Crickets chirped in excitement closer by. Leaves and bushes rustled as Meaghan pushed through the otherwise slumbering forest. She had slowed to minimize her noise, but the effort would not matter. She could have a dranx's power of silence and Faillen would still have no trouble finding her. She would never hear him, or the flight of his knife as it sought her heart.

She chased the thought from her head and refocused her energy on her power. He could kill her, but she had to believe he would not. She had never sensed malice in him before, except toward Garon. Even when he had held her at arrow point the first time they met, he had not wanted to take her life. He had only wanted to protect his family.

Something stirred within her and she paused, recognizing it. The emotions felt distant, but their intensity made it easy for her to separate them from each other. Distrust, anger, guilt, and despair suffocated her like thick blankets. Caution, curiosity, and anticipation coupled the darker emotions, and she understood the source of

317

them. Faillen watched her, and followed. Or more likely, he hunted her.

She continued, maintaining the same pace as before. Her nerves spiked and she tucked her hands inside her cloak to keep them from shaking. She needed to talk to him, which meant she needed to hide the fact she had sensed his presence until he came close enough to hear.

His anger increased, and the strength of it almost stole her courage. She forced a breath, using the cold air as a salve and kept going. Faillen's emotions worried her, but until she felt malice or hatred in him, she would not run.

A mouse scurried across her path. She jumped, using the surprise as an excuse to stall a little longer, and then gasped when a dark shadow dropped from the tree next to her. It swooped, silent and deadly in front of her face, and then it disappeared again. It took her a moment to recognize the glint of talons in the hazy moonlight, and a moment longer to see the white body of its prey struggling within its grip. The mouse broke free, fell, and then became captive again. This time, she saw something else that gave the bird a name. She saw gold.

"Scree," she said, drawing a hand up to her heart. "You survived."

"No thanks to you," Faillen responded behind her.

Meaghan turned, her hands raised and empty. She knew he had approached. His emotions had swelled and closed in on her when Scree dove for dinner, and she had let him come. Now she would discover if her trust had been misplaced.

The tip of a blade hovered inches from her face, its sharp edge flashing a threat by the moonlight, and her faith waned.

"I didn't start the fire," she whispered. She had wanted to sound assertive, but her voice would not cooperate. She curled her fingers into her palms and tried again. "If that doesn't matter to you and you mean to avenge Ree's death with my life, your time is now. I brought no one with me."

"I know. I've been following you since you left the cave."

Faillen turned the knife in his hand. His eyes flicked to her throat and she swallowed the fear choking her.

"You should have brought someone," he told her. "I could kill you. I'm as much your enemy now as Garon."

"If you were, I'd be dead already and we both know it. I've come to help you."

"I don't need your help. I don't need anyone."

"You need your son," she said, lowering her hands. "He needs you. Now more than ever."

Faillen looked away. Guilt surged through him. "Where is he?"

"Neiszhe's watching him."

"Cal's wife," Faillen said and withdrew the knife from Meaghan's neck, though he did not return it to his belt. "I didn't know she was his second."

Meaghan nodded. "His first wife was a member of the castle guard. Garon killed her."

"Is that why Cal won't talk about the attack on the castle?"

"It's one of the reasons. He was also close to my father, and to a lot of other people who died that day. But Cal isn't the only one to find grief in this war. Garon's taken from all of us. He murdered

Nick's father in front of him. He sent Mardróch to Earth to kill James and Vivian, the people I knew as my parents." She drew in a shuddering breath. Her own grief mixed with what she felt from Faillen. "And recently, he destroyed Neiszhe's village."

"And now he's taken Ree," Faillen said. He tightened his fist on the knife. "As well as my son."

"Not for long. We're going after him."

"Because you're worried about what he could do to your war," Faillen spat out, his anger building again. He brought the knife back up, his eyes seeking hers across the blade. "You're no better than Garon."

"The Elders want to do it for that reason," she admitted. Taking a step forward, she cut the distance between them, forcing him to choose between using the blade and lowering it. It wavered in his hand, an inch from the base of her throat. "But they don't know you. I do. I know your boys, and I knew Ree. I want revenge for what Garon did and for what he's doing to Zeiihbu."

She stepped forward again. The tip of his blade touched her skin, and then Faillen swore and threw it. It lodged into the ground at her feet. "Are you insane, or do you want me to kill you?"

"Neither," she answered. "I want you to face the truth. You know who you are. Don't let Garon change that. Don't betray Ree's memory of you."

Faillen stared at her. Pain flooded through him, into Meaghan, and then he walked away. She watched him disappear into the trees before reaching down to dislodge his knife from the soil. She followed him, catching up a hundred yards deeper into the woods.

"Leave me alone," he told her. She laid a hand on his shoulder and he turned from her. "Leave me in peace."

"You aren't in peace. You suffer. And we all suffer with you, but no one more than your son." Faillen said nothing. She reached behind her back to grab the book she had hidden in her waistband and handed it to him. "Aldin asked me to give you this if you came back. He cried out for you when he went to sleep tonight. He thinks he's lost you, too."

Sparks had scarred the book's leather cover. Smoke had stained its pages. It reeked of ash, and charred wood. But Faillen grasped it like a treasure. "Ancient Æren," he read from the spine and trailed a finger down the words. "Aldin hasn't been without this since you visited last. He hated it before that day, before Nick talked to him. I was proud of him for finally wanting to study."

"Nick cares about him."

"I know. Aldin begged Ree to help him with his language studies every day after. When Ree didn't have time, he'd take the book outside and try to figure it out himself. He really wanted to make fireworks." Faillen breathed out a half-laugh and flipped open the book, staring at the top right corner where heat had curled the edges. "I can still hear her reading the words to him. I can also hear her screaming for me in the smoke. I couldn't find her. Despite all the things I'm supposed to be capable of, all the things that made me worthy of her love, I couldn't find her." He sank to his knees and stared up at Meaghan. "I couldn't find her when she needed me most. I failed her."

Faillen's anguish drowned Meaghan, filling her eyes with hot tears until she turned her power inward to silence it. She lowered to the ground beside him. His tears fell on the book, so she closed it and set it aside. Then she took his hands in hers. In her best act of friendship, she stayed beside him while he drained his emotion.

"You didn't fail her," Meaghan told him after he had let go of her hands. "You stood strong when Garon threatened you, and by doing that, you saved her boys from him. It was what she wanted."

"She died for it," Faillen said. "She died because of my decision."

"She died protecting her family. Ree wouldn't have wanted it any other way. She wanted her sons to make a difference. They will now. I promise you."

Faillen nodded and lowered his eyes to the book where it lay on the ground beside his knees. "Garon wants you. I released Scree after the fire started. She returned tonight with a note from Zeiihbu. They've taken Caide to my tribe's village. They've promised to release him if I bring you."

"They won't. They're lying."

"I know," he said, picking up the book. "Did you tell the truth when you said you'd rescue him?"

"I did. Nick volunteered to lead the rescue party, but I don't want him to go. I'd rather take his place. And if Garon wants me in Zeiihbu, it'll be easier for me to get close without his army suspecting."

"Suspecting what?"

"That I'm not as naïve as they think."

A genuine smile crossed Faillen's face. Behind it, Meaghan felt a spark of hope. "You have a plan, don't you?" he asked.

She shrugged. "It's more like a loose idea and probably a bad one at that, but I'm open to suggestions."

Faillen laughed and stood, then offered her a hand and drew her up beside him. "Nick's right to want to go in your place. He's your Guardian, and you're the rightful ruler."

"I may have the blood of my ancestors, but I don't have Nick's heart. I don't have his head. And ultimately, he's best for Ærenden."

"Perhaps," Faillen said. "But you'll never convince the Elders of that. They'll protect you over Nick."

"Not all of them will."

The response came from the darkest shadows of the forest, and Meaghan whirled toward it, yanking Faillen's knife from her belt before she recognized who had spoken. Her heart sank. She had not yet convinced Faillen of her plan, and now she would lose any progress she had already made.

Cal stepped forward. Although moonlight illuminated his body, his face remained dark. He fixed his eyes on Meaghan. "I can think of one Elder who'd prefer to finish you off right now. It would simplify things."

Despite his words and the threat he did not bother to hide, Meaghan smiled with relief. He had returned. His cloak had been singed in places, and large chunks of material had been lost in others. His beard appeared wet, either from sweat or water. Soot streaked across his cheeks. He ran a hand over the top of his head and ash rained from his hair. But he appeared to be uninjured, and more importantly, he was alive.

She launched a hug at him before he had the chance to block her.

Pressing a kiss to his cheek, she wrinkled her nose at the odor clinging to him. "You're okay," she said after letting him go. "I was worried."

"You could've fooled me. After taking off like you did, I'd guess you were more interested in worrying others than being worried yourself."

She dismissed his comment with another smile. "How's the rest of your team?"

"Fine. Zellíd suffered a few nasty burns, but he's being healed at the moment, as I should be."

"You're hurt?" Meaghan asked, and then spotted the bandages showing through the holes in his cloak. They covered his left forearm and his right thigh. She reached for one. "Why didn't you—"

Cal's hand latched onto her wrist, cutting off her question. He twisted it, bringing her arm up to get her attention. "Because you decided to take off without telling anyone. What else was I supposed to do? Nick's frantic. Miles is ready to send everyone in the caves out to search for you, and I'm furious. I don't like pain and these burns aren't exactly tickling me." He twisted her arm one more time, treating her to her own bout of pain, and then let her go. "Why did you come out here exactly? I told you to leave Faillen alone. He needs time."

"We don't have time," she said, pressing her wrist into her other hand. It throbbed, but she thought better of complaining. "The Elders want to send a rescue party to find Caide. It leaves in two days."

"And?"

"And Nick volunteered to lead it."

Cal stared at her. "Why would he do that?"

"Because they said only one of us could go. He wants to make sure it isn't me."

"He's still afraid Abbott's prediction will come true," Cal said and raised a hand to her shoulder. "So why not let him do it?"

"Because he can't. Garon wants me there. I'm afraid of what he'll do to Zeiihbu if I don't go. And Nick," her voice broke. She closed her eyes. "There's a good chance he won't make it back. He deserves to be King, Cal. He'll be a better ruler than I will."

"Is that the only reason you want him to stay?" Cal asked, and despite the seriousness of the conversation, she thought she heard humor in his voice. He tilted her chin with his fingers so she looked up at him when she opened her eyes. "I suspect otherwise, but that's a discussion for another day. Nick will have a hard time forgiving me if I side with you on this. You know that, don't you?"

She nodded and wiped a tear from the corner of her eye.

Cal sighed. "All right. Let me talk to him once we convince the Elders. I'll see if I can make him understand."

Surprised, Meaghan sucked in a breath, but Cal did not wait for her to react any further. He turned to Faillen. "If Meaghan is risking her life for your son, then I expect you to do something for her in return. You'll take her offer. You'll lead her army when you return from Zeiihbu, even if she doesn't make it back. Swear by it."

Cal extended his right hand toward Faillen, palm down. Faillen stared at it.

"Do you need any more proof?" Cal asked. "Can you honestly

question her selflessness now?"

"No." Faillen's gaze rose to Cal's. "No, I can't." He brought his right hand up, intertwining their fingers and then covered their fingers with his left hand. He waited for Cal do to the same. "From my lips to the death," he recited.

"From my lips to the death," Cal repeated, finishing the Zeiihbu promise.

Faillen released Cal's hands and turned to Meaghan. "A new pact for a new war," he told her and bowed. "I am at your service, my Queen."

CHAPTER THIRTY-FOUR

THEY APPROACHED the entrance to the caves with a plan. Cal and Faillen would talk, and Meaghan would remain silent. Though insulted that they thought she would mess up the conversation with the Elders, she had to admit her record backed the possibility. She had met with the Elders twice already, and both times, she had angered them. If it happened a third time, she suspected they would throw her in the path of danger just for the chance to get rid of her. Cal only chuckled at the suggestion.

"You're a lot more valuable than you realize," he told her, then gestured for her and Faillen to stop as voices drifted toward them through the foliage. Meaghan recognized Nick's first. Miles and May's followed. Although Meaghan's power remained muted, their frustration became clear as soon as she understood their words. A debate raged about whether they should send out a search party or keep looking for Meaghan on their own.

"She'll be fine," she heard Sam say. "I think we should block the cave entrance and lock her out for the night. That would teach her a lesson."

"You'll risk her life if you do that," Nick argued. "And your own if you dare mention the idea again."

"Threatening him isn't necessary," May said. "He wasn't serious."

Sam sighed. "Of course I wasn't. This is just too reminiscent for me. I had this conversation over and over again with the Elders when a certain ancestor of hers used to disappear."

"I know," Nick responded. "I've heard she's a lot like Adelina."

"Adelina?" Sam scoffed. "As difficult as Adelina could be, she had courtesy for other people. I meant Ed. He was practically a leaf in the wind most days. Cal seemed to be the only one who could manage him."

"Did I hear someone say my name?" Cal asked, stepping out from behind a tree to join the conversation.

"We were talking about Ed," Miles told him.

Cal chuckled. "Making comparisons no doubt. Meaghan has the best parts of him."

Sam raised an eyebrow. "Only if you consider being hotheaded, impulsive, and careless to be good traits."

"I do. She's brilliant, too. It's a great combination if you want to get things done."

"Or get yourself killed," Miles muttered. "Did you have any luck finding her?"

Cal nodded. "That I did. And she had luck finding Faillen. They'll be along shortly."

"She went after the man who tried to kill her this afternoon?" Sam asked. "Is she insane?"

"She might be a bit of that, too," Cal said, then turned as Meaghan stomped her feet, making more noise than she normally would. "Let's see if she at least apologizes."

Meaghan cleared the trees and feigned surprise to see the group staring at her. The intensity of their anger made her acting more convincing. At least the embarrassment was real. "I'm sorry," she said, taking Cal's cue. "I thought I'd be back before anyone realized I'd left. I didn't mean to scare you."

"Do we look scared?" Miles asked. "Or should I wonder if you sense it?"

"You asked me not to use my power on you."

"It's nice to know you pay attention to some of our requests," May commented, crossing her arms. "Although we'd get a lot more sleep if you'd pay attention to more of them."

"You have no idea," Nick grumbled. He studied Meaghan for a moment before he spoke again. "Are you okay?"

"Of course. You know Faillen wouldn't hurt me."

"I do," he said. "But there are worse things in the woods than Faillen. Around here, there's a creature known as a black daggercat. I'm sure you can figure out his special talent."

Her mind painted an image she hoped did not match reality and her heart raced with the thought. "I guess I wasn't thinking."

"It's a habit with you. Max tried to warn you, but instead of listening, you took off. He's been through enough, and now he's pacing the caves, worried about you. Do you realize how selfish you've been?"

Meaghan swallowed, hurt by the rage in Nick's voice as much as by the truth. "Look, Nick—"

"This is an argument for a more private place," May interrupted, placing a hand on her son's forearm. "I'm sure you have a lot to discuss, but for now," she nodded at Faillen, who stood beside Meaghan. "You understand if we let you back in the caves, you can't repeat your behavior from this afternoon. If you do, you'll be arrested. The only reason you aren't now is because we all understand grief."

"I appreciate your generosity," Faillen said. "I lost myself for a moment. It won't happen again."

"I'm sure it won't," Cal said. "Your son's inside. He's looking for you."

And with those words, he signaled the start of the dialogue they had planned.

"I look forward to seeing him," Faillen responded. "But there's a matter we need to discuss first." His eyes flowed from Cal to the faces of the people he had not yet officially met. "You're the Elders, correct?"

"We are," Miles said. "I'm Miles, the Head Elder. Those under me are Cal and May, who you know, and the longest appointed of us, Sam."

Faillen inclined his head in greeting before returning his focus to Miles. "I recall my father telling me the Elders and the Queen share responsibility in decision making, especially when decisions bring risk to the royal family. Is that true?"

"It is," Miles replied. "As Guardians, we're tasked to protect the royal line."

"Or at least it's something we try to do," May added and cast a pointed look at Meaghan. "It's not always as easy as it should be."

"I'm certain it's not." A smile of amusement touched Faillen's lips when Meaghan huffed beside him. "I'm afraid I'm not going to add to that ease, though. I need help. I believe only Queen Meaghan can provide it, but there's risk involved."

"Our Queen is hardly adverse to risk," Sam remarked. "As I'm sure you've noticed. Should I assume you've made your request to her already? Given her recent attitude, I'm surprised you'd come to us at all, even if it's protocol."

"She asked me to respect your authority on this."

"Did she?" Sam asked and lifted an eyebrow in Meaghan's direction. "This must be an interesting request."

"As I said, it's not without risk," Faillen responded. "My father sent a message tonight. Garon is holding Caide hostage in Zeiihbu. He's wants Meaghan in exchange."

"Never," Nick insisted, and his cheeks blazed red with his anger. "We'd never sacrifice—"

Faillen held up his hand. "I'm not suggesting we do. I think if we're able to convince Garon we intend to trade her, we have a chance of taking back Zeiihbu and my son."

"There's a lot to gain," Cal said and stroked his fingers through his beard. "If we agreed to this, would Zeiihbu fight with us? Not just along the borders, but truly fight Garon's army?"

"They would," Faillen promised.

"You aren't seriously considering this," Nick said. "What would be the point of reclaiming the throne if Meaghan didn't survive to use it?"

"The point is saving Ærenden," Sam responded. "If we put together the right rescue team, Meaghan has a shot of returning."

"A shot?" Nick stared at Sam, and then threw up his hands when the Elder did not respond. "You're willing to risk her life on a *shot* she might return? This is ridiculous."

"I'd gladly accept your help instead," Faillen told Nick. "But we can't get close enough to Garon's army without Meaghan."

"I won't allow it."

"I'm prepared to accept your offer," Faillen added. "You'll have my warriors and my leadership."

"Not under these conditions."

"What offer?" May asked. She frowned at Nick. "That's the second time Faillen's mentioned it. What offer did you make?"

"It's nothing," Nick clutched his hands into fists at his sides. "It's withdrawn."

"The Queen doesn't think so," Faillen said. "She agreed to it."

"To what?" May prompted.

"To use my expertise as a Zeiihbu warrior to lead the army. She and Nick made the offer to me when I saw them last."

"Did they?" May's lips flattened into a thin line. "Was this your idea?" she asked Meaghan.

Meaghan nodded, attempting to maintain the vow of silence she had made to Cal and Faillen. She laced her fingers together in front of her.

"I see," May said. "Are you aware the Elders control the army?"

Meaghan nodded again.

"So you knew you didn't have the authority to make the offer and you did it anyway?" Miles asked. "What gives you the right to think you can bypass us?"

Meaghan tightened her grip, controlling her anger. She looked at Nick over his mother's shoulders. Though he had long ago come up with a response for the question, he would not meet her eyes. To prevent her from going to Zeiihbu, he would sacrifice their plan. She had no other choice. She had to answer. She opened her mouth, but closed it again when Faillen stepped forward, drawing the Elders' attention.

"I don't wish to interfere with your duties," he said. "As the Guardian army proved to my people in the Zeiihbu War, their methods are beyond reproach. I believe Nick and Meaghan wanted to mobilize a second army, one comprised of villagers. I can train them, and I can share Zeiihbu strategy with you. Our combined knowledge might give us the edge over Garon's army."

"The people have been through enough," Miles said, his voice curt. "It's our job to protect them, not command them into harm's way. They'd be slaughtered."

"They're being slaughtered now," Cal countered. "If we train them, they might stand a chance of surviving."

"I agree," Sam said and addressed Faillen. "Are you saying you'll only do this if Meaghan accompanies you to Zeiihbu? I'm afraid we won't be able to reach a consensus if the two issues are attached."

"I'm sorry," Faillen responded. "But I intend to try to rescue my son no matter what you decide. Since I doubt I'll succeed without Meaghan's help, I won't make a promise I can't keep."

"Makes sense," Cal said. "Let's put it to a vote."

Nick shook his head. "You can't—"

"It's not your say," Miles interrupted. "This is for the Elders to decide, though my vote is no. Faillen's help isn't needed, and I don't see the point in placing Meaghan in danger." He turned to Cal. "Shall I assume your vote is yes?"

"It is," Cal answered. "And since Nick can't go with her, I'd like to volunteer to be her Guardian on the mission."

"If the vote passes, I'll allow it," Miles said. "Sam, what about you?"

"I vote yes."

"May?"

May pressed her lips together and Meaghan realized she struggled with the idea of sending her son on a mission that could be his last. If she voted yes, she would sacrifice her son's wife. If she voted no, she would sacrifice her son. May mulled it over in silence for several minutes and then shook her head. "I don't think either of them should go. We don't have a solid plan in place, so I'm voting no to both."

"Only one vote is up right now, May," Miles told her. "But taking your vote into account, we have a tie. I'm afraid without a consensus the vote is equivalent to a no. I'm sorry, Faillen, your request is—"

A screech pierced the night air, cutting off the remainder of Miles' words. The sound descended, fast and loud. Faillen wrapped his cloak over his arm, extending it as a streak of feathers shot through the sky. Sharp talons grabbed the perch Faillen provided.

"Hello, lovely," he said. Scree turned her head to stare at him, and then screeched again. Faillen retrieved a piece of meat from the leather pouch on his belt and handed it to her. "Did you have a nice hunt?"

She twittered, flapping her wings in a blur of brown and gold before settling. Turning her attention toward the meat, she clutched it in one claw, tearing chunks from it with an eager beak.

"It can't be," Miles whispered, and his eyes seemed to double in size. "He's extinct."

"She," Faillen corrected. "And I assure you, she's as real as we are."

"A gildonae," Sam said. His voice rose in pitch in his excitement. "The Gildonae Alliance."

"It appears that way," Miles agreed. "This nullifies the vote."

"You can't," Nick protested. He turned to his mother. "You've already decided."

May laid a palm against his cheek. "I'm sorry, Nick. This is out of our control."

"I don't understand."

"The gildonae is the sign we've been waiting for. She's in the prophecy."

Nick stared at his mother for a moment before his face stiffened and he stepped back from her, severing their connection. "I still don't understand."

"I don't either," Cal said. "What prophecy?"

"The Aurean Prophecy," Sam answered. "Vivian found it when she was a teenager. It contains five verses, though the fifth was lost ages ago. Only a few words could be deciphered."

"Which words?"

"Death. Day of dark. Æren sleeps."

Cal grunted. "So nothing useful. What do the other verses say?"

Miles reached inside his cloak to withdraw a book. "This is the first verse," he said and began to read, *"After brick and fire fall and dark upends these lands; Near decade twice will come to pass in wait of child's hands; Through Earth and toil, through battled hue, through Aurean's impart; This child's hands will helm the hope, rend darkness soon apart."*

"Brick and fire," Cal said. "Anybody who was at the castle knows that's how the war started. The 'near decade twice' part is also easy enough to figure out. It's been a little over fifteen years since the war started. That's the better part of two decades. Should I assume the child is Meaghan?"

"We think so," May told him. "The Aurean reference has been a little harder to decipher."

"What do you mean?" Cal asked. "It's obviously referring to the prophecy. Isn't that why Vivian named it that?"

"She named it that because the ancient Seers wrote it," Miles said. "But that doesn't mean the Aureans were referring to themselves. We think they might have been referring to Vivian's vision of Meaghan and Nick's wedding."

Cal nodded. "So the Aurean in question is Viv. What does the second verse say?"

Miles continued reading, *"Await the sign, the noble plume, the gold of colored grace; Upon the perch by which it lands, the leader of this race; Rethink thy bounds, embrace the cry, the Gildonae's implore; Alliance born 'tween child and man will end the war of wars."*

"These things are always obvious after the fact," May said. "We've been trying to decipher that verse for some time. Of course, we didn't know the gildonae weren't extinct."

Sam chuckled. "If we take the whole thing literally, it simply means the man the gildonae perches on is meant to be the leader in the war, and we need to embrace Meaghan's alliance with him."

"Which we will," Miles said. "Against my better judgment. The third verse seems to pair with the second, *From mountain top to water deep, with ghosts at last in tow; The promise made will come to pass; the seeds of friendship sowed; In death, in strife, in battle bound; in beastly shadow's doom; The whispers born from rhyme and rift will bring a Master's boon.'* We can probably assume the Master is Caide, which would make this verse about his rescue."

"And the fourth verse?"

Miles returned his eyes to the book once more. *'Prepare the way, this sign doth show, beginning to the end; Upon the loss of child's heart, freedom doth depend; Beware the words of troubled times, beware the truths of old; The answer hides in buried lies, the Reaper now will sow.'* He looked up again. "All we can really decipher is that for the end of the war to come, Meaghan has to lose her heart, whatever that means. The only Reaper we know about is the amulet, and it doesn't fit in this context."

Meaghan knew of another, and so did Nick. She locked eyes with him for a breath before he looked away. She would go to Zeiihbu. The second verse ensured that.

And if the fourth verse and Abbott's dream aligned, death would collect her there.

CHAPTER THIRTY-FIVE

NICK SLAMMED his hands against the cave wall, embedding sharp pebbles into his palms. The sting helped clear his mind, but only for a moment. He could not believe Seers had predicted Meaghan's death twice now, and the Elders had still authorized her mission. They needed to keep her alive. They needed to keep her here. And if that failed, they needed to hog-tie her until she realized her stupidity.

He sighed and chased away the grief threatening to grip him. He would not give up hope. He had to believe there was another explanation for it all—for Abbott's dream, for the prediction. He only needed to come up with it. He closed his eyes and pressed his forehead against the wall to steady himself. Cold shale pressed into his skin. Water eased across his brow and dripped down his face. He willed his brain to focus, to use logic and reason, but only one answer came to him. He would lose her. Before he ever earned her love or had the chance to build a future with her, he would lose her.

It seemed as if shards had broken from the wall and burrowed into his heart, shredding it, and he hated her for it. He hated them all for it. His friends and family had promised to protect her. Instead, they had turned her into a bargaining chip for more soldiers.

"Nick."

He spun around and stared down Cal with the venom coursing through his blood. "Go away."

"Not until we talk."

"What is it you think you can say to me?"

"She's not dead," Cal responded. "You have to remember that."

"She's not dead *yet*," Nick corrected. "She will be soon."

"You can't be certain."

"I can." Nick leaned his back against the wall. "Abbott's dream came from Vivian. She was never wrong."

"Maybe not, but Abbott only saw that Meaghan wasn't at your coronation. There could be many reasons for that. Adelina missed Ed's birthday party once because she was assisting May with a birth in the castle. It happens."

"It isn't likely," Nick said and slipped his hands into his pockets. "Not when you add the fourth verse of the prophecy to Vivian's vision. I have no other choice but to realize what it means."

"Prophecies are impossible to understand sometimes. Even Vivian couldn't figure this one out. Otherwise, she would have stopped Garon's attack before it happened."

"She couldn't figure it out because she didn't know yet."

"About what?"

"The Grim Reaper," Nick told him. "On Earth, he's a fictional creature who collects souls from the dead. A soul is the heart of a person."

Cal stared at him, his eyes unblinking for a moment before he responded. "I'm sure it means something else here," he said, though his voice lacked conviction. "We might not know what, but it does. She won't die on my watch."

"Sure," Nick said, and closed his eyes, letting his anger dissolve into pain. "I keep saying the same thing. And every time she sneaks off to do something risky, or she fights, or she gets injured, I realize I have no real control. She'll invite death to meet her, and all I'll be able to do is watch it happen."

"Nick—"

"I'm sorry, Cal. I don't mean to take this out on you. I know you'll protect her, and I appreciate that. Just give me time to sort through this."

"Nick," Cal said. "Look, I didn't—"

"I know." Nick straightened up, refusing to look at Cal. "You did what's best. I understand the strategy behind the mission. I understand the need. We have to do this to win the war. And I also understand the woman I've wed. She can't sit by when she knows she's able to help someone. It's one of the reasons I fell in love with her on Earth." He dragged a hand over his face. He would do anything to take her back there again, to keep her there until no threat remained. "Unfortunately, it's the same reason I'll lose her in Ærenden."

"Nick—"

Nick shook his head, then turned away and disappeared into the darkest parts of the caverns.

§

HE FOUND his way deep under the earth, winding through mazes and into rooms that had not seen a human in thousands of years. He got lost, met dead ends, and backtracked until the familiar found him again, only returning to his tent when early morning neared. He expected to find Meaghan sleeping, but the blankets remained undisturbed, her pillow unrumpled. He suspected she had not wanted to face him any more than he had wanted to face her.

He spent the day wandering again. Occasionally, he spotted friends from his village camped among the other refugees and stopped to talk to them, but his conversations never lasted long. His mind refused to be distracted from Meaghan's impending departure. Anxiety commanded him. He wanted to burn off energy. If he found the Elders, he had no doubt they would assign him a task to fulfill his need, but he could not speak to them yet. His anger needed distance.

By evening, hunger drove him to seek out his first meal. He found Max's tent tucked into the back of the sleeping cavern, and his friend invited him to share a batch of reheated rabbit stew. Max had already heard the news and offered no false words of comfort. They ate in silence, the companionship more welcome than conversation could ever be.

At bedtime, Nick retired to his own tent. Meaghan had not returned, so he lay down and tried to sleep without her. Though his nightmares shattered his dreams at first, he eventually found solace through the weight of his weariness.

Meaghan slid into place next to him sometime later. He reached for her. Her hands sought his. The warmth of her body greeted him, and then he drifted off again. In the morning, she had disappeared.

The schedule for his second day started much like his first. He wandered, pretended to be interested in conversations, and then gave up and hid in his tent. Word spread that Guardians from neighboring villages had arrived to join the rescue party. Some came by invitation. Others came looking for a chance to be included in the new adventure. The latter left without consideration. Selecting who could be trusted needed both care and control. Nobody wanted to take the chance a volunteer might be a spy.

When the neighboring children squealed and ran with excitement to the front of the cave, Nick knew the horses had arrived. He paused as reality broke through his numbness. Meaghan would be going soon. The animals always came the day before departure.

His eyes swept her side of the tent, looking for any hint of her plans, any sign he would have more time before he lost her. He saw nothing but a slightly ruffled quilt. He ran his hand over it, surprised when his fingers bumped into something hard, and stripped back the cover to reveal the Writer's book. He picked it up. The original story appeared, as always, but the other pages remained blank. He thumbed through them, unfeeling as they fanned his face, and then stopped when black flashed in front of him where it had not been before. He only managed to scan the words *Chapter Three* before a voice interrupted him.

"Is there a new story?"

He looked up at Meaghan. His heart leapt as it used to when she surprised him on Earth. She smiled, reached for the book, and he closed it, tightening his grip on the spine to prevent her from taking it. "Please don't," he said. "I haven't read it yet. I don't want it to disappear."

She nodded and sat next to him. Drawing her knees under her chin, she wrapped her arms around her legs, and he realized she did not know what to say.

"Are you done planning?" he asked.

"For now." She stared down at the ground. "Cal wanted to say good-bye to Neiszhe, and Faillen needed to spend time with Aldin."

"And you?"

"I wasn't sure if you'd want to see me." Her eyes met his, and he saw pain in them. Sorrow had darkened her face more times than he cared to remember, yet he had never seen this type of pain from her before. It matched the grief he had been burying for two days. He brought a hand to her cheek. She pressed one of her own to the back of his hand.

"I'm sorry," she whispered. "I really am. I don't want this, but the prophecy—"

"Is a suggestion." He brought his other hand to her knee, and then folded her into his arms. "Prophecies and predictions aren't guarantees, Meg. They're potential roads among many. We can change the future."

"Can we?" she asked. "It feels more like I'm on a collision course. I don't see how I can stop it."

"Don't go. Just don't go and it'll stop."

"At what cost?" She pressed her face into his shoulder. Her lashes brushed his skin and her breath warmed his neck. "How many lives would be exchanged for mine?"

"There has to be another way. Tell me you won't go and we'll find it."

"I'm sorry," she said again, but the words sounded hollow to him. He only wanted to hear that she would do what he asked, that she would do what mattered most to him.

"You can still change it," he told her. She lifted her head to look at him. "Never give up. Be smart. Be careful. But above all, listen to Cal." He drew his fingers to her brow. "Do you remember the first time we went ice skating together?"

She nodded. "You'd never done it before."

"I loved it," he told her. "But I was scared at first. You took my hand and pulled me out on the lake anyway. I was freezing. I hated walking on thin metal blades. And I could swear I saw fish below the ice, their eyes frozen open in terror."

She laughed. "You did fine. Better than that, in fact. You didn't need my help at all by mid-afternoon."

"I always need you," he said and pressed his forehead to hers. "It was because of you that I found my courage. It was because of what you said."

"What was it? I don't remember."

"You told me that no one does anything alone. To succeed, we have to let someone else teach us, and we have to remember to lean on the people who give us strength." He paused, scanning her face in an attempt to memorize every detail. "Take your own advice. Lean on Cal and Faillen. Make sure you come back to me."

"I will," she promised, though she looked away, and he knew as well as she did that the promise might be impossible to keep. He traced a finger along her jaw, bringing her eyes back to his, then tilted her chin and kissed her. She no longer fought him or resisted, and for the moment, they found their way back to a place he thought had long ago been lost. She sighed when they parted, and stood.

"I have to get back," she said, her voice taking on an authority that told him she had already returned to whatever business shadowed her mind. "Faillen asked me to make a request of you."

"What is it?"

"He wants you to start training the villagers while we're gone. Is that something you can do?"

"I think I can manage. Compared to training you, it should be easy."

She laughed and pressed her fingers into his shoulder. "I'll miss you," she said, and then left him once more.

CHAPTER THIRTY-SIX

"SHE'S SO beautiful," Ed whispered. He leaned down to press his lips to the top of his newborn daughter's head. "You did an amazing job with her."

Adelina smiled. "Meaghan's not just mine. Your part in this was equally important."

He chuckled. "My part was brief. And a lot easier. I've never been so amazed by anyone in my life. First you carry her for nine months, and then you spend two days birthing her. I think I'd choose to go into battle for a sleepless week rather than go through that myself."

"So would I," Adelina said, laughing, and then smoothed a thumb over the baby's cheek. Meaghan pursed her lips, instinctively searching for food. "She was worth it. I think she's my greatest achievement."

"Mine too." Ed settled onto the blanket beside his wife then nodded toward the foot of the bed when he saw a quick blur of movement. "We have company."

"I see that." Adelina covered another smile with the tips of her fingers when a tuft of blonde hair poked above the end of the bed and then disappeared again. "Nickaulai, you don't need to hide."

The blonde hair popped up again, followed by two sets of small fingers that gripped the edge of the bed. Finally, a pair of blue eyes peered at them. She patted the bed next to where Ed sat. "Come here, dear. Come meet Meaghan."

The child ducked below the edge of the bed once more. A moment later, he poked his head up again, then scurried to her side and climbed onto the bed as Adelina requested. He grinned as he focused on the baby in her arms.

"Does your mother know you're here?" she asked him.

He shook his head, and reached out to stroke the baby's arm, snatching his hand back when her mouth opened in a yawn.

"Don't be frightened," Ed told him. "She's just sleepy. Do you want to hold her?"

Nick's eyes drew from the baby to Adelina. "Can I?"

"Of course. Come a little closer."

He did as she requested, nestling his knees against her side before pressing an index finger to the baby's cheek. "She's pretty. Pretty Meaghan."

"Yes, she is," Ed said. "She's also fragile, so you have to hold her a special way. Do you want to learn how?"

Nick's head bounced up and down. "Momma says she's mine. She says I have to protect her."

Ed chuckled. "Someday. For now, hold out your arms like this." He extended his arms, palms up. Nick mimicked him and Ed removed Meaghan from his wife's arms. "Now watch me," he instructed. He tucked the newborn into the crook of his arm, supporting her head. "See how I have her against my body with her head sturdy on my arm? Can you do that?"

"Yeah."

"Good." Ed placed the baby into Nick's outstretched arms and smiled when the boy drew her against his side, holding her as Ed had shown. Meaghan turned her eyes toward Nick and gurgled.

"She likes me," Nick said, grinning broadly. Then he disappeared.

Adelina stared at the empty space on the bed before reaching a hand out to where the boy had been. Her fingers coursed across the blanket, then gripped it. "He," she began, and then drew her eyebrows together. "What happened?"

Ed leaned over to kiss her. "Meaghan's okay," he assured her. "Nick only started teleporting last week. He's not strong enough to go far. I'll find him."

Adelina nodded, and then closed her eyes when Ed rose from the bed. As he had predicted, the young boy remained near. He sat on the couch in the living room, the baby nestled in his lap. Ed sat down next to him.

"You shouldn't do that," he said. "You scared Adelina."

Nick looked up at him, frowning. His arms tightened around the baby. "She's mine. Momma said so."

Ed smiled and laid a hand on the boy's shoulder. "She will be one day, but right now she belongs to Adelina and me. It's our job to watch out for her."

Nick's eyes filled with tears. Meaghan began to cry and the boy looked down at her. "It's okay," he said, planting a kiss on her cheek.

The baby calmed and he grinned at Ed. "See, I can keep her safe."

"I know that, son," Ed replied and lifted the baby from Nick's arms. He moved to the floor so the boy could still see her. "And when you're old enough, I'll be proud to have you guard her. But now isn't the time. You're too young."

"I'm a big boy," he said. "I have powers now."

"So I saw. But you can't do that again. Promise me you won't."

Nick's lip trembled, but he did not cry. Meaghan began to fuss again. "I promise," he said, then stroked the dark hair on Meaghan's head. "One day, Meaghan."

"Nickaulai!"

Nick dropped his hand, jumping from the couch at the sound of his mother's voice.

"What are you doing here?"

His eyes grew wide, pleading with Ed for escape. Ed patted him on the shoulder and stood, facing his wife's redheaded Guardian with a smile. "He wanted to see the baby, May. He did a good job holding her."

"Is that all?" she asked. "He's been trouble lately."

"That's all," he assured her and looked down at the frightened boy. "Right, Nick?"

Nick nodded a bit too enthusiastically, and May narrowed her eyes, looking between Nick and Ed for the truth. Neither of them offered it, so she sighed, then sat down on the couch and drew her son to her. "It's time for you to stop coming to the castle," she told him. "Now that you're getting your Guardian powers, you need to attend school with the other kids."

Nick's eyes turned from his mother to the baby and back. "I like it here."

"I know," May said and though her son did not catch it, Ed heard a hint of sorrow in her voice. "The Elders have decided it's time for you to train to be in the Guardian army. Don't you want that?"

"But," his eyes found Ed's. "But Meaghan's mine."

His mother smiled, a gesture also laced with sadness. "When Meaghan is Queen, you'll protect her in the army. For now, it's time to go home. Say good-night."

"I don't want to." Nick's eyes filled with tears again, and this time they spilled over. Meaghan began to wail. "I want—"

"That's enough," May said. "You've upset the baby."

Nick sniffled and wiped his nose on his sleeve, obeying his mother.

"Now say good-bye to Ed and Meaghan and then go say good-bye to Adelina. And say you're sorry."

Without bothering to ask what he should apologize for, he nodded. Ed crouched in front of him again, giving him the chance to see Meaghan one more time. The baby calmed.

"See you soon," Nick told her. He planted a kiss on her forehead, and then scurried from the room.

"What happened?" Ed asked when the boy could no longer hear. "I thought Nick was supposed to guard Meaghan. Why is he training to be in the army?"

May sighed. "I shouldn't have said anything to him. I just assumed he'd be following tradition. My family's been watching Meaghan's for generations, after all, but the Elders decided to enact the rule."

"What rule?"

"An old one that states a Guardian can only guard someone of the same gender."

"Miles guards Adelina's sister," Ed pointed out.

"I know. And she's the reason they're enacting the rule again. They don't want to risk the chance of another abdication. Especially if Meaghan's the purpose of your prophesied wedding."

"That makes no sense," Ed said. "It's not like they can keep Meaghan away from all male Guardians until she's wed. And it's not like Istera wed Miles. She wed someone from the army. If Nick and Meaghan are meant to fall in love, Istera's already proven that stationing him there won't stop it."

"It will if they assign him to border patrol," May muttered. "I'm sure that's their plan."

A miserable demotion for the young boy, Ed realized, and frowned. "I guess there's no arguing on this," he said, though he hated to admit it. He trusted no Guardian more than May, and he knew his daughter would be safest under the care of May's son. "We'll have to wait and see what happens. What do we do now?"

"We keep them apart. I don't want Nick to get attached to Meaghan any more than he already has."

"Agreed," Ed said and shifted the baby in his arms when she started crying again. "I should get her back to Adelina."

May nodded. "I'll return after I take Nick home. And then you can tell me what really happened with him."

Ed simply chuckled and left the room.

§

NICK AWOKE to the heavy darkness of the cave. A rare quiet surrounded him, a sign the world had long since fallen under sleep's command. He closed his eyes again to focus on the dream. He remembered it as he had seen it in the book that afternoon, but he could not feel it the way he wanted. He could not relive the emotions or the sensations of seeing and touching Ed and Adelina as he had when he read the words. He could only see the images as they still existed in his mind. Soon even the vividness of those began to fade, dissolving into the dark as fast as the words had disappeared from the pages.

He wished he had had more time with the story. As soon as he had finished reading it, Meaghan had come to pack. They said little as he closed the cover over the pages. Then she left again. He had not remembered the day Meaghan had been born, nor did he remember his strong need to protect her from such a young age. It had consumed him, and as he grew older, it had overtaken him again.

His mother had not told him about his army assignment. She had continued to train him as a personal Guardian at home. It had been a gamble on her part, but it had paid off when Nick and Meaghan's matching powers surfaced.

Or rather, when everyone realized Meaghan's power had surfaced. She had cried when Nick grew upset and calmed when he calmed. Watching the past had made it clear to him. Meaghan had not been colicky as an infant. Her empath power had shown up at birth. She had been reacting to the overload of emotions surrounding her and had stopped fussing after a month only because she had learned how to focus her power on those closest to her.

He reached out to hold her and to tell her about his discovery, but his arms only met her pillow. He could not sense her anymore. Cal now had the honor of her guardianship, which meant they had left.

Nick tightened his hand into a fist, clutching the fabric of her pillowcase between his fingers. He could no longer protect her. He could no longer prevent the future from coming. And in that failing, he knew her spot in bed might remain empty forever.

CHAPTER THIRTY-SEVEN

MEAGHAN'S HORSE whinnied. She calmed him with a gentle hand to the neck, and then cast a glance over her shoulder, toward the cave. In the soft glow of the full moon, she could make out the dark rock lining the entrance, but nothing more. She knew when she returned from Zeiihbu, if she returned, their home would be elsewhere. But she etched the view into her mind and her memory just as she had etched Nick's last words into her heart. It hurt to leave. It hurt more to realize the pain she had caused him—and the anger he harbored for her. Though he hid it from her, he could not hide it from her power. She had wanted to honor his request to stay, but she stood firm against him because she had no other choice.

He had always protected her. Now came the time for her to protect him.

"Are you ready?" The question came close to her ear.

"Yes," she answered, and though she had barred the tears from her eyes, she could not keep them from shaking her voice.

"He'll forgive you," Cal responded. He laid a hand over hers in understanding. "When you return to him, he'll forgive you."

"Will he?" she asked. Her horse pawed the earth, ready to move, and she tightened her hold on his reins. The ambercat gloves stretched taut across her knuckles. "And what if I don't return?"

"You will, or we both won't. And frankly, I intend to see my son, so not returning isn't an option."

Meaghan smiled, her determination renewed with his decree. A bird whistled, long and low from a distance to the right and she pointed her horse in that direction. Faillen waited, as did the others. It was time.

Turning once more in her saddle, she cast a final glance toward the cave, and then pressed her knees into her horse's sides and vanished into the night.

The adventure continues with

ÆRENDEN: THE ZEIIHBU MASTER

Coming in 2014!

ABOUT THE AUTHOR

Born in Bangor, Maine, Kristen Taber spent her childhood at the feet of an Irish storytelling grandfather, learning to blend fact with fiction and imagination with reality. She lived within the realms of the worlds that captivated her, breathing life into characters and crafting stories even before she could read. Those stories have since turned into a wide range of short tales, poems, and manuscripts in both Young Adult and Adult genres. Currently, she is working on the Ærenden series from her home in the suburbs of Washington, D.C.

Learn more about Kristen and her work at <u>www.kristentaber.com</u>.

CPSIA information can be obtained at www.ICGtesting.com
Printed in the USA
BVOW01s1850170114

342258BV00006B/35/P